MW01515490

A Man's World

Part two of A Woman's Touch series

To Liz xoxo

Delaney Foster

By Delaney Foster

Copyright © 2015 by Delaney Foster

All rights reserved. No part of this book may be reproduced in any form or by any means without the prior written consent of the author, excepting brief quotes used in reviews.

This is a work of fiction. Names, characters, and incidents either are the product of the author's imagination or are used fictitiously. Any resemblance to actual persons or events is entirely coincidental.

CHAPTER ONE
Heidi

You know when you're watching a movie and you know something bad is about to happen but there's nothing you can do about it? So you just sit there on the edge of the sofa and wait for it to be over. Yeah. That's pretty much how I would describe what just happened. Taylor Montgomery was determined to make sure Nick wanted nothing to do with me. Well, she got her wish. Although I bet she never thought this would be how it played out. I knew when Alex followed me upstairs after she tore my dress nothing good would come of the situation. I am just too stupid to connect my thoughts with my vocal chords. I should have told him to go back downstairs. I should have told him I had it handled. And I never should have asked him to help unzip my dress. Another stupid move. In my defense, it's not like I asked him to take it off or anything. As a matter of fact, I remember specifically telling him to unzip and leave. That's when I realized how drunk he was. And how hurt.

Alex is a really good guy. We had a good thing. Until I met Nick Knight. Nick is like gravity to me. I am pulled to him. Whether I want to be or not. I don't have a choice. I'm not sure I ever did. It's been one month since Nick came into my world and flipped it upside down. And now he's gone. Alex is bruised and bloody. And I am standing here in a $1200 dress that looks like a family of rats got a hold of it. Not exactly the way I had imagined this evening going.

 I am a whirlwind of emotions right now. Surprise turns to worry. Worry to afraid. Afraid to want. Want to need. Need to pain. The look in Nick's eyes when he walked in the room was like nothing I had ever witnessed. Not when Trey would get angry and flip shit. Not even when I told Cole I was leaving. This was different. This was deeper. Darker. Some crazy combination of emotions I've never seen before. When he approached me after wailing on Alex. So slowly, so calm, it was all I could do to just stand and wait for him to make his move. I wanted to reach out and touch him. Soothe him. I need to tell him he's thinking some really crazy shit right now. Beg him to listen. But one look, one touch, and I knew that would be pointless.

3

He needs time. So I watch the man I don't think I can live without walk out of this room. Without asking him to stay. Without following him. I don't think my heart can take hearing him tell me it's over before it's really only just begun. I lean my head back against the thick post and slide my way down until my butt hits the floor.

Alex coughs and pulls me out of my trance. Oh god. He looks horrible. Why didn't he fight back?

It's not like he doesn't know how. I have watched him beat shit up every Tuesday night for the past three months. "Ohmigod Alex!" My eyes pop open and my hands fly to my mouth when he turns to face me. There's blood spilling off the top of his right brow where the skin is split open and he has a nasty cut and there's some decent size swelling going on right at his cheekbone. His lip is busted and bleeding.

"Come on, love. It's not that bad," he says, attempting to smile. He winces at the action so I'm guessing it *is* that bad. He scoots toward me and leans against the side of the bed, letting the mattress support his weight.

"You keep telling yourself that, champ."

Alex makes another attempt at smiling. It hurts me to look at him. "Come here. Let me look at that."

He does as I ask and scoots closer to where I am sitting. I lean in and inspect the damage. It's hard to tell if he needs stitches or not because there's so much blood. I move to get a closer look. Our faces are just centimeters apart and he's giving me this intense look. I've seen that look before. God, what have I done? "Alex, I'm so sorry." He brings his hand to my face in an attempt to comfort me. The gesture is gentle. Sweet. I can't do this. Instinctively, I look over my shoulder at the door.

"He's not coming back Heidi," Alex tells me, his expression apologetic.

"I know." And I do. As much as I want him to barge back in here and admit he overreacted. To hold me and kiss me and tell me we'll work through this. I know he's caught in a place somewhere between hurt and anger. I've been in that place. And even though being there alone probably isn't the best route to take, it's the one way to ensure things aren't said. Things that will be regretted later. Things that emotions can disguise as truth.

I stand and reach for Alex's hand. "Come on. Let's get you cleaned up."

I don't know if it's the cold water or my touch but he shies away the moment the cloth touches his skin. With one hand I hold his head in place while I blot and dab at his wounds with the other. Once the bleeding has slowed, I hand him the towel. "Are you okay to drive?" It's the cut on his eye that has me concerned more than the amount of alcohol he's consumed. A run in like the one he just had is enough to sober anyone up. Especially when it involves your best friend.

"I bet you're a great mother," he tells me, completely ignoring my question. *What? Where did that come from?* And as if he read my thoughts he continues, "You have a gentle touch. And a genuine concern. Your son is a lucky little boy."

Why did he have to bring Hudson into this? And of all times, now. As if I don't have enough emotional stress to deal with, now he's drudging up all the stuff I have going on with my son. That's actually how this horrible day began. With an email informing me that I have no venue to hold his fundraiser. Without a fundraiser, I have no way of paying for the necessary heart surgery he has to undergo within the next few weeks. No. I'm not a great mother. A great mother would have a way to fix this. A great mother would be more focused on a solution to her child's issues and less on her own relationship drama. Regret and guilt consume me. I've wasted enough time chasing my hormones. I need to get my shit together and focus on the priorities. "Thank you," is all I say. I have a million things on my mind right now. Hudson is just one of them. My job is another. Shit. My job. This is my party. I have to get out there. "Can you help me find a safety pin?" *Or five.*

"Probably in Nick's office," Alex replies. *Great.* Not what I wanted to hear. I do a few quick touch ups to my make up before I put on my badge of courage and hope to goodness that Nick did not go to his office. I'm not asking Alex to go with me. The last thing he needs is another encounter with Nick. So I head out of the bathroom and toward the stairs. He follows me. Is he asking for trouble? Idiot. "Alex, I've got it from here. Go home," I plead.

He stops walking and looks at me, his expression defiant. "I'm not leaving until you do. I want to make sure you're okay."

I appreciate the gesture but really, I've had all I can take for one day. I just want to fix my dress, wrap up this party, and go home. Maybe when I wake up this will all be a bad nightmare. I rub my temple with two fingers to try to ease off the impending migraine. "I'll be fine."

He's not listening. "And I'll be right here. Making sure of it," he pronounces.

Fine. You have a death wish? That's your dumb ass.

Thankfully Nick is not in his office. Or anywhere in the house from what I can tell. I fumble through a couple of desk drawers until I find some paperclips. This will have to do. I conjure up a couple of makeshift safety pins with the clips and fold the skirt of my dress under, pinning it in place at the seam on my waist so you can no longer see the rip. I actually didn't do half bad a job. It's dark and most everyone is drunk. I doubt they'll notice. Except that instead of floor length, my dress is now a few inches above my knee. Oh well. A girl's gotta do what a girl's gotta do.

Alex is standing watch, I assume, in the hall. When I come back into view he stares for a brief second and then swallows hard. "And I thought that dress couldn't get any better," he says with a sly grin.

I cock my head to the side and glare at him. Now is not the time for flirting. I walk past him without commenting. When we get to the doors leading onto the patio I place my hand on his chest to stop him from going any further. "You should probably just wait here," I warn. "I won't be long. And then we'll go."

His expression is one that suggests he doesn't believe me. "I promise," I assure him. "Ten minutes."

He nods and opens the door for me. I don't know why he insists on waiting. He really should just go. The only reason I'm still here is to save my ass. Since Nick so graciously informed the entire congregation of guests that I am responsible for this whole affair. Okay maybe that was a bad choice of words. *Function*. That's better. I find the guy I hired to man the fireworks display and tell him to lock and load. I don't care that we're thirty minutes ahead of schedule. Then I make my way through the crowd to the tent with the stage and wait until the band finishes their song before I take center stage.

"Hello ladies and gentlemen. I hope all of you have had a good time tonight. I know both Senator Knight and Mr. Chastain appreciate all your support." The crowd turns their attention to where I stand and I'm suddenly a little self-conscious. I wonder where Nick is. And if he's watching. I remind myself it doesn't matter because I have my reputation and business to think of. "We have one final surprise for you before we conclude the evening's events. Please turn your attention to the river for a one of a kind fireworks display to celebrate our nation's independence. Once again, thank you all for coming out. Please remember we offer a designated driving service for those of you who wish to take advantage. Enjoy the display!" I beam my best superficial smile and wave goodnight as I move to exit the stage.

Graham Batiste is standing at the edge, hand extended to escort me off. I politely accept. Even though I'd rather trip and fall on my face in front of all these people than let this asshole touch me. But here we are again with the reputation and saving face.

"Nice legs," he comments. *Gross.* I think I just threw up in my mouth a little.

I roll my eyes at him and he snickers. "You don't like being complimented?"

"I don't like being objectified," I reply.

His eyes grow wide along with his smile. "A woman with caliber. And looks. I can see why Nick is so infatuated."

I'm not in the mood for conversation. Especially not with Graham Batiste. "Speaking of Nick, have you seen him?" I ask, hoping to deter him from wanting to continue this….whatever it is.

He shakes his head and scans the crowd. "Not in a while. But if I do, I'll let him know you're looking."

I smile and nod. "Thanks."

"Heidi," he calls out as I turn to leave. I look over my shoulder without turning my body to face him. "I'm not as bad as you think I am," he utters. And instantly I feel bad for judging him. He probably isn't a bad guy. I can't imagine Nick would be such good friends with him if he were. I smile, genuinely this time, and nod my head at his declaration.

"I'm sure you aren't," I tell him. "Enjoy the rest of your night. I need to find Nick." It's a lie. I'm not going to find Nick. Mostly because Nick doesn't want to be found. Instead I go find Alex. And let him walk me to my Jeep so I can go home.

CHAPTER TWO
Heidi

Saturday, July 5

So much for waking up to last night just being one big fat nightmare. I slept in Hudson's bed. I guess I thought it would make me feel closer to him. And I needed to feel something. Anything. Other than pain and regret. It's six in the morning and I am wide awake so I decide to go for a run, something I haven't done in....well, now this is embarrassing. I can't remember the last time I went for a run. I make it through two miles without dying then come back inside for a shower.

An hour later I'm at my desk sipping on my second cup of coffee. The store isn't open yet but it doesn't have to be for me to go in. Being the owner has its advantages that way, you know. And I haven't exactly been focused on work the past week or two so I have a lot to catch up on. Since Hannah quit, I have my design projects plus her events to plan. Thank goodness Meghan has the organization jobs under control. I would have to add more hours to the day to be able to do it all. I plan on training Ashton to take over the event coordinating starting next week. It's one of the services I offer but it's my least favorite to head up so the sooner I can pass it off, the better. My heart is in design. That's what I love to do. If I could afford it, I'd do it for free. Have my own little non-profit design service. Everyone deserves to come home to their own little slice of heaven. So our little group of five has become an even littler group of four.

Shelly is the first to show up after me. When she walks in my office and finds me at my desk, she seems surprised. "You either woke up too early or are going to bed too late. Why are you not sexing it up with Senator McGorgeous?" *Get straight to the point why don't you?* She never has been one to beat around the bush. I'm one of the few who can appreciate her honesty and not think she's a complete bitch. I see it as part of her charm. And when I don't want to hear it,

I just tell her to shut up. It's not often that she listens, but I tell her anyway.

"In case you haven't noticed, I haven't exactly been getting much work done lately," I reply. I'm trying not to look at her. She knows me too well. She will figure out in a heartbeat that I'm full of crap.

"Is it the blonde bitch? Because I will totally kick her ass if you need me to." *Now that's a good friend.* Her comment actually makes me laugh. Partly because she's serious and it's cute. Shelly is all of 5'3 and couldn't kill a fly. And partly because of the irony. If Taylor hadn't ripped my dress with her hooker heels, I never would have gone inside. Alex would never have followed me, and I'd be in bed with Nick right now. But the truth is, as much as I would like to put this all on her, Taylor didn't screw this up. I did. I should have told Nick about Alex the minute I found out they were best friends. He would have either: listened and been okay with it or he would have written me off right then. At least then I might have had a chance to get out of this thing with no bruises. Now, it's too late. I've already fallen.

Ashton and Meghan interrupt our conversation with their arrival. I use the distraction to my advantage. "Hey I need you two to head the clean-up crew for the Knight event," I tell them as they walk by. All three girls look at me like I have a bomb strapped to my chest. *What? You've never heard of a boss telling her employees what to do?*

"Did I say something wrong?" I inquire. Ashton and Meghan shake their heads and purse their lips.

"Nope. Nothing wrong," they both reply as they first eye each other, then Shelly, before looking back at me.

"I have a lot of work to catch up on," I explain. "Hannah really left me in a bind." I hope I'm convincing. "I've already lined up a cleaning crew and the guard at the gate is expecting you."

Ashton is the first to respond. "What time do we need to be there?"

"Ten. So you should probably get going," I advise. Shelly is watching me closely as I continue to pretend to read my emails. Ashton and Meghan take down the address and go about their business.

Once they're gone, Shelly turns to me and glares. "Now you can tell me what happened. And don't give me that *I have a lot of work to do* crap."

Well I do. "Nothing happened. And I *do* have a lot of work to do." I persuade her.

She scoots back in her chair and gets comfortable. "Good thing I don't have plans. I can wait."

I growl at her. She's way too persistent. I guess it's better to get it out of the way so we can both get something done today. I hmmph and close my laptop. "Fine," I say, giving her an irritated scowl. "Nick and I had our fun and now it's over. Moving on."

"Moving on? Just like that?"

"Yes." She sits up, her body language indicating she is waiting for more. I roll my eyes. "You are relentless! He's not the first guy I've ever slept with and you never cared whether or not I talked to any of the others afterward," I remind her.

"He's different and you know it," she says.

"Different or not, it doesn't matter. He found out about Alex." I say that as if it's supposed to just explain everything.

"Oh," she says simply.

"Yeah. *Oh.* And he didn't stick around long enough for an explanation so there you have it."

"How did he find out? Oh god. Don't tell me you and Alex....*you know*...after you and Nick...*you know...*"

"No! God no," I say, exasperated. "Alex and I were talking and he walked in." I think for a second. "Well that's not *exactly* how it happened, but that's pretty much it." Shelly's eyes widen and she nods her head forward, urging me to expound. I let out a long huff. "I had a rip in my dress. Couldn't reach the zipper. Nick was busy."

"Soooo you thought it would be a good idea to just have Alex undress you?"

Well it sounds horrible when you say it out loud. "Not undress me. Just start my zipper. But he hadn't even done that yet when Nick walked in. He hadn't even touched me. Nick jumped to conclusions." I roll my eyes at the memory. "So he asked if Alex and I had...ever..." I can't even finish the sentence.

"And you told him? Are you stupid?"

"That's kind of a big deal. And I wasn't going to lie."

Shelly closes her eyes and shakes her head in disbelief. "Did you at least explain that it was before you knew him?"

"We didn't get that far. Something related to *'get the fuck out'* followed shortly after."

"So you just left?"

"Yep."

"Without trying to talk to him?"

"Yep."

"You have to tell him what happened." Shelly's tone is determined. Like if I don't tell Nick, she will. *Please don't.*

"He doesn't want to hear it Shelly. Look, it was great while it lasted. Time to move on. Shit happens."

"That's a great attitude. Someone should put that in a greeting card. So positive and encouraging."

I glare at her and open my laptop again, hoping she takes the hint that the conversation is over. Thankfully she does, but instead of just getting aggravated and walking out of my office like she normally would, she walks around to where I sit and gives me a hug. "We'll fix this. You two have to work. Giving up is not an option. Getting drunk is, though. Maybe you should go for some whiskey amnesia tonight. Five shots. I hear it's a great painkiller." She kisses me on the cheek and goes back to her desk in the front of the store.

A few minutes later I smell cookies baking. Yum! The girl knows how to cheer me up.

Three hours later I have finished as much work as my brain can handle and decide to close up for the day. We don't typically stay open all day on Saturday anyway. Ashton and Meghan haven't made it back yet and I let Shelly go home an hour ago. I have the radio blasting and I am singing Ed Sheeran to the top of my lungs when my phone rings. "I see you're still speaking to me," Alex says when I answer.

"Of course I'm speaking to you. Why wouldn't I be?" That's just ridiculous.

"You mean, apart from the obvious?"

I don't blame him for what happened last night. He was drunk. Drunk people say things. I should have been honest with Nick from the moment I found out he and Alex were friends. There's no one to blame but myself. I am woman enough to admit that.

"Don't do that. Last night was last night. Today is a new day. How are you feeling?" I think about his cuts and bruises and what he must look like. And feel like.

"I've been better," he says. "And I've been worse." I can't imagine that, but if he says so...

"What do you have planned for tonight?" he asks.

Oh no. I think he's confused. I said I was okay with talking to him. Never said seeing each other was a good idea. As a matter of fact, it's probably the worst possible idea right now.

"Shelly suggested maybe having a drink." It's not a lie. She did say I should have a drink. Although she didn't say she would be having one with me like I am making it sound. I know he wants to apologize. Or talk. He always has been a talker. Me? Not so much.

"A drink might not be a bad idea," he says. "Let me know if your plans fall through. I'd like to see you."

He means *'I'd like to have a semi-serious conversation with you and make this awkward for both of us'.*

"Okay," I say. Even though I have no intentions on seeing him tonight. My plans are to stop by Rouse's, grab a bottle of whiskey, and take Shelly up on her five shot challenge. According to her after the fifth shot, you forget why you started drinking in the first place.

Just as I get off the phone with Alex, Meghan and Ashton get back from Nick's. Meghan walks in my office and slaps an envelope down on my desk. "He said to make sure you get this," she says.

I arch an eyebrow at her and slowly open the envelope. God I hope it isn't a letter. That's about as bad as sending a text. It isn't. It's a check. For two thousand dollars. I have to look at it twice. Even *if* I had planned on invoicing him for the event, which I hadn't, his total bill was only a little over a thousand dollars. Why would he pay double? And how did he know what to pay to begin with? "What is this?" I ask just before Meghan turns to walk out.

She looks at me like I have just asked her what my name is. "Um, it's a check. You take it to the bank and they give you money for it," she explains with a smirk.

No kidding. "You don't say!" I tease. "I meant, why did he send it? And how did he know what amount?"

"I don't know what happened with you two, but you both have some serious shit to work out."

That doesn't answer my question.

"From the little that I did understand of what he was saying, he didn't care what you were charging him. He said if that's not enough, send him a bill. I'm pretty sure he was drunk. So most of what he said didn't make any sense," she continues.

"Drunk? At ten in the morning?" Well he's got me beat by a few hours. Then again he is a little more familiar with whiskey than I am. And he doesn't have clients and timelines to worry about.

"Yeah. Pretty sure. Anyway, we're going to head out. You okay?"

"Why wouldn't I be okay?" I'm wondering if he said something. Why else would she say we had stuff to work out? "Did Nick say something else?"

She shrugs. I don't move my eyes from hers. She gets the hint and spills. "I told you he just rambled. He asked why you weren't there. If you were sick or something. I told him you were at the office catching up on work. Then he started laughing and saying something about "not finishing what you started" and "reviewing your contract" and how he should call your lawyer. Then he laughed again and mumbled on about killing a mother fucker. Like I said....serious shit to work out. I have a lunch date with Josh. Are we good?"

"Yeah, thanks. Have fun on your date." I replay her conversation with Nick in my head, processing what he told her. I assume he was taking a shot at Alex with the whole "call my lawyer" comment. I can't believe he was drunk already. Way to act like a grown up, Senator. At least I am waiting until *after* work to hammer down the whiskey.

~~~~~~

Since Shelly ditched me for her boyfriend and I am stuck knocking back shots by myself, I decide to share the experience with her via Snapchat. In a series of videos. I know. I didn't really think it through.

Video One: I am sitting at my bar. Bottle of Jack in one hand, shot glass in front of me.

"According to my best friend Shelly, whiskey gives you amnesia. So here's my five shot challenge....Let's see if she's right." I down the first shot. *Oh god! It burns! This is horrible.* My eyes squint shut and my lips pucker as the liquid gold settles. "Woah. That was...not good."

Video Two: Still sitting at the bar. I pour another shot. "Maybe it's supposed to get better as you go. Shot number two. Bottoms up." *Nope. Not much better. Lungs still burning.* I stick my tongue out and exhale loudly. "People actually drink this on purpose? What the hell is wrong with them? What the hell is wrong with *me*?"

Video Three: I pour my third shot. Still sitting at the bar but having a little trouble sitting up straight on the backless stool. I adjust myself and sit up straight. "As you can see, Shelly, I am *so not* enjoying this. But I am not a quitter dammit!" I throw back the shot and scowl at the camera. It only burns for a second this time. "And as for you, Mr. Know-it-all, I *do* finish what I start. See?" I hold up the empty shot glass and flash a sarcastic grin.

Video Four: I have decided to move my party of one to the living room. It's a little more comfortable here on the floor. Not as far to fall. *If* I should happen to fall. I place the shot glass on the coffee table and pour, spilling a little over the top. "Oh shit! Oops!" I wipe the spill with my hand, not realizing I've only just made it worse. A lone strand of hair has fallen out of my bun and is hanging in front of my eye. But I don't care. I just blow it out of the way so I can take my fourth shot. "Almost there!" I hold the glass up like I'm toasting the camera. "Shell-eeee! You're missing all the fun. Cheers!" Right about then an upbeat song about shaking off players and haters comes on the Pandora station and I immediately start singing along. And dancing. Dancing wasn't the best idea. I can't help it though. Who wouldn't want to dance to this song? The beat is contagious. I spill the whiskey. My mouth falls open and my eyes grow wide as I stare at the wet spot on my shirt in exaggerated disbelief. "Better get a refill." I pour another shot and quickly down it before I have another accident. This one goes down pretty easily.

Video Five: "Last one Shelly. I did it!" I pour the last shot. Without spilling. I smile proudly. "And you're right. I don't remember why I'm doing this. Are you even watching?" I look into the camera as if I'm trying to see if Shelly is somehow going to be on the other side of the lens. The song mentions something about heartbreakers and I suddenly remember the *why.* I point at the camera. "You are *not* a *Knight* in shining armor." I chuckle to myself at the pun. "You're just an asshole in tin foil. And you are a heartbreaker. But I don't have to tell you that. You already know. It's what you do. And I'm the dummy who fell for you." I hold the shot glass up. "But now I'm forgetting. Forgetting *allll* about you." And I take the last shot.

Strong, bare arms and a warm chest hold me close. I'm being carried. And I'm naked. What the hell? I blink twice and try to focus on the face in front of me. I try to wiggle my way out of his arms. He just pulls me closer. "Ssssh. I'm just giving you a bath, love." *Alex.* Why? How? Huh? Did I let him in?
I hear the faucet running and know we're in my bathroom now. Alex lowers me into the tub of warm water. Oh yes. This feels nice. I could sleep here. I sink down further into the water. I finally open my eyes all the way and look at him. He has taken his shirt off and is kneeling on the floor in front of me. His lip is better. Just a small cut. But the gash above his eye is still pretty bad. Wait. Are those stitches? His cheek is bruised and still bears the evidence of last night. I reach out to touch his face but he halts me. He shakes his head "no" and places my hand back in the tub.
"How did you get in? Why are you here? And *why* did you just stick me in the bathtub?" I realize it's a lot of questions at once but hopefully he's sober. He can catch up.
His mouth spreads into a wide grin. "You let me in. I've just witnessed an incredibly interesting series of videos. And.....you have what I assume to be vomit in your hair." *Oh god.* That's embarrassing.

I move to sit up so I can inspect the damage but again, he stops me. "Lie back. I'll do it."

"I can wash my own hair, Alex."

He fills a cup with water from the tub and begins pouring it over my head. His hand is at the back of my neck, holding me still. *Okay have it your way.*

He continues pouring until every lock is saturated. I hand him the shampoo, a silent act of permission to continue. He smiles and squeezes the liquid into his palm. He massages my scalp gently. It's very intimate. My body is suddenly hyper aware of its nakedness. But the feeling of his fingers kneading through my hair is too good for me to ask him to stop.

When he's finished rinsing out my hair, he sets the cup on the floor and stares at me. Just briefly though. He waits for the dirty water to drain before he starts running more. Once the tub is full, he reaches for my pouf and covers it with my favorite body wash. I watch intently, my heart pounding, waiting on his next move. *Touch me.* No, don't. *Or do.* Crap, I don't even know any more. My brain is fighting with the whiskey. And the whiskey is winning. Thankfully, Alex is in his right mind because he hands me the lathered up pouf. "Just call for me when you're ready to get out." And then he stands and walks out of the room. *Whew.* That might have been bad.

CHAPTER THREE
Heidi

 I made it through drying off and slipping into some pajama bottoms and a tank top all by myself. I smile proudly to myself as I walk out of my bedroom into the living room where Alex is sitting on my sofa. He's focused on something on the screen of his phone. Shortly after the bedroom door opens, he looks up. "I thought I told you to call me when you got out," he says.

I look around the room before narrowing my eyes at him, as if I'm trying to remember, even though I never actually forgot. "Did you? Hmmm."

He stands and walks into the kitchen, grabbing a glass from the counter. He meets me back where I am standing, watching him, and holds the glass out. "Here, take this." He moves to place a small pill in my hand.

"Are you trying to give me roofies?" I kid.

He eyes me warily. "Of course. Because you aren't quite drunk enough for me to take advantage of." There's a slight hint of amusement in his tone and his eyes twinkle a bit. I don't entertain it. "What? Didn't think that was funny?"

I shrug nonchalantly. "Eh, jury's still out." I catch the double meaning behind my statement and laugh at myself. Like hysterically. Though I'm pretty sure it's not that funny. In between deep breaths I say, "Oh god that's so funny. See? Because you're a lawyer. And I said 'the jury's out.' Like in a courtroom? Get it?" I'm slapping his shoulder as I speak.

He just stares at me, trying to appear unmoved, but I see his mouth twitch. He wants to laugh. He just doesn't.

"I forget you're a lawyer. But I guess it does explain a lot. Like the loft, for one." I have stopped laughing and caught my breath now. "I mean, I kind of wondered how a guy who teaches kickboxing classes could spring for a loft like that but hey....who am I to judge?" I start laughing again. "Judge. Oh goodness. No wonder there are so many bad lawyer jokes out there. It's so *easy*."

He remains stoic. I grab the glass and the pill from him, mimicking his unrelenting expression. I let out an exaggerated huff. "Fine. Give me the drink." I swallow. "What's it for anyway?"

He chuckles. "To help with the headache you're bound to wake up with."

Well that's thoughtful. "Oh. Thanks," I tell him, downing the rest of the cranberry juice. I guess he wants to make sure I'm peeing properly too.

Alex takes the empty glass from my hand and puts it in the kitchen. I'm still standing in the spot where he left me when he comes back in the living room. He lifts me up and carries me into my bedroom like a groom would carry his bride on their wedding night. He gently lays me down on the bed. "You know you're supposed to wait for the pill to kick in before you throw me in bed?" I tease.

I notice the corner of his mouth twitch like he wants to smile again but holds back to prove a point. "Get some rest Heidi," he says as he pulls the white down comforter up over my body. I snuggle into my pillow. I never noticed how cozy my pillows are. My blanket too for that matter. Wow. I have a really comfortable bed. I pull the covers up to my chin and look at Alex imploringly.

"Stay with me," I petition him. My bottom lip pokes out and I bat my eyelashes. He looks at me with that calculating expression he gets when he's thinking of the right thing to say to me. "I don't want to be alone." This time I'm not joking or teasing him. It's the cold, hard truth. I'm drunk and I'm weak. The only thing I want to do right now is the very last thing I need to do right now. And that is call Nick. I'm not sure if I would cuss him out or beg him to come see me. Before I assaulted that bottle of whiskey, all I could think about was what I would say to him if I were to call him. Or see him. No. I don't want to be alone. Although I can't believe I actually admitted it. Out loud. I blow out the breath I've been holding in.

Alex looks at me apologetically. "I'm not the gay friend who holds you while you cry yourself to sleep," he begins. "I can't be responsible for the way my body will react to lying next to you all night, love," he explains. "It's just not a good idea."

I hear what he's saying, but I refuse to listen. I pull back the comforter and pat the empty spot next to me. Then I nod my head toward the pillow. He closes his eyes and tilts his head back, running his fingers through his curly hair.

Reluctantly he walks around to the other side of the bed and climbs in, fully clothed, and lies with his hands behind his head as he stares at the ceiling. I'm guessing it's a tactic he's using to make sure he doesn't touch me. I grin proudly to myself.

It's been a few minutes since I switched off the lamp beside the bed. Neither one of us has moved. Neither one of us has spoken. But somehow just having him here makes me feel better.

"Mind if I ask you something?" he finally says, breaking the silence. I roll over to my side so I can face him. "Nope. Go for it." I wait for something intense and personal. He hesitates a moment before continuing.

"Did you have salad for lunch?"

Did I have salad for lunch? I think for a second. "No. A burrito. Why?" *Oh god. No.* I immediately remember him washing vomit out of my hair. Followed by a memory of some pretty intense throwing up on the living room floor. And then the dry heaves. Those are the worst. I'm pretty sure it was right after that, that I blacked out. He had to have seen it. He washed it out of my hair for crying out loud. Gross. Well, this is embarrassing. I groan. "Ohhhh mannnn. Alex. Oh god I'm sorry you had to see that."

He laughs. Just a short chuckle, but it's cute. Even though it's dark, I can picture his wide grin. "It was incredibly disgusting," he says. I can tell by his tone he's just giving me a hard time. But I still feel bad. "Okay! I said I'm sorry…"

He chuckles again. "And the smell…."

I smack his chest playfully. "Alex! I already feel bad enough."

He brings one arm down and places it under my head, pulling me to his chest. Then he places a soft kiss on the top of my head. And just as quickly, as if I had burned him, he pulls his arm away again. "Shit," he swears under his breath.

I know the gesture was strictly instinct and I can't blame him for that. I'm an asshole. I shouldn't have asked him to stay. Maybe this was a bad idea. Or maybe I should take the opportunity to get it all out in the open. I can always blame it on the alcohol. I mean, I *have* already maneuvered through the four stages of drunk. I started at angry drunk. Moved on to vomiting drunk. Then nonsensical drunk. And now…emotionally honest drunk.

I scoot closer to him and nuzzle my head against his shoulder. "It could have been you, you know," I confess. He inhales a deep breath through his nose but doesn't say anything. "The one who broke me. It could have been you. If I had just let you in. It would have been easy." *Way to go heartbreaker.* Oh well. The words are out. Can't take them back now. I close my eyes and wait for his reply, hoping maybe by some miracle he didn't hear me. Or maybe he's asleep. Kind of like how when you were little and you thought a monster was in your room so you hid under the covers, thinking that if you couldn't see it, then it couldn't see you. Maybe if I just lay real still and quiet…..

Alex lets out the breath he inhaled and swallows hard. *Oh crap.* Here we go. Me and my stupid word vomit. The crazy thing is, I think I meant what I said. Not that I feel about Alex the way I feel about Nick. Not even close. Night and day. But I could see myself getting comfortable with Alex before I met Nick. It wouldn't have been as fierce and as passionate as what Nick and I had. But it would have been good.

"You aren't broken," he tells me. "Because you aren't the type of woman to let herself become broken. You're cracked. Not shattered. And you will be okay. Because you are strong. And you are not alone."

I want to believe him. I want his words to be true. But I don't feel strong. I feel shattered. But one thing I don't feel is alone. And that's a good enough start.

He runs his fingers softly up and down my arm, soothing me, coaxing me to sleep. He is warm. And strong. And completely selfless. My mind is exhausted and my eyes are getting heavy. I don't have the energy to respond. I just want to sleep.

Sunday, July 6

I wake up alone, although I could swear that's not how I went to bed. Did I imagine Alex being here? I try to muster up a play by play of last night's events. Oh no. The videos. I check my phone in a panic, cringing at the thought of what responses I might find. What if Nick saw them? Surely he would have called by now if he had. Or maybe he's really mad enough at me that he doesn't care.

I scroll down until I've gone all the way back to three days ago and no videos. What the hell? I check the videos on my phone. Nothing. Not from last night anyway. Am I losing my freaking mind? Maybe I forgot to hit record? Shelly says whiskey gives you amnesia. I say it gives you hallucinations.

Either way, I'm thankful for Imaginary Alex and his magical little pill. I don't have a headache. Or an upset stomach. But I am starving. Probably because I emptied the contents of my insides all over my living room floor last night. Or maybe I dreamed that too because there are no signs of my Burrito Grande anywhere to be found.

After I fry myself an egg and some bacon, I spend the rest of the day eating homemade brownies, watching Lifetime movies, and hating happily ever afters. Halfway through the third movie I get a text from Alex.

Alex: You know you snore when you're drunk.
Me: I do not!
Alex: Oh you definitely do. How's the hangover?
Me: There isn't one. I made Jack Daniels my bitch.
Alex: So you're ready to have another go at it then?
Me: Taking the day off.
Alex: That's probably for the best. Hungry?
Me: Overdosing on chocolate as we speak.
Alex: We should discuss rehab.
Me: Rehab is for quitters. I'll just have to double up on my kickboxing ;)
Alex: Are you flirting with me?
Me: Goodbye Alex
Alex: We were just getting to the good part.
Me: This is reality. There are no good parts.
Alex: I've got plenty of good parts ;)
Me: Okay, now you're flirting. Bye Alex.
Alex: You scared? Say you're scared.

I choose not to respond. Alex had managed to make me smile for the first time today. And I prefer to sulk and hate people who smile at text messages.

Monday, July 7

I've already been at work about a half hour when Shelly walks in. The plan is to be out of the building by the end of the month so I have a few projects to wrap up before we take our mandatory leave of absence. I will continue to work while we set up shop at our new place, which I have yet to find. I'm just going to have to go back to the good old days when my sunroom was my office and Shelly popped in once or twice a week for updates. I'm a big girl. I can handle it. It actually works out well because I will need to be home with Hudson for a while once he has his surgery. Dr. Collins assured me the recovery time for this type of heart surgery is only a few weeks and Hudson will bounce back just fine. Easy for her to say. It's not her child they're patching up. I still haven't figured out how I'm going to afford the down payment, but I will. Hey, maybe Nick has a few lonely senator friends who need a "date." Close your mouth. You watch the news. We all know it happens. If you're gonna be a *date for hire*, you might as well be a high class one, right? I know. I know. That's crazy talk. I'm kidding anyway. Besides, I've slept with enough of his friends already. Oh god. Why does every thought I have lead to Nick Knight? I'm going to drive myself crazy.

Shelly walks into my office and plops down in the chair in front of my desk. She's smiling an over-enthusiastic smile and watching me type. Her bright red lipstick makes her teeth look extra white today.

"Whatcha doin?" she asks cheerfully.

"Making money," I reply just as cheerfully. Only my tone is fake. I wonder if she noticed.

"Did you kiss and make up with Senator Six Pack?"

I roll my eyes and shake my head. "Not quite. I took your advice and had a date with a guy named Jack."

"Go get em party girl!" She sits up straight and moves her arms in circles over her head like she's dancing. Or twirling a lasso. However you want to look at it. I can't help but laugh at her movements.

"Party of one maybe," I reply.

Shelly stops moving and cocks her head at me. "Damn. So no witnesses?" She looks disappointed.

"I may have posted a couple of videos to my story. Alex saw them and staged an intervention. He showed up at my apartment just in time to wash what was left of my lunch out of my hair. Woohoo! Party time!" I exaggerate the last part for dramatic effect.

She has slouched a little in her chair and I have her full attention now. Her smile is gone and her expression tells me she's still processing what I just told her. "Ew. That man is a saint."

"Tell me about it." I close my laptop and lean back in my chair. For just a moment I look up at the ceiling, collecting my thoughts. "You know the thing is, I *know* Alex is a great guy. He makes me smile. He shows up when I don't want to be alone. He cleans up my puke and puts me to bed. But I wanted it to be Nick. So much. The whole time, I wished it had been him. Is that horrible?"

When I look back down to face Shelly, she is leaning forward over my desk, reaching for my hand. She sighs a sympathetic sigh and sticks her bottom lip out in a pout. "No babe. That's what we who actually participate in the dating world call normal. Go talk to him. Just explain what happened."

I let go of her hand and look at her like she just asked me to tell the Queen she has spinach in her teeth. There's no way I can do that. "Right. And he's going to actually sit through the whole thing, hear me out, and forgive me immediately. Because that's how it works in fairy tales and the movies." My tone is sarcastic and my words are short. I don't mean to lash out at Shelly. She's just trying to help. Because that's what best friends do. I make sure to soften my tone before continuing. "You didn't see him the other night. He was…..done. Past angry. Past hurt. It was like it made him physically ill to look at me. How do you fix that? How do you take that back?" I feel myself cringe at the thought of never seeing Nick again. Never speaking to him. Never touching him. Life was much easier when I made myself numb to all of this.

"I don't know," she says. This is Serious Shelly. Not Sarcastic Shelly or Witty Shelly. This is my lifelong best friend who cries when I cry and hurts when I hurt. "But I do know you have to try."

24

I want to try. I need to try. I owe it to myself to at least try. "You know that feeling you get sometimes? You go to school. You start a career. Do something with your life. You keep yourself busy enough. Go out with friends. Spend time with family. And for the most part, you're happy. But at the end of the day when you lie in bed, just before you fall asleep, there's this feeling. Like you have more to work for. More to do. More to find. *Something* is missing." I look at Shelly to try to mentally convey the emotions I can't quite put into words. "When I found Nick, that feeling went away. I stopped looking for more. I had everything I needed. I felt like for once, I was whole. Nothing was missing. I had found the *something*. Without even trying or knowing *what* it was that was missing. He was it."
I blink back tears, regain my composure, and a thought occurs to me. "What if he doesn't want me to try? What if he's already past it? *'Oh well, didn't work with the designer. Moving on'* What if I'm not his *something* like he is my *something*?" A million things go through my head at once. None of them positive. "What if that's why he sent extra money? Just in case. To make sure there were no loose ends. To be done with me. Because that's what he wants." The thought of him writing me off so easily makes me sick to my stomach.

"You're overthinking it Heidi. Stop sabotaging your own happiness. A man doesn't just sit in a woman's office for three hours waiting for her to come in, if she's not his *something*."
I remember that day. It was the day after I found out he and Alex were best friends. I wanted to end it all right then. I tried. I was ready to make a clean break from both of them. And then Nick showed up in my office. With his irresistible smile and that magnetic force that makes it impossible for me to stay away from him.
"Okay genius, how? How do I explain? Sure, I could tell Nick what happened with Alex was before I had ever even met him. And that would be easy…If I hadn't pretended not to even know Alex. And now I'm supposed to tell Nick that I was already having sex with him? *Hey Nick, I know I lied about not knowing him before, but I swear I'm telling the truth this time.*"

I prop my elbows up on my desk and fold my hands together, using them as a chin rest, while I wait for a response. It's all a matter of which lie he should believe. And either way, the truth is, I lied. Let this be a life lesson- lying sucks. No matter what reason you have for doing it.

Just as Shelly was getting ready to dish out some more of her infinite wisdom, a young man peeks his head in the door. "Heidi Lemaire?" He's holding a large gold envelope. He's probably no more than twenty-one years old. And I really hope he didn't overhear the last part of our conversation. I stand to greet him. "I'm Heidi. How can I help you?"

He stretches out his hand, extending the envelope to me. "This is for you."

CHAPTER FOUR
Nick

All it took was one look and I was done. One look at those beautiful bright green eyes. Her contagious smile. That fucking perfect little mouth. Her spirit, her determination, her fire. It was all there in that look. One look and Heidi Lemaire had captured my soul. Falling for her was like stepping in quicksand. The more I fought it, the deeper I went. So I stopped fighting. And she consumed me.

Ironically, it was also with one look that she destroyed me. No words. I realized all I needed to know when she looked at me. The apology. The regret. The truth. It was all there. When I asked if she had slept with Nate. That one look was my answer.

I wonder what his girlfriend would think about all this. By the way he talked about her I would have bet all my chips on him being totally whipped. That goes to show how much I know. I might just have to fuck her. Let's see how he feels about *that*. I remember the day Nate first met Heidi. It was in my office. She left distracted that day and I didn't hear from her until the following day when I tracked her down at her store. Is that when it started? Was it a one-time thing? Of course not. I know from experience one time with Heidi is never enough.

Watching them while I gave my speech at the fundraiser, the way he looked at her, I knew in my gut something was up. Shit I can't blame Nate. Heidi isn't an easy woman to say no to.

I said I can't blame him. That doesn't mean I have to forgive him. After I handed Nate the ass whooping he deserved, well he deserved more than he got but I stopped myself for Heidi's sake, I spent the rest of the night on my boat. Which probably wasn't the best idea since all I could think about was the day I had Heidi grinding on my thigh until she came apart right there in front of my eyes. Going inside the house didn't help much either, since I had some pretty explicit memories of her on the kitchen counter, in the bedroom, in the bathroom, and right here in my office bent over this very desk.

This is why I don't bring women outside of the guest room. I don't need constant reminders. Everywhere I look, there she is.

I'm on my second bottle of Johnnie Walker in forty-eight hours. I'm the drunkest I've ever been and Monica is standing in my fucking door way staring at me the way she stares at her daughter, Olivia, when she's disobeying. Well I'm not a kid and she's not my mother so she can fuck off. I'm not in the mood to listen to her bullshit.

"Snap out of it asshole," she tells me.

I'm leaning back in my chair with my bare feet comfortably propped up on the desk in front of me. I don't even think about what I look like. I did manage to shower Saturday night. My hair is left exactly the way it dried and I'm pretty sure I'm not wearing underwear underneath the jeans I threw on. Fuck a shirt.

"Have a drink, Monica. Lighten the fuck up." I offer her the bottle. When she glares at me, I shrug and pour more into my half empty glass.

"Why don't you *grow* the fuck up? You can't drink all your problems away, Nick. This is ridiculous. You weren't even this bad when Elise left."

Like I said....not in the mood for her bullshit. "Unless you're here to have a drink, or suck my dick, find something else to do. You're my housekeeper, not my therapist."

If she could shoot lasers from her eyeballs, I'd be toast. "You're pathetic."

I wink at her as I take another drink. I laugh to myself as I watch her walk out of my office. Like I offended her or something. Her mouth didn't have a problem with my dick when *she* was the one broken hearted and fucked up. Oh well. Her loss.

Maybe I do have a habit of drinking away my demons. So what. It helps. It keeps me numb and it helps me sleep. Which is a whole hell of a lot better than walking around pretending like nothing ever happened. Or worse, walking around constantly reminding myself that it did.

I wasn't sure whether to be relieved or pissed off Saturday when Heidi didn't show up to take down the decorations scattered across my backyard from Friday night's fundraising event.

Part of me was hoping to see her. Even though I have nothing to say. Just to *see* her. To remind myself she's real. That the whole thing wasn't some fucked up nightmare. Or maybe I wanted it to be a nightmare. She would walk in and tell me none of that shit with Nate really happened. But she didn't show up. And not only did she not show up, her assistants told me she's fine. Just fucking peachy. Back to work as usual. Like nothing happened. Like she didn't fuck my best friend. Like she didn't take my world and shake it up, throw it down, and stomp on it.

I sent a check back to her office. She never sent me a bill, but her assistant was pretty good at guessing on a total. I made sure to send extra, a lot extra, thinking either one of two things would happen. One, she would get offended that I assumed what she was worth and call and cuss me out for paying without a bill. She likes to run her business by the book. Very professional. I remember the way she would call to confirm her appointments with me. That seems like forever ago. Or two, she would get offended that I sent extra and call and cuss me out. She did neither. I didn't hear from her. Not even a text. I almost dial her number three times but change my mind. Monica is right, sitting here staring at my phone is pathetic. So I just keep drinking. Until I pass out.

I'm not sure how I got in my bed or how long I slept but at some point in the middle of the night I went downstairs and made myself an egg sandwich. I really need to get my act together before leaving for Washington D.C. on Tuesday. Nothing a glass of water and some aspirin can't fix. That's when I remembered setting up a meeting at my office with Halliburton.

Thank goodness I doubled up on the aspirin. When I woke up this morning I felt like death. I can imagine what I'd have felt like if I hadn't gotten a head start.

When I get to work, Candace has a message for me from Elise. She's been calling me for a month now. At first it was two or three times a day. Now it's more like once or twice a week.

I'm not even remotely curious what she wants. Her texts say she just wants to talk but I know that's bullshit. No one ever *just wants to talk*. There's always a motive behind every conversation and I don't have time to find out what hers is. Elise dropped to last on my list of priorities when I found out she had been fucking my best friend Matthew. That was over four years ago and I'm over being mad or even giving a shit, but that doesn't mean we're going to start hanging out on the weekends. I'm starting to believe I need to keep any future girlfriends away from my friends. *Girlfriend. Was Heidi my girlfriend?* I don't know. I do know everything was different with her. And it wasn't just Heidi that was different. I was different because of her. From the first day she walked out of my office, there wasn't a minute of the day I wasn't thinking of her.

Finding out about Elise and Matthew was painful, but over time I have come to think it was more about being pissed off for taking a shot to the ego than anything. Here was this woman I had given everything to, done everything for, and promised to be with forever….and it still wasn't good enough. With Elise I never looked back. I never thought twice. It was like flipping a switch. When it was over, it was over.

Finding out about Heidi and Nate was different. It was like finding out Santa Claus isn't real or the sky isn't blue. Like I'm not ready to accept it yet. Like I need more proof. I had been living in this fantasy world with this perfect fantasy woman and I would have dared a mother fucker to tell me it wasn't real. I had found the one thing I didn't even know I had been looking for. It was more than just being comfortable or having a good time. More than two people liking the same things and holding a decent conversation. Every time I was near Heidi, and even the times I wasn't, there was this unseen force pulling us together. I felt her touch before she ever laid a hand on me. I inhaled her scent before she ever came close. And I tasted her before our lips ever touched. I respected and admired her as a woman and a mother. I wanted to know all of her secrets. To tell her all of mine. I wanted to share her laughter and heal her pain. I had only just begun to show Heidi what I could give.

All of that was stolen from me. Snatched right out of my hands. And there's not a mother fucking thing I can do about it. I want it back. I want *her* back. Fuck pride. Part of me wants to take Heidi to some far away fucking place and show her why she should choose me. Part of me is screaming back that her choice has already been made.

She's a grown woman and knew what she was doing when she spread her legs for my best friend. But most of me wants to beat the holy hell out of Nathan Alexander for ever touching her. My mind goes back to Friday night. The moment I walked in my bedroom and saw him standing behind her. Whispering in her ear, touching her, looking at her the way I look at her when I want her.

Pride wins. I'm not calling her. I'm not taking her anywhere. From this moment on, I'm going to do my best to forget her.

Two hours later my wallet is half a million dollars heavier thanks to a new partnership with the guys at Halliburton. I'm wrapping up a radio interview when I hear yelling outside my office near Candace's desk.

My first thought is of Heidi and I'm suddenly anxious. So much for forgetting her. I want to see her about as much as I don't want to see her. And I have no idea what would come out of my mouth if I did actually see her.

Grow some fucking balls Nick and stop hiding behind those doors.

I take a deep breath and open the double doors to my office.

"Nick. They told me you weren't here."

She's standing there in a pair of skin tight jeans, heels, and a long sleeve, white shirt that buttons up, only she's left the top three undone to display her ample cleavage. Her long black hair falls over her shoulders and she's smiling at me like we're reuniting on Oprah.

Elise. I mentally kick my own ass for not returning her phone calls.

"Because that's what I pay them to do," I say flatly as my eyes move over her body, taking in her obvious effort to appear seductive. "But I've apparently underestimated your determination."

She giggles and looks up at me, batting her unnaturally long eyelashes. Just another part of her that's fake.

"Come on Nick. You know me. When I want something....." She trails off into thought at the end of her sentence and licks her lips. If she thinks she's turning me on she's fucking crazy.

I look over to Candace, who has one hand on the phone receiver. I assume she's preparing to call security. My expression is apologetic. I feel sorry for anyone who has to deal with Elise. "Thank you

Candace. I'll handle it from here." She nods and puts the phone down.

I open the door to my office, inviting Elise inside. "Since you're here, you might as well come in and tell me what you want." She brushes against me when she walks past and I shudder. God I hope this is not why she's here.

She takes a seat in one of the chairs in front of my desk. She looks exactly the way she did when I left her. I sit back in my chair and wish I had a drink. "So. What is it?" I ask. "It's obviously important since you can't seem to take the hint and leave me alone."

She pokes her bottom lip out and cocks her head to one side, staring at me with wide eyes. This over exaggerated expression lasts a few seconds before she lets out an exasperated huff and rolls her eyes. "Tell me you're not still mad at me."

"I'm not still mad at you."

She leans forward, her arms squeezing her breasts together. I'm guessing she thinks I give a shit about her tits. I don't. "Good. I miss you."

I knew this was coming. "What happened? Bad play on the stock market? Matthew lose all his money?"

She looks offended. "That was rude. And no. He didn't. Is it so hard to believe I just miss you?"

I stand and start to walk around my desk toward the door. "Well thanks for sharing that. It was great seeing you. Take care." She's wasting my time and I don't have the energy to entertain her. I am still fighting a hangover and I have to go home and pack.

She reaches out and grabs my arm. "Nick, wait. There's another reason I want to talk to you."

I close my eyes and pinch the bridge of my nose. Games. She's still playing her fucking games.

I open my eyes again and find her fidgeting. She's nervous. Elise is never nervous. I loosen up hoping it will help her relax. "I'm listening," I tell her.

"It's about Monica," she starts. She takes in a deep breath then continues, "We know you've been taking care of her." She says this like I'm harboring a fugitive or holding her captive or something. Like it's a horrible thing to do. "I never understood why you thought she was your obligation anyway." She shakes her head as if she's trying to erase the thought. Like her brain is an etch-a-sketch.

I stuff my hands in my pockets and wait for her to get to the point. "Well she graduates soon and she has to know her gravy train is about to leave the station."

Gravy train? Nice. I don't expect her to understand why I do what I do for Monica and Olivia. The good thing is, I don't have to explain it to her, or anyone else. It's my choice to help them and I don't need anyone's approval.

"Did you know she took Matthew to court?"

What the fuck? No, I didn't know that. Why? He's never done anything for her or his daughter. Why would Monica think he would start now just because she has a piece of paper from a judge?

"I've been busy. We haven't had much time to talk," I reply, realizing the harsh truth in my answer. Monica usually has dinner ready for me the nights I fly in from Washington. She has my laundry done and my bags packed when it's time for me to leave again. I spend Saturday afternoons teaching Olivia how to swim or to play the piano. But this past month I have been so wrapped up in Heidi, I haven't had more than two conversations with Monica. So no wonder I don't know what she's got going on.

"They went last month. She thought she was going to just flash her pretty smile and get what she wanted." Elise rolls her eyes in disgust.

"Since when is wanting a father to take responsibility for his child such a bad thing?" I unintentionally raise my voice a notch. This conversation is not going in her favor. She's just going to end up pissing me off. She stands and glares at me defensively.

"It's not. When the man you're dragging through the mud actually *is* the father."

Hold on. There's no way I heard her right. "What the fuck are you saying Elise?"

She shrugs and smirks at me. "Matthew isn't Olivia's father. The judge ordered a paternity test."

Elise places her hand on my shoulder in a gesture to calm me as she continues. "She's been playing you Nick. The whole time you've been taking care of her out of some twisted sort of guilt over what

33

happened. It seems Matthew wasn't the only one in that relationship with wandering eyes. She had been screwing around on him too. She's a manipulative little bitch. Don't take it personal. She had us all fooled."

This changes everything. "I need you to leave," I demand. I can't even look at her. There's no way Monica knew Matthew was not Olivia's father. No way she lied to us all on purpose. No way she let me take on an obligation that wasn't mine, knowing what she had done. No way she let me feel this guilt for four fucking years when she was just as guilty as he was. No way she's been using me all this time. Elise is a fucking liar. And women worry about trusting men? You think we're the lying, cheating assholes? Take a look in the mirror baby.

"Nick..."

I stop her. The conversation is over. "Now."

Thank god Elise is not a complete idiot. She leaves without another word. I grab my keys and tell Candace I'm gone for the day and I'll see her when I get back in town.

CHAPTER FIVE
Heidi

The envelope is flat and thin. It almost feels empty and I wonder if this is some kind of joke. I look over at Shelly who is just as curious as I am.

"Well...open it," she demands.

I sit at my desk and study it for a minute before deciding to pull apart the silver prongs that secure the flap, and see what's inside. It's a cashier's check. Along with a single letter stating that Graham Batiste appreciates my cooperation and wishes me the best in my future endeavors.

So that's it? A one hundred thousand dollar check and a thank you? He thinks he's getting off that easy? I owe more than that on this building. One hundred thousand dollars doesn't do squat for me.

I can feel my face heat up. There are so many emotions consuming me right now. I am shocked, disappointed, panicked, confused, and mad. Like blow shit up mad.

I look up and realize Shelly has been calling my name for the past two minutes but all I could hear was the sound of all my blood rushing to my head.

"I'm sorry. What?"

She gets up and walks over to my desk where I have placed the check. Yea, she's nosey like that. I guess she figures after twenty five years of friendship we're past the point of having secrets. "Woah. That's a lot of zeroes," she says.

I pick up the check and the letter, shove it in my purse, and pull out my keys. I have to go. There's no way I'm letting this happen. "I have to take care of this. I'll be back later," I inform Shelly. She's looking at me like I'm a stray dog that she's not sure whether she should pet or be afraid of. "It's nothing you need to worry your pretty little head about. I'll be back in a minute," I say as I fake a smile and rub the top of her head.

I hop in my Jeep and say a silent thank you to whoever invented the navigation app because I have no idea where Graham Batiste's office is even located. All I can think about is how this happened. What made Graham think a hundred thousand dollars would do all the things he promised….all the things Nick promised. *Nick.* I think back to the night in my apartment when he first saw my sunroom-slash-office. When I told him how far I'd come and he told me everything would be okay. I remember the day I went on his boat. *Damn, that boat.* We came back to my office and I signed my life away. He told me he was taking care of me. He took care of me alright. That's what I get for trusting someone I barely even know. He smiled his sexy, crooked, little smile and I just handed him the keys to my kingdom. Like I had nothing to lose. Then a thought occurs to me…I pull out my cell phone and call Alex.

He barely gets out a full "hello" when I'm grilling him.

"Alex, I need to ask you a serious question and I need you to be honest with me when you answer."

"Good afternoon to you too, love," he replies. Normally I would apologize but my brain is not running on *normal* right now.

"I'm serious."

He clears his throat and I picture him sitting up straight, looking amused. I'm never serious with Alex so I'm sure he's intrigued. "Go ahead then."

"How do Nick and Graham Batiste know each other?"

He doesn't answer right away. I'm no detective but I watch enough television to know stalling means he's thinking of the answer he thinks I want to hear rather than the one that is true.

"What makes you think they know each other?"

I let out an exasperated sigh. "Because I'm a woman and we have an incredibly natural talent for intuition."

He chuckles. I guess he doesn't realize I'm a woman on a mission. And you don't chuckle at a woman on a mission. "Why does it matter?"

Lawyers and therapists. Always answering a question with a question.

"Because it matters. Please just answer me." I'm already aggravated. Traffic sucks, and Alex is playing dodge the question.

"They played baseball together in college," he says hesitantly. *I knew it.* I knew when I watched them at the fundraiser that they weren't just recent business acquaintances. Graham was so bold with Nick, and Nick isn't the type of man to let just anybody get bold with him. College buddies, then. My head is spinning and my gut is telling me Alex isn't telling me everything.

I urge him on. "And?"

"And?" He repeats the question.

Some dickhead cuts me off so I growl and curse him under my breath. "Yea. I know there's more. You're just not telling me."

This time it's Alex who lets out an exasperated sigh, which lets me know I'm on the right track.

"You aren't going to let this go, are you?"

"Nope."

He pauses briefly, trying to figure out the explanation most likely *not* to cause me to flip shit.

"BKG is a primary contributor to Nick's campaign," he finally admits.

I purse my lips and move my eyes around, giving my brain a moment to process what exactly that means. "Meaning: Graham writes Nick a big fat check and in return, Nick makes sure BKG gets whatever it wants. Isn't that how it all works?" I hear my voice easing up a notch with every word I say. I feel myself beginning to hyperventilate at the reality of what I've just discovered.

"Heidi," Alex warns. "Whatever you're thinking, I can assure you it couldn't be further from the truth."

"I have to go," I tell him as I hit the red button and throw my phone in the passenger seat. It immediately begins buzzing when Alex calls me right back. I turn the radio up and press the gas. I can't get to Graham's office fast enough.

~~~~~~

The whole way there, all I can think about is how completely betrayed I feel. And stupid. Let's not forget stupid. It all makes perfect sense. Graham hires Alex to do his dirty work, knowing I would take it to a higher level when I got no response from his office. *Did Alex ignore my messages on purpose?* Doesn't matter. What matters is that he did ignore them. So I did go for help. That's where Nick comes in....the big bad wolf waiting for the stupid, stupid girl to take his bait. I never even questioned when he said he would take care of it for me. I didn't even read the freaking contract! I just believed him. Like a lovestruck idiot. I initialed and signed my little heart out, not ever giving it a second thought. All because he smiled that crooked smile and got my panties wet. I wonder how much I was worth to him. How much Graham gave him to play me like a fool. How many times they have pulled off this little scheme. It's actually a brilliant operation they have going when you think about it. I wonder if Alex was in on the whole thing or if that part was just a coincidence. I mean, was the plan to have them both seduce me so that all the bases were covered? You know, just in case I didn't go to Nick for help, then Alex would just screw me stupid, literally, until I signed on the dotted line.

My heart falls to the pit of my stomach at the thought of being nothing more than part of a business deal to Nick. A means to an end. Isn't that ironic? Most of my life, that's all men have been to me and now that I found one who actually matters, that's all I am to him.

For the first time in my life, I hurt. Like physically *hurt* when I think about how I feel for him. I am too shocked to cry so I just stare. I don't see the cars passing me by or hear the music blaring through the speakers. I just see us. Him. Pretending like I was different. I should have known from the minute he took me to that restaurant for lunch and told me that's where he does all of his *business* deals. God he's good. He sure had me fooled. And here I am feeling like crap for what happened with Alex. I eventually get angry with myself for letting this happen. Then I just get plain old pissed off....because I can damn well guarantee that Nick Knight got more than one hundred thousand dollars out of this deal.

I turn down a long road that looks like it should actually be a driveway. On either side of the driveway-road is a line of beautiful oak trees that follows the path all the way to its end. About a mile down, the road opens up into a massive parking lot in front of a huge office building made entirely of glass. I am a little surprised at the location. I would have thought a man as arrogant as Graham Batiste would want his office on the corner of Royal and Canal, for everyone to get a glimpse of his success. Not hide it in the middle of nowhere down a two mile driveway. There are bright red steel beams framing each corner and you can see through the glass to a background of rich red walls. As I approach the entrance, I see the reception desk off to the left and an obnoxiously large and wide staircase made entirely of teak wood to the right.

Directly in front of the reception area, centered on a soft, white, shag rug, are two charcoal gray leather sofas. The sofas face each other and there is a buttery yellow ottoman in the center of them. This is where I sit while I wait for the receptionist to finish dealing with the UPS guy. Once he leaves I walk up to the counter and introduce myself.

"Hello. I need to see Graham Batiste. You can tell him Heidi Lemaire is here." I wait for the woman to call him or buzz him or whatever it is she has to do.

"Of course Ms. Lemaire. Do you have an appointment?" She is a lot more pleasant than Thing One and Thing Two were the first time I went to Nick's office. Her smile is actually comforting. And after the way my blood has been boiling for the past thirty minutes while I drove over here, I could use a comforting smile.

"I don't, actually. But I really need to speak with him if that's at all possible." I try my best to be considerate and patient, but inside I am bursting at the seams.

The woman smiles but I can tell she's probably thinking *"Great. Here's another idiot looking for special treatment because she forgot to make an appointment."* She speaks loudly and deliberately into the receiver, for my benefit no doubt. "Sorry to bother you sir but a Ms Lemaire is here to see you."

Like I care if I'm bothering him. She's lucky she's over forty. Otherwise I wouldn't have been so polite in asking for him. She nods and smiles at his response. *He can't see you, you idiot.* She looks up at me knowingly and I immediately feel bad for mentally calling her an idiot.

"Mr. Batiste will be down in just a moment."

That might not necessarily be a good thing. Shit's about to get real and I doubt he wants an audience. But who am I to tell the great Graham Batiste what to do. So I sit back on the sofa and wait.

CHAPTER SIX
Heidi

The receptionist, whom I now know as Pauline, offers me a bottle of water or cup of coffee while I wait. I ask for a glass of wine instead. She doesn't look amused. I shrug. Oh well, it was worth a shot. Speaking of shots, I could use one or two..or four, right now. Maybe I'll call Joel and we'll go have drinks later. I am about to reach for my phone when I see Graham walking down the monster steps. I'm telling you, that staircase has to be thirty foot high and twenty wide at the base. It's absurd. The steps get narrower the higher up you go, but they're still crazy big.

He is actually a really attractive man...on the outside. He is tall with dark hair and a five day stubble. Perfect teeth and a sculptured jaw. His eyes are a piercing bright blue, a sharp contrast to his jet black hair. He is wearing a black suit jacket, loose black slacks, and a white v-neck t shirt. He's also wearing a cocky grin that gets wider I swear with each step he takes. *Asshole.*

The bigger he smiles, the angrier I get. I don't wait for him to get to the bottom. I meet him halfway up the staircase.

He rakes his eyes over my body, his smile now more of a closed-mouth, tilted, *I know something you don't know*, smiles.

"Stop looking at me like that," I snip at him.

He arches a brow and tilts the corner of his mouth. "How am I looking at you?"

"Like I'm a big juicy steak and you haven't had lunch."

Graham throws his head back and laughs out loud. "Now Heidi, you make it sound like I'm the villain here." His tone is condescending. Like he really believes he hasn't royally screwed me over.

I move up a few steps so we're eye to eye. "Well you're definitely not the hero."

"Aren't I?" he asks. *Seriously?* He has got to be effing kidding me. He thinks he's a *hero?* I should kick him. In the knee. Hard. Right now. Or maybe I should kick him in the balls. Yea, that would probably make me feel better.

I pull the cashier's check from my purse and hold it out in front of him. "I don't need your charity, and I'm damn sure not taking your insults. You can have your stupid money back." I shove the check against his chest as I turn to go back down the steps. My adrenaline is pumping and I feel like I am about to cry at any given moment. Not because I'm hurt, but because there are too many negative emotions running through my veins right now and something's gotta give. I am furious. And the longer I stand here, the more furious I become. Oh my god, the nerve! I could scream. Like literally just belt out a big ole psycho scream right here in his face. I make it two steps down then stop and turn back to face him. "Oh, and tell your partner in crime I hope his dick rots off."

As soon as I start down the rest of the stairs, a strong hand grabs my elbow, halting me from going any further. I jerk my head around and look down at the hand on my arm then back up at Graham, daring him to keep touching me. He pulls me back up the steps until we are once again face to face.

"In my office. Now," he demands. The smirk is gone and there is a deep indignation in his eyes. I am angry, but I'm not stupid. I don't argue with him. I do, however, yank my arm free. I don't need him dragging me around like a scolded child.

I follow him up the stairs and down a wide hallway. At the top of the stairs, both to the left and the right, are cubicles in a loft type setting that overlooks the main lobby. But immediately at the top of the staircase is a long, wide hallway with offices on both sides. At the end of this hall is an elevator and a small desk with a young woman behind it. This is where Graham leads me.

He smiles and makes small talk with the girl while we wait for the elevator. When it opens for us, he places a hand on the small of my back and urges me inside. The gesture gives me goosebumps. And not the good kind. I don't want this man's hands anywhere near me. He is the enemy. The man who literally robbed me of my dream all because he thinks his dream is worth more. I remember the hallway we just walked down. In a single line, all the way down the hall, right at eye level on either side, were framed photographs of buildings. Hotels, restaurants, casinos. You name it. There must have been thirty or forty of them altogether. I am assuming they all belong to him. And here I am, all I have is one little two thousand square foot building. A building it took me two years to acquire and another six months to renovate. A building that may just be brick and mortar on the outside, but it's so much more on the inside. And not just to me but to Meghan, Ashton, and Shelly too. We have all put our hearts and souls into my business. And this man….who probably can't even count how much money he has….is stealing it away. It's such an arrogant asshole thing to do. And Nick helped him do it. I want to cry. This time because it does hurt.

The elevator doors close, snapping me out of my trance. "Those photographs in the hall…those are all properties you own?" I don't know why I asked. I already know the answer. I guess I just wanted confirmation that he is as big of a dick as I think.

He stuffs his hands in his pockets and leans against the rear wall of the elevator. "Yes. Impressed?"

By the amount of restrain I've managed to show by not punching you in the throat? Yes.

"And yet you are still able to remain so humble." I shoot him a disapproving glare and then return to my sulking.

He laughs again only this time not quite as loud as before. This time it's more of a chuckle than full blown laughter. "You don't care for me much, do you?"

"I don't even know you."

Graham removes his hands from his pockets and inches toward me, his blue eyes twinkling.

"Well maybe that's the problem. You just need to get to know me."

Seriously? I already gave him the check back. Nothing left to take from me. So that means now he's just being a pervert. I jut forward, poking a pointer finger into his chest. I am fuming now so there's no filter.

"Maybe *that's* the problem," I tell him, poking him with each word. "You and your group of obnoxiously good looking friends think you can just run around seducing people into handing over whatever you want from them. You don't care who you hurt. You just rip through women's lives like tornadoes, not even looking to see what kind of mess you leave behind."

The elevator opens but that doesn't affect our conversation. Graham looks thoroughly confused and I begin to wonder for a moment if I spoke clearly.

"What...the fuck....are you ranting about?"

I narrow my eyes and glare at him. "Are you really going to play dumb right now?" I don't give him time to answer the question. I roll my eyes at him and speak slowly and deliberately. "Your whole little setup....keeping me preoccupied with Alex...then making sure Nick slept with me so I didn't bat an eye when you slipped right in and took what you wanted. I have to admit, it's pretty brilliant...but you're all assholes for doing it and I hope it all comes back to bite you in the ass."

I push the button to close the elevator doors and go back downstairs. I said what I have to say and now I'm ready to go. Graham is staring at me like I just told him I shot his dog. *Truth hurts huh dickhead?*

The elevator is silent for a moment. Then I decide to finish this thing off. I have to know. It's eating at me. "I just have one question," I say. He keeps his eyes on mine as he waits for me to continue. "I got one hundred thousand dollars....which doesn't do shit for me by the way. Doesn't even pay off what I owe on the building, much less get me into a new one. Anyway....How many zeroes did Nick's check have on it? What was I worth to him?"

He cocks his head and eyes me curiously. Not long after, his lips part and his eyes widen as realization hits him. He smiles a half smile. "Holy shit," he says. "You think I *paid* Nick to fuck you? So you wouldn't give me any trouble?"

He closes his eyes and laughs. "Oh my god. Heidi. *That* is rich. Seriously. I mean, it's a hell of an idea, but I can promise you....." He stops talking as he inches toward me until I'm backed against the elevator wall. He places one hand on the wall just above my head and looks down at me. "He fucked you because he wanted to. And my guess is he wanted to because you are a beautiful..." he brings his other hand to my cheek and runs a finger along my jaw. "Smart..." He leans in an inch closer so that his face is just inches from mine, "and incredibly sexy woman," he finishes, "especially when you're mad."

I bring my hand to his crotch, where he is sporting a semi. I stroke him once through his trousers then rest my hand on his rapid growing erection. He closes his eyes and leans his head back. He's actually enjoying this. What an ass. The elevator doors open and I choose this moment to squeeze. As hard as I can. His eyes pop open but he isn't able to say anything. He just stares at me, jaw dropped and in shock. Now I'm the one with the cocky grin.

"Don't ever think you can touch me like that again," I say as I walk out. He leans against the wall of the elevator, still speechless and rubbing his dick. I press the button for him to go back up, but right before the doors close I manage one final remark. "We should do this again sometime. Come by my office. It's the one right there on the corner of *Eat a dick* and *Fuck you*."

By the time I get back to the store, I am feeling pretty damn proud of myself and not near as worked up as I was when I left. Hudson's dad, Cole, called me to remind me that they will be gone for a week, starting tomorrow. Every year Hudson's baseball team travels to compete in a World Series. This year the team voted to go to Orange Beach, Alabama. He didn't need to call to remind me. There's no way I'd miss it. I booked my condo over a month ago.

"Pack your bags. We're going to the beach!" I exclaim as I walk into the store.

Shelly slowly looks up at me, eyebrows arched and lips pursed in curiosity. "Is that where you've been? Spending all those zeroes on a beach vacay?"

Way to spoil the moment. "No," I say flatly. I work on finding my happy place again. I was just there a minute ago. Surely it's not that far away. "Come with me. Five days." I sing my next words, hoping they'll seem more appealing that way. "It's the be-each. And it's free-ee." I walk over to her desk and grab her hands. "Pleeease."

She is looking at me the way I look at Hudson when he asks me for something I know I'm going to give him but want to make him sweat it out first. After a few seconds she finally responds with a sigh.

"Fine. But I have to ask my boss," she jokes.

"I think I can put in a good word. Now....Let's go shopping."

Shopping always makes me feel better. I'm female. It's what we do.

For the rest of the day, the only thing I let stress me out is deciding which bathing suit to buy.

Tuesday, July 8

I'm expecting a typical day at the office. Clients freaking out about making the wrong paint color selection. Brides needing me to put the smackdown on overly dramatic, and un-cooperative bridesmaids. Setting appointments with some possible fundraising venues for next week. You know, as normal as it gets around here. As soon as I get back, I need to get Hudson's surgery scheduled and down payment taken care of. It will take about four to six weeks for him to be ready for normal activity so I want to make sure we do it in plenty of time for school.

I'm in my office returning emails when someone knocks on my door. Shelly never knocks and I gave Meghan and Ashton the rest of the week off with pay, so I have no idea who is going to appear once I say "Come in."

It's the same guy who brought me the envelope yesterday. *What the hell?*

He takes a couple of awkward steps forward before I let him know it's okay to come all the way in. He places the envelope on my desk, thanks me, and turns to walk back out.

"Wait," I say, halting him.

He turns to face me. "Yes ma'am?"

"Who sent you? Who do you run for?" I assume he is a runner. Who else goes around dropping off documents all day every day.

He smiles. "He said you would ask that."

"Well then he's a smart man. Did Graham Batiste send you?"

At that very moment a familiar voice echoes from the hall outside my office. "Not a bad guess." The runner nods at the man then takes off. Graham leans against the doorway, holding out a white handkerchief. "May I come in?"

God, he's persistent. I thought for sure the whole crotch squeezing ordeal would keep him away. I smile a painted on smile. "Of course."

He takes a seat in the chair in front of me and crosses his long legs. There is nothing but silence for a moment while he figures out what to say to me. I don't need to think about it. I have nothing to say to him. He looks around my office, floor to ceiling, wall to wall, then back at me. "You have a nice set up Heidi," he compliments.

"You mean *you* have a nice set up? In a couple of weeks it doesn't belong to me anymore. Or did you forget?" My tone is snarky and short.

He sits up straight in his chair and slides the envelope in my direction. "Open it," he commands.

My eyes fall to the envelope then move to meet his. His expression has softened. I see none of the cocky, self-absorbed jerk from yesterday. I see the man who helped me off the stage at Nick's party. A man I can bet many people don't ever see.

I open the envelope and pull out its contents. It's a document with a single paragraph highlighted. At the end of the paragraph is a short line with my initials on it. I remember signing this. Correction: I remember Nick making me sign it. Is he here to rub my stupidity in my face? I look around the room, agitated, then at Graham. "I get it. I signed. Sealed the deal. Whatever." I slide the paper to his side of the desk and sigh. "Why are you here Graham?" I guess I was wrong about Nice Guy Graham.

He slides it back to me and taps the paragraph. "I don't think you do get it," he says as he gets comfortable in his chair again. "When you left my office yesterday, I thought about everything you said. None of it made any sense. Granted, you were ranting. You're angry….for what, I don't know. That's between you and Nick." He props an ankle up on his knee and leans back. "But even with all your ranting nonsense, I still couldn't figure out what you meant about *one hundred thousand dollars*…blah blah blah. So I went back and reviewed our agreement."

He waits for me to interrupt with something sarcastic, but I'm actually interested to see where he's going with this so I sit tight and listen.

He grins when he realizes he's got my attention.

"I agreed to give you fifty thousand dollars *and* pay all relocation expenses," he states. He points to the paragraph again. "Right here," he nods his head at the document, encouraging me to follow his finger. "You signed this Heidi. You mean to tell me you never read it?"

So stamp *dumbass* on my forehead. Nick said trust him, so I did. "Not really, no. I just trusted Nick to handle all that," I explain. I am sure he is probably thinking I'm an idiot. I am thinking it. Why wouldn't he?

"You trusted him with something as major as this, and now you aren't even speaking to him?" *Who died and made you judge of all things appropriate?*

My answer is a silent shrug. He shakes his head and moves his eyes toward the ceiling, as if asking for help from above.

"The fifty thousand dollars is to cover any money you'll lose during the transition. It's not the final total. Never was. I'm still taking care of everything else. Whatever you decide to do from here, whatever you want, just send me the bill. Think of it as a fresh start. With unlimited resources. I told you Heidi, I'm not the bad guy. I want us *both* to win here."

I scan the paper and find that's exactly what it says. I mess with my cuticles for a moment before looking up at him apologetically. "I'm an asshole. I made all those accusations. I'm sorry. I really am." Hey, I'm woman enough to admit when I'm wrong and apologize for it. Then I realize he keeps saying *fifty* thousand. "You said fifty thousand dollars. But the cashier's check was for one hundred thousand."

He smiles as he stands, placing a brand new cashier's check on top of the document on my desk. "When you said you thought Nick got paid to work this deal, you couldn't have been further from the truth. Think about that." He winks and walks out of the room.

I swallow back the lump forming in my throat. I don't want to process what that means right now. I hurry and try to catch Graham before he leaves.

"Graham," I say just as he reaches the front doors. He turns to face me and cocks his head in question. I bunch my eyebrows and wrinkle up my nose like I've just witnessed something painful happen to someone. "Yesterday. The elevator. Sorry about the crotch thing," I tell him.

He chuckles and shrugs. "No big deal. I deserved it. See you later Heidi."

CHAPTER SEVEN
Heidi

What the hell was *that?* A big fat reality check, that's what. *Literally.*

Graham left another check on my desk. Only this time I didn't shove it back in his face. I'm still wrapping my head around the fact that there's more where that came from. He didn't even blink an eye at the idea of helping me get back on my feet once I move. Not to mention there's a whole fifty thousand dollars in this check unaccounted for, and the way he suggested that Nick may have had something to do with it. It's like someone just told me the Joker isn't really the bad guy, but the hero. There's no way he meant everything he said. No way he's just going to let me have my way. Just like that. I call Alex to request a copy of this contract I let my body sign in place of my brain. He promises me I was well taken care of and have nothing to worry about. *Thanks, but I'll see for myself.* I'm still a little gun shy, even though Graham waltzed in my office with a million dollar smile and a sugar-coated explanation. Before we get off the phone, Alex invites me to dinner. I decline. Politely of course, explaining that I have to get ready for my trip to the beach, which opens up a whole other line of questioning. *What is he, my dad or something?*

I agree to cook for him when I get back and he lets up. *There you go. Good boy.* Just like giving a pacifier to a baby.

I spend most of the rest of the afternoon packing and all of the evening staring back and forth between the clock and my phone. I want to call Nick. I have an excuse now so technically I could get away with it, right? He probably wouldn't answer anyway. This is the conversation I have with myself for three hours before I finally take a hot shower and go to bed.

Wednesday, July 9

49

Shelly begged me to let her bring Emmett, her boyfriend. As if I need to be reminded that I am alone. It looks like me and my wine will be spending a lot of time at the beach. Shelly is not shy about letting her freak flag fly, and I am not listening to that for the next five days.

First stop after I unpack- Hudson's condo. He, Cole, and Cole's new wife, Michelle, are staying at a different complex but it's on the same road as the Turquoise, where I am staying, so it's really not a big deal.

He runs and jumps into my arms as soon as I walk through the door. "Mom!" he exclaims. I sweep him up and squeeze him tight. It seems like forever since I've seen my little man. Days without him are like days without sunshine. My heart warms every time I see his smile. He smells like sunscreen...and Doritos. I kiss his cheeks at least twenty times and then rub my nose against his.

"Hey there handsome! I sure have missed you," I tell him.

He squeezes my neck once. "I missed you too. I'm really glad you came. I was getting mom-sick."

I smile at his made-up word then set him down. He reaches up and places his little hand in mine and leads me into a nearby bedroom.

"This is my room. You can sleep right here," he says, patting the side of the bed near the window as he says the last two words.

I shake my head and kiss his forehead. "I'm not sleeping *here* silly. I have my own condo. Right down the road." He still has a lot to learn about how this whole divorce thing works.

He drops his head and looks defeated. I pick his chin up and make him look at me. "But you can come sleep in *my* room if you want." His expression immediately changes and he lets go of my hand and runs into the kitchen where his dad is. "Dad! I'm sleeping over at mom's tonight. You've earned a break, pal," he says while pats his dad on the back. Cole chuckles and nods as he pops a grape in his mouth.

"Gee, thanks," he replies.

"Okay mom, let's go. Can we get Shakes on the way? Pleeeease?" he begs. Shakes is a local place we always get frozen custard from when we're here. It's kind of a tradition and I knew Hudson wouldn't let me forget it. If you've never had custard, take this as my personal recommendation to try it. Yum. If you like ice cream, think of custard as its hot, older brother. Melt in your mouth good. We're definitely going to Shakes.

I look over at Cole, who is admiring the little boy we share almost as much as I am. "Are you sure you don't mind?" I am not the *I'm-his-mother-and-it-doesn't-matter-what-you-think* type.

This is technically his time with Hudson, so I feel it's only respectful to ask.

"Not at all. Just have him at The Wharf at 5 for opening ceremonies." I give him a thumbs up and head to the room to help Hudson pack an overnight bag. Then we go get custard.

Opening ceremonies are Hudson's favorite part of the World Series. Each player gets a pin and they spend most of the afternoon walking around meeting players from other teams and trading said pins. The rest of the ceremony is spent listening to a man on a stage introducing each team. It's hot and I am thirsty. I wonder how Hudson hasn't passed out yet. He says it makes him feel "*Major League*" so I don't argue. This is his time to shine so I sit back and bask in the glow.

I give Shelly and Emmett the death glare when Hudson and I make it back to the condo two hours later. Not that I think they would do anything with my son here, I just wanted to make sure they knew I would not be a happy momma if they did. We all pop some popcorn, have a pizza party in the living room, and watch *Big Hero 6*, which is pretty sad for a cartoon. I thought cartoons were made to make you laugh. What the hell? That night after Hudson tells me about everything he's been doing the past week, I hum to him until he falls asleep next to me.

Thursday, July 10

It's four o'clock and Shelly, Emmett, and I are on our way back to the condo. We've been at the baseball park since nine o'clock this morning. Hudson had two games to play today. His team won both of them so naturally they were all pretty excited. He decided to go back with his dad while he and his team mates play musical condos over the next few nights. Even though he is the smallest on the team, he has the loudest roar of all of them. He is the one on the field calling the plays and cheering his team mates on. And they all love him. It makes me so happy to see him with his friends.

When we finally make it back to Turquoise, Shelly and Emmett go straight to their room to change, although I'm sure I'll be finished long before they will. I throw on my bikini, pour some wine in a plastic cup, grab my beach bag and my kindle, and get ready for an afternoon alone with the sun, the waves, and a new sexy book boyfriend. I haven't even pulled out my phone since I called Cole yesterday to let him know I was coming to see Hudson. I plan on not thinking about anything outside of this beach until Sunday. I glance over at it on the nightstand, tempted to check it, then opting not to. I know I'll just be disappointed when there's nothing there.

Just as I get ready to get cozy in a chair, the umbrella guy comes to the section I have chosen as my sanctuary. He closes all the umbrellas and picks up all the cushions from all the chairs in my row, right up until he reaches mine. I'm pulling my hair up into a bun when he approaches. I don't have time to be hassled by him about not having paid for my chair, so I just reach for my bag to get him my card. "I know. You have to reserve the chairs..." I start, not even looking up at him as I dig.
"It's five o'clock. I'm not worried about a reservation," he says. His voice is deep and firm. It's enough to make me look up at the man behind it. I'm sure I look like I've just been bitch slapped. I was thoroughly expecting a...well I'm not real sure what I was expecting, maybe some skinny but unnaturally tan eighteen year old kid. Definitely not this. This is a man. Dark, handsome, and a six pack my grandma could have washed clothes on. He runs a hand through his dirty blonde hair and smiles down at me with perfect white teeth.
I raise my sunglasses to confirm my vision. Yep. Sure as shit. Milk has positively done his body good. I'm talking like two glasses a day, good. And I'm pretty sure he's legal. "So, then you don't want my number?" I ask, placing the tip of my index finger at the corner of my

mouth and biting gently on the nail, while holding up my debit card in my other hand. Yes, I'm flirting.

He licks his lips and half-smiles back at me. "Oh, I definitely want your number. But not the one on that credit card."

I give myself a mental high-five. He's flirting back. *Score.* I pull my finger from my mouth, drag it over my chin and down my throat before I grab a stray hair at the back of my neck and twist it in my fingers. "Go ahead and finish what you started. You know, with the umbrellas. I'll be here when you're done." I pull my sunglasses back over my eyes and settle in my chair, not giving him another glance. What? It's not rude. I'm flirting, not begging. He'll be back. They always come back.

Umbrella Guy lets out an amused but curious "hmmph" then goes back to the business of picking up chair pads and folding umbrellas. I wait a few seconds before turning to look at him again. When I do, I find him looking right back at me. I flash him a sexy smile then slowly bring my head back around. I take out my wine-in-a-thermos and my kindle and wait.

As soon as I slide the little lock on the screen, I'm reminded of Nick, and all the nights I read to him. His little inquisitions after every chapter. The way it felt describing to him some of the very things I would have died to feel him do to me. Hearing the way he would get jealous of the man in the story, not knowing that there was never a face other than his own that I would put with that character. I take a sip of wine and search through my library for something that won't make me think about Nick Knight.

Twenty minutes later I'm two chapters into *Jane Eyre*, my little plastic cup is empty, and I'm just about to dip my toes in the ocean when Umbrella Guy makes himself at home in the empty, wooden lounge chair beside me. He looks over at me with a confident grin as he places his hands behind his head and stretches his legs out. This guy is seriously hot. You could bounce quarters off his abs and his calves are just...amazing. Don't even get me started on his biceps. And that tan. He works on the beach, what do you expect? He is wearing a pair of dark green swim trunks with a navy blue string that ties at the waistband. I didn't miss the way they hang just right around his hips, emphasizing the perfect "V" and very slight exposure of well-trimmed hair. Yea, he's sexy and he knows it. I don't care. He can be as confident and cocky as he wants to be. I'm not interested in his personality anyway.

"1109," I say as I stuff my kindle and my cool cup back in my beach bag.

"That's it?" he asks as he watches me stand.

"You wanted a number. There you go," I reply with a smirk. "Unless you plan on getting in the water with me," I continue.

I don't elaborate nor ask him again. I just make my way to the edge of the water. Holy crap, it's cold.

Slowly, I make my way further out until I'm just about waist deep. The waves aren't overbearing but they aren't small either. Every once in a while one will smash against my back, pushing me forward. Umbrella Guy watches me from his chair for a minute or two until he finally realizes, I guess, that I'm not coming back up there to fawn over him, although I'm sure that's what he's used to. Instead, I creep out a little further into the water. Soon he's right here beside me just in time to grab my waist when a wave smacks me in the back, making me lose my balance. No sooner are we back on our feet, than an even bigger wave crashes over us, sending us both underwater. Through the whole debacle he never manages to let go of my waist. We both come up with a mouthful of salt water. I smooth my hair out of my face and start laughing.

"Oh my god! This is crazy! Whose idea was this anyway?"

He laughs with me. "Well since you decided running from me was a better idea than talking to me, I'd say yours."

I feign shock. "I was not running from you. I was already planning on getting in when you showed up."

I start wading my way back to the shore and he follows.

"You're doing it again," he says.

I grab my towel and wrap it around my freezing body. "Doing what?" I look over at him and find he's eyeing me curiously. I see little goosebumps all over his body and realize he probably doesn't have a towel. Because he probably never planned on getting in the water. I instantly feel bad for him.

He arches a brow and replies, "Running from me."

I unwrap my towel and move behind him. Without saying a word, I begin to dry his back and his shoulders. Then I move to his front and wipe down his chest and abs. He is watching me with a smile as I confidently step back and give him a *who's running now* look. I wrap the towel around my body once again then reach for my bag.

"You're wrong, Umbrella Guy. I'm not running. You know exactly where to find me."

"Do I at least get a name?" he asks as I am walking away.

"1109," I yell over my shoulder. Then I blow him a kiss and continue back to my condo, mentally doing the running man and cabbage patch, at the same time, all the way there. The artist formerly known as Heidi is back in action.

I take my shower and throw on a pair of running shorts and a t-shirt. Shelly and Emmett left for the beach right as I got back. I have Pandora playing on the Bose sound system and I'm just about to pour myself a glass of wine when the doorbell rings. I smile victoriously to myself. God it feels good to own my own life again. No more wondering where Nick is or what he's doing. Or if he's going to call.

I open the door for Umbrella Guy, who has now changed into khaki chino shorts and a white button up with the sleeves rolled to his elbows. Typical beach wardrobe. He's got his hands behind his back and I silently pray he did not bring me flowers. His face beams when he smiles and under any other circumstance, a girl would be feeling like the luckiest woman in the world to have this man at her door. But we've all established I'm not your normal girl, and I didn't invite him over to play Scrabble and eat pizza.

You see, for me, sex is like a drug. It takes me away from the real world, even if for just a little while. It helps me forget the pain of rejection, or failing, or loss. It fills a void. For a little while. This isn't something I'm proud of. It's just the way it's always been. In a world where I once felt like I did everything wrong, that was the one thing I knew I could do right. So now, when I lose a client, piss off an architect, fight with Shelly, or watch the man I care about walk out of a room and never speak to me again: this is how I choose to handle it. There's a chase involved in the flirting, a game of sorts. This way I feel like I've at least won something. Even if the feeling is only temporary.

So I invite Umbrella Guy inside and get started on my fix. "Want a drink?" I offer as I walk toward the kitchen.

He pulls his hands from behind his back to reveal two green glass bottles. *Thank the heavens it's not flowers.* "Thanks, but I brought my own." He extends one of the bottles in my direction. "One for the lady?"

I arch an impressed brow at him. "Stella, huh?"

He smiles in response. I grab the beer and a bottle opener and lead him into the adjacent living room. The condo is furnished with upscale slightly modern décor. There is a glass top dining table with six rattan side chairs and two linen upholstered head chairs, bar stools to match the side chairs along a granite top island that separates the kitchen from the rest of the open living and dining areas, and a decent-sized wet bar with glass shelves and a mirrored back. In the living room there are two tan club chairs and a cream colored sectional centered around a large fireplace with a slate tile surround and a flat screen television above the lacquered walnut mantle.

I sit on the sectional and pat the empty spot next to me. "I figured you for a Budweiser kind of guy," I tease as he opens our bottles. "You've got good taste," I continue.

Umbrella Guy nods his head in my direction, "Obviously."

I'm pretty sure I blush. Even as often as I have done this, and as confident as I am in my ability to lead men around by their penis (I'm totally convinced that's why God made them external organs that stick out the way they do, by the way), I still don't handle compliments well.

I take a long swig of my beer. He does have good taste. I'm not much of a beer drinker, but this is really good. Or maybe I'm just really nervous. Either way, I wash away Nervous Nancy with another swig of beer and set the bottle on the cocktail table. He settles his bottom into the seat cushion and begins to make small talk. "So do you spend a lot of time at the beach or is this your first time?"

I lick my lips and tilt my head as if he's just said something amusing. "Well this is definitely not my first time." His eyes move to my mouth and I watch as his Adam's apple moves when he swallows hard. I part my lips and gauge his reaction. Immediately his lips part in return. My imaginary scoreboard flips one for the home team. I move around to straddle his lap, looking him directly in the eye. I guess now is as good a time as any to be honest. "Look, we both know you're not here to pop a cold one and watch the game."

His mouth twitches in one corner and his eyes narrow as he sorts through his options of what to do next. He adjusts himself in his seat and I can feel him getting hard between my thighs. "Why don't you tell me why I'm here then?"

Oh you know damn well why you're here. I give him the benefit of the doubt and play along. "I'm an adult," I say as I lean forward. "And you're an adult," I continue as I inch closer to his face. "We'll figure something out."

My lips are just centimeters from his, waiting for the perfect moment to close the gap between us, but he takes control and presses his mouth against mine. His tongue snakes in and tangles with mine. His kiss is smooth and calculated. Almost practiced. I'm sure he gets lots of beach body booty calls. He tastes like beer and spearmint. Like he was chewing gum before he got here. My body rejects the flavor. It wants cinnamon and whiskey. Dammit. Now I'm frustrated. I slowly pull away from the kiss, hoping he doesn't notice. He doesn't. His hands slide underneath my shirt, his fingertips grazing the skin on my back as he whispers in my ear. "Tell me your name," he pleads.

I tilt my head to the side, allowing his skilled mouth access to my neck. He takes advantage and begins placing soft kisses just below my ear. Oh god. That's the spot. *The* spot. I run my fingers through his blonde hair, encouraging him to keep going.

And that's when Shelly bursts through the front door.

CHAPTER EIGHT

Nick

I've only been in Washington DC since Tuesday and I have voted on more platforms and attended more committee meetings in two days than I have all session so far. I've managed six radio interviews and one magazine article. Hell, at this rate I might just run for fucking president. Anything to keep my mind off the seriously screwed up pile of shit that is my life right now. I packed enough for three weeks, left instructions for Candace, and took off without leaving Monica so much as a "Fuck You" on a post-it note. I haven't thought about how I'm going to approach Elise's little revelation about her yet. But you can bet your sweet ass I'm going to approach it.

 My whole life I've known women to be great actresses. They pretend to like sports or calamari, just because you do. They put on their make-up and spend hours changing the color of their hair, all so you never see their true selves. I got a fine introduction to how the mind of a gold digger works at a young age. My father was a politician. He also owns two shopping centers and seventeen rental properties. It wasn't always like that for him though. He told me stories of his childhood in Cuba and how he came to America when he was eleven with a dream to play baseball. At the age of twelve, he was adopted by some bi-polar, manic depressant asshole and spent the next five years hiding in his room until he could use college as an excuse to get the hell out of there. The day he walked out the door, he vowed to be someone who never had to step foot back through it. I don't know the details of what went on in that house. That was something he never liked to talk about, but I know it was enough to make him want to be someone who could make a difference. *"You have to make your own luck, because sometimes life deals you a bad hand,"* he used to tell me. He met my mother at a golf tournament during his first term as state senator. He fell in love with her wicked ways and she fell in love with his checkbook.

 For years I watched her smile and kiss him goodbye then sit in the courtyard and cry to her friends about how miserable she was. I watched her flirt with his friends at dinner parties when she'd had too much vodka. I witnessed the metamorphosis from avid sports fan when she was in the living room with him, to eye-rolling football nazi as soon as she stepped into the kitchen. I heard her tell him lies about where she had been or how much money she had spent.

I suppose the life altering moment though, was when she took me on a day trip to the beach. I hate the goddamn beach. I was thirteen. She told me to read a book or build a sandcastle while she talked to her friend Shaun. Mom and Shaun went out into the ocean and stayed there for what seemed like hours. Maybe that's just because I was bored as fuck and ready to go home to play ball with my friends. I didn't realize it at the time, but my mother fucked Shaun that day. Right there, in the water, while I sat on the beach. I can see them so clearly in my mind. I remember watching and wondering why they had to be so close to each other. What they were doing out there in the waves. Now that I'm a sexual being of my own, I know exactly what they were doing. I have experienced two types of pain in my life. The type of pain that hurts you. I mean physically. Like the time I broke my ankle sliding into third base playing college baseball. And the type of pain that changes you. Watching my mother hurt my father for all those years and slowly realizing she was never the woman I always believed her to be, falls in the last category.

You see, it was my father who taught me not to be afraid to go after what I want and never give up, even when it seems hopeless. To make my own destiny. But it was my mother who taught me that women don't want the good guy. They don't want the man who buys them jewelry and rubs their back after a long day. They don't want men like my father. They want men like me. Men who give them what they need. Men who don't require all the false enthusiasm because we don't stick around long enough to give a shit.

I have made incredible efforts to keep women like my mother out of my life. My parents are still married, and I'm sure she still screws around, but that's not a conversation I care to have with my father right now.

I never would have pegged Monica as the devious, gold digging type. I genuinely felt sorry for her. I felt guilty even. I suppose she knew that and fed right into it. If I had seen what was happening with Elise and Matthew when it started, I could have ended it all right then. I could have called them out and squashed the whole fucked up mess. Monica could have gotten out with nothing more than a broken heart and moved on. Instead, it went on for months and she ended up pregnant and alone. So I helped her pick up the pieces that Matthew left lying on the ground. And now I know it was all a lie. I have to say though, I don't regret knowing Olivia. She is a beautiful little girl regardless of who her parents are. Maybe now at least it's not too late for her to have a chance to know her real dad. Maybe he won't be a royal douchebag. I really hope Monica doesn't screw that up for her.

I think of Heidi and her son. I respect the way she has her rules about not having men around him, even though it was extremely frustrating at times. I know from experience shit like that can screw with a kid's head. I think back to the day I saw her with him at the restaurant. Who the fuck was that guy with them? Could that have been Hudson's father? Why was she having lunch with him? I remember the little boy saying he had been at the hospital. And the band aid on his arm. The way he said his mom worries about him. *Fuck.* Is he sick? No. She would have told me. I laugh at myself. *She didn't tell you about Nate.*

What makes me think she would have told me everything about her life? Why do I even give a shit? *She fucked your best friend.* I have to stop thinking about this woman. And I know the perfect way to start.

A couple of the other representatives and I take a trip to a local gentleman's club. It's bottle service only so you can be sure not just anybody is walking through those doors. We take a seat in a private section to the right of the main stage area and are greeted by a tall, leggy brunette who likes to be called Charla. I order us a bottle of Pappy Van Winkle and wait for the show to begin.

Charla seems to have taken an interest in me, but I'm more interested in this bottle. She is standing directly in front of where I sit, her ass in my face as she bends over and runs her hands up the insides of her long legs. She stops when she reaches the spot between her thighs to peek her head around and steal a glance at my reaction. I take a sip of the whiskey and nod for her to continue. She smiles and brings her hand to the edge of the material covering her most intimate parts. Slowly, she pulls the material to the side, revealing a completely shaved and dripping wet pussy. She wiggles her butt in front of me like a woman waving a pork chop in front of a hungry dog. I'm not impressed. I've seen pussy before. I pull back my hand and smack her on the ass. Hard. She yelps and stands upright, turning to give me a curious glance. "So that's what you're into?" she questions, her expression now amused.

I respond with a half-smile of my own. "Did you enjoy it?" Not that I had to ask. I already know the answer. Charla moves closer so that her legs are now straddling my lap. Her hips are gyrating and I can see her pupils dilating. She's practically salivating at the mouth. She leans forward and licks the rim of my ear. "Yes," she whispers. I'm pretty sure there are rules against this type of thing. No touching or some shit. But Charla is damn near ready to pounce on my dick and I'm one drink away from letting her.

"Then that's what I'm into," I reply. I lock eyes with her, not making any further moves. The next one is hers to make. She leans forward a little more so that her bare breasts are no more than two inches from my mouth. I lift my drink and am just about to drown her tits in whiskey when she jumps.

One of the other guys is obviously feeling left out because he has reared back and smacked her ass too. "You like that baby," he sneers obnoxiously. The other men laugh at his ridiculousness. This is what happens when you mix alcohol and testosterone.

Charla stands back up and gets back on her little platform. She gives me a look that says "To be continued.." and I just arch a brow in response. An hour later, Charla is gone and we are being entertained by a petite blonde they call Sami. I've finished my bottle and am ready to call it a night. Tomorrow is Friday and the senate floor is closed for the weekend. Normally I'd be flying home right now, but I'm not ready to face that giant yet so I have decided to stay in DC. Charla left me her number on a napkin. Along with what I assume to be stamped on lipstick. I fold it up and stick it in my pocket. A month ago I wouldn't have bothered with a number. I would have had

Charla on her knees in a broom closet or a bathroom stall. That was a month ago. That was before I ever laid eyes on Heidi Lemaire.

The Denali drops me off at my apartment where I vow to take a long, steaming hot shower until I am ready to fall into my bed. All night long I thought of Heidi. I wondered what she would think of my plans for the evening. I wondered what it would be like to watch her dance for me. I wondered if she would like it if I smacked her ass. I wondered what she was doing. I can't get escape her. She's right there, in every thought. Charla is beautiful and sexy and very, very ready. But I want Heidi, and dammit that pisses me off. Why did I let her in my head? I climb into bed without even getting dressed and try to explain the sinking feeling I have in my gut. What if she's using the same remedy I chose to? What if she's out with someone else? What if she's with Nate right now? The mere thought makes me more jealous than I can stand.

Sometime in the middle of the night I wake up and swear Heidi is next to me. My body senses her. My soul feels her. And I'm fairly certain I heard her whisper my name. I roll over to find there's no one there. Damn. I really need to quit drinking.

CHAPTER NINE
Heidi

I hop off Umbrella Guy's lap and pull myself together. Shelly introduces herself and Emmett to my guest, who no doubt is embarrassed. I would be too if I didn't know Shelly as well as I do. We were roommates for a while right after high school, before I left for college. Everyone knows what those years are like so I'm sure you can imagine we're beyond being modest.

The rest of the evening Shelly goes to great lengths to keep me as far away from Umbrella Guy's lap as possible. She starts by asking me to help her in the kitchen. Then she busts out a freaking board game. Like we're fifteen instead of thirty-two. I did learn his name is actually Rowan. I didn't have a problem calling him by his nickname, but I don't think he liked it very much. He ended up learning my name as well, which made him smile victoriously. At one point I finally get him alone in my room but that moment doesn't last long thanks to Shelly. Apparently she can't find the ibuprofen. And it's an emergency. I'm starting to think it's more like a conspiracy than an emergency though.

I give him an embarrassed shrug when I finally walk back into the room. "She's a little high maintenance," I explain.

He chuckles and walks toward the door way, where I am currently standing. "It's okay. She's just being a good friend. You know, *stranger danger* and all," he jokes. His hand runs from my shoulder all the way to my wrist. He takes my hand in his and pulls me close. His lips press against my forehead. "I had a great time and I'd like to see you again," he says. *Oh no. This was not a date. Please don't think this was a date.* What was supposed to be a thirty minute pick-me-up is turning out to be a two day diversion.

I don't want to hurt his feelings so I smile and agree. "Of course. I'm a firm believer in *finish what you start*," I reply flirtatiously. My mind immediately goes back to Nick's comment to Meghan last Saturday about me not being at his house for the clean-up. I feel a lump in my throat and I'm sure the shift in my mood is a noticeable one. I give Rowan a weak smile as I walk him to the door.

As soon as he is gone, I look around for Shelly but she is nowhere to be found. Of course. *Thanks for the booty call break-up.*

Once I'm in my pajamas, I crawl into bed and snuggle with one of the extra pillows. It's not a hard warm body but it's all I've got so it will have to do. A few hours later, when I roll over, I feel him. My body responds immediately. My skin is on fire. My core is throbbing. Craving. I can smell him, vanilla and musk...and whiskey. He's been drinking. I move my hips in anticipation of his touch. My lips part, preparing to meet his. I snuggle closer, my body searching for the warmth of his. Then I open my eyes. And he isn't here. I instantly feel the loss. Like a punch in the gut that stops you from breathing. "Nick," I whisper, as if I believe I could just conjure him up with the mention of his name. For the first time since the all of this happened, I cry. I cry because I miss him. And I cry because I let him become someone I would miss. The reality of it all sinks in: Nick Knight is going to take more than a couple of beers and a one night stand to get over.

Friday, July 11
Shelly comes into the kitchen as I am finishing up a bowl of cereal before leaving for Hudson's second day of baseball. She is smiling proudly. I glare at her.

"Good morning sunshine," she sings.

I growl.

"What? Somebody pee in your cheerios?"

"Cock-blocker," I say flatly.

She scrunches up her nose and shakes her head disapprovingly. "You don't even have a cock," she says matter-of-fact.

I tilt my head, bringing my chin down, and look up at her. "No thanks to you."

Shelly laughs and takes a sip of my orange juice. "You'll thank me later. When you go for your yearly and are one-hundred percent disease free."

I snatch my glass back from her hands.

"What?!" she calls out. "You're a comfort sex-er. Some people drink. Some people eat. You sleep with random men. That's not going to make you feel better. Sure, maybe for twenty minutes or so, but not permanently. I'm just trying to help you work through your issues here." She pats me on the shoulder. "That's what best friends do, you know."

Is she for real? "Well I am officially revoking your best friend card," I tell her as I stand to put my bowl in the sink.

Her mouth falls open in false shock. "Under what grounds?"

"Failure to give good advice due to extreme sarcasm."

She stands in front of me, blocking me from leaving the kitchen. "That's not fair!" she exclaims. "I wasn't being sarcastic. Besides, you know I'm right. And that's why you love me. You want advice? Real advice? Call Nick. Get it over with one way or the other, so you can get on with your life."

I place a hand on both sides of her face, squishing her cheeks, and kiss her on her forehead. "I will. As soon as I get home."

I don't know how much truth is in that statement but she's right. She usually is. I need closure. Whether it's good or bad.

Another day down at the ball park and I am hot and tired. Hudson's team won a game and lost a game today.

I stay at the pool the rest of the afternoon in order to avoid Rowan. It's always awkward when the one-night stand you had worked out so perfectly in your head doesn't work out so perfectly in real life. I have come to learn sometimes men need more. They need to feel like we want to chase them. Like they are a prize worth winning. Unfortunately for Rowan, I don't have the time or the energy for a chase right now. Don't get me wrong, he is hot and any woman on this beach would jump at the chance to have him rub her down with hot, greasy tanning oil. But with me, it's not about any particular conquest. It's about the conquest in general. See in this whole situation, it's not about *Rowan.* It's about me. You can call me selfish. I call it self-preservation. I've spent enough time chasing men who aren't interested in chasing me back. All men are replaceable now. A means to an end. All but one. One discovered a crack in my armor and found a way to seep in. All the way to my very soul. I have to make sure I don't let that happen again.

CHAPTER TEN
Heidi

Saturday, July 12

Hudson has three games today. I have come to the conclusion I will get a tan and not ever spend more than thirty minutes at a time on the beach. I get all the sun I need right here at the baseball field. I wouldn't trade it for the world though. Watching him run around out there like all the other kids on his team and seeing how happy it makes him to be a part of it all makes me happier than anything else in the world. No one in this crowd of people would ever guess in less than a month he will be having open heart surgery. I often wonder *why him*. Why put such a remarkable burden on such an amazing child? He has such an incredible spirit. He is always so happy and full of love. Then it hits me: *That's* why. Because he cannot be shaken. He will not be broken. Through everything Hudson has been through, he remains unmoved. He keeps on singing and dancing. He keeps on playing and laughing. He has never questioned why. He has never wished it all away like I have. Even at such a young age, he is so much stronger than I.

Tonight is my last night here so I ask if he'd like to spend the night again. Of course he's too wired up and excited to spend a boring night with mom. I don't argue. He deserves this.

They win two of the three games, putting them in the championship playoffs first thing in the morning. He won't sleep a wink tonight.

I purposefully continue to avoid the beach at all costs when I get back to the condo. Until it gets dark at least. An awkward run-in with the Incredible Hunk is the last thing I want right now.

Shelly and Emmett cook stir fry for dinner then we mix margaritas and sit on the balcony, watching the ocean. Well, I'm watching the ocean. They are in their own romantic world. She's sitting on his lap and they're talking and laughing. Shelly says something that obviously amuses him because as soon as she finishes speaking, he leans forward and bites her boob. She squeals and holds herself in mock pain. I can't watch any more of this so I go inside and pour myself a glass of wine, deciding it's dark enough now for me to brave a walk on the beach. I could use some time in my own head just my thoughts and the sound of the waves crashing. I make the mistake of pulling my phone out of my purse. The only time I have used it over the past four days is when I have called Cole to check on Hudson. I have three missed calls from numbers I assume to be clients since they aren't programmed in my phone, two missed calls and four texts from Alex, and one text from Meghan. I respond to Meghan's text and contemplate whether or not to return the four from Alex. I slip on a long sleeve shirt and a pair of flip-flops and make my way to the beach. Halfway down I decide I could actually use some company so I call Alex.

He picks up on the second ring. "Wanna take a walk on the beach?" I ask him.

"Heidi? Is that you"

Silly Alex, who else would it be? Of course, I do hear loud music in the background. Then I remember it's Saturday night. He's probably at Jackson Street Pub. I suppose no one told him he's supposed to sit at home in his pajama bottoms and wait for me to call.

"Come on, Alex. It hasn't been *that* long since you've talked to me."

"It's been long enough," he says, and I catch a hint of something unusual in his voice.

I didn't realize it until now but I've missed that voice. His sexy little accent. The way I can hear him smile when he speaks. *Stop it Heidi.* The music seems further away now and I realize he must have walked outside.

"It's a bad time. I didn't think about you being out. We can talk later," I tell him.

Right about then I hear a woman's voice in the background call his name and inform him she has his beer. *Talk about shitty timing.* Why did I even call him? Some twisted part of me must enjoy self-torture. I really need to figure out what part that is so I can tell it to fuck off.

It's not like I expected Alex to actually be waiting on my phone call. I haven't given him any reason to think he should, and I don't plan on it. I have no business leading him on. He is a man. And a man's got needs. I get that.

"I should let you go," I say, not even recognizing how much truth that statement actually bears.

"That's not necessary," he tries to persuade me.

It's completely necessary. I find my confidence and manage to tell him goodbye.

"Heidi," he starts, but I cut him off.

"I'll be home tomorrow. I'll call you then." *No. I won't.*

Alex isn't a crutch for me to lean on. He isn't 'home base' for me to tag and be safe. It's time for me to put on my big girl panties and move on. Time for us both to move on.

I take my time walking back to the condo. By the way Emmett was latched onto Shelly's boob like a breastfed baby, I can assume they've moved on to a more adventurous playground by now. Alex has text me twice since we got off the phone. *"Please call me back,"* was the first text. Then, *"Heidi…"* was all the last one said. I sit on the sand and stare blankly at my phone. I almost tap the screen by Nick's name twice. This is ridiculous. I have never been afraid of a man. Well, not in the way that I am now. Trey scared the piss out of me, but that was because he drank too much, did too much coke, and used me as a human punching bag afterward. Never have I been afraid of simply picking up the phone and dialing a number. I think it's more the rejection I'm afraid of with Nick than the actual man himself. What if he doesn't answer? Or worse: what if he does answer and just doesn't want to talk to me?

I hop to my feet and head back to spend another night alone.

Sunday, July 13

Hudson's team loses their first game by one point. He looks so defeated. And tired. He looks really tired. I am sorry they lost but glad at the same time. My little man needs some rest. After the game he finds me in the stands and wraps his little arms around my waist.

"You did great out there slugger," I encourage him.

He looks up at me like I've just called him by the wrong name. "Mom," he says matter-of-fact. "We lost." He looks so serious. "If you're not first, you're last."

Well that's a pretty crappy outlook for a six year-old. I hope his coach didn't tell him that. I run my fingers through his sweaty hair. "How about we say: It's not about winning or losing. It's about not giving up."

He curls his mouth to one side as if he's considering what I said. Pretty soon he smiles and shakes his head up and down. "Yeah. That's a good one mom. You're the best." He gives me another hard squeeze before letting me go. I guess he's too big to have his teammates catching him hug his mom. I don't care. I kiss him anyway. On the cheek. I'm not *that* embarrassing.

"I'm going home now. You sure you don't want to come with me?"

"Nah. I'm spending some quality time with dad. He's showing me how to be a man," he informs me.

I fight back a laugh. "Is that right?"

"Yep. We shaved last night. And tomorrow he's teaching me to ride a dirt bike."

"Well I wouldn't want to get in the way of you becoming a man." It's hard for me to keep a straight face.

He takes my hand in his and gives me a sincere look. "Someone's gotta take care of you mom."

Annnnd my heart just melted. He thinks it's his job to take care of me. "No, no my sweet, sweet boy. It is my job to take care of you."

"I love you mom. I'll see you next week."

"I love you too my baby." I lean forward to give him another kiss but he takes a step backward.

"Can we just fist bump this time? You already kissed me."

And now he's six again. I laugh and reply, "Of course," as I hold my hand out for an official fist bump.

CHAPTER ELEVEN
Heidi

Monday, July 14

I wake up in the exact spot I fell asleep in. I don't think I even moved last night. So many thoughts running through my mind: Hudson's surgery and how I'm going to juggle being home with him and packing and moving my store, if I should suck it up and call Nick or just go balls to the wall and go by his office, what is up with my sudden need to cling to Alex, and then Umbrella Guy.

Shelly handed me a note from him when she got out of the Jeep last night. Apparently he had stopped by the condo while I was out having my moment of epiphany on the beach.

"Why didn't you tell me he came by?" I had asked her. *"Because you would have called him,"* she stated simply. *"And as your best friend, it is my duty to make sure you make good decisions."*

She's right. I would have called him. The entire week I was in dire need of a distraction and he had the goods to provide one. Last I checked, I am an adult and my decisions are mine to make. Since when has Shelly decided to become a big, fat road block on my way to Fornicationville? The note was simple and to the point. *If you're still ready, I'm still willing.*-followed by his name and a phone number. I crumpled it up and tossed it in the trash can. No need for it now.

Now, here I am, lying in bed at nine o'clock on a Monday morning like I have nothing to do. I have longed to dream of Nick the way I did three nights ago. To feel him here with me. Every time I fall asleep, it's all I hope for. But it never comes. I get up and make a mental "to-do" list. I have resolved to take a field trip to the senator's office today. It's all or nothing, right? I pull out and discard every decent outfit in my closet. Fifteen minutes later, I have come to the conclusion I should have gone shopping before deciding to go all Braveheart, running to Nick's office after not seeing him in over a week.

I settle on a black tank top, long black maxi skirt with a slit up one side, and a wide brown belt with a turquoise buckle that hangs loosely on my hips. I want him to look, but I don't want to overdo it. I leave the panties at home. They'll just end up wet before it's over with. I'm thinking positive and hoping I won't need them anyway. It's only been ten days since we've seen each other and my body hasn't forgotten how it responds to him. I feel the heat rise between my thighs just at the thought of it.

First on my agenda for today, however, is making sure Hudson's surgery is taken care of. Thanks to Graham and his generosity, I am able to make the colossal down payment with no hesitations. It's crazy how quickly your life can change. Two months ago, I was a single mom who got up and went to work every day. I was a mother who hummed her child to sleep at night, not fearing what the morning might bring for him. I was a woman who never thought about things like how it felt to miss someone's touch or the sound of their voice. A woman who didn't spend her nights wondering if that someone was thinking of her too.
But here I am today, pulling into the parking lot at Dr. Collins' office, preparing to write a forty thousand dollar check in hopes of saving my child's life. My back seat is full of boxes as I start the reconstructing process for my small business and my heart is racing at the thought of seeing Nick Knight. That's life for you. A perfectly imperfect storm. Calm one minute, blowing you completely off balance the next.

Dr. Collins was pleased to see me. *No shit Sherlock. You just bought her a car.* But, I feel like even despite the money, she genuinely cares about the children she works with. She had already assembled a stack of papers for financial assistance in the case I couldn't come up with the money. She could have told me about all that two weeks ago and saved me a few sleepless nights and a boatload of headaches. She assured me once more that this is the right decision and that I will be amazed at the transformation in my son when it's all said and done. He will eat more and gain weight. He can stay active without tiring so quickly. He will have color in his cheeks and his eyes will get back their sparkle. She is so determined and optimistic when she speaks of the impact the surgery will have. It thrills me to think of Hudson this way. *Normal.* I feel like I've just won the lottery. Suddenly, I can't wait until next Tuesday.

With that out of the way, I feel on top of the world. Nothing can bring me down. I am invincible. Now is the perfect time to talk to Nick. He has no idea why, because I have never shared Hudson's illness with him, but I need to thank him. Whether he had anything to do with the other fifty thousand dollars in that check or not, he is the reason I got the money to begin with. Without Nick I would have gotten nothing more than an eviction letter and a middle finger. I was wrong for ever thinking anything different. Graham made me see that.

Nick has affected my life in ways he doesn't even know. My heart swells at the thought. The same man who gives me butterflies, the man whose mere presence awakens every cell in my being, the man who has me submissive at nothing more than a tilted smile- That man has helped me save my son. And made sure I can continue to care for him by also saving my business. All of a sudden, the past doesn't matter anymore. What happened with Alex seems so obsolete. All that matters is seeing him. Letting him know I need him.

The building looks so much bigger than I remember. As I make my way through security and past Thing One, my pulse begins to race. Oh god. I'm really nervous. What if Taylor Montgomery is in his office for one of her weeklys? What if Alex is here? The thought makes me wonder if he's spoken to Alex since last Friday. So many scenarios run through my head before the elevator doors open on his floor. I take in a deep breath and blow out slowly before I exit. Here goes nothing.

Candace is on the phone as I approach her desk. She smiles politely at me and holds up a finger, indicating she wants me to wait just a moment.

"Heidi! Hello," she shrieks as she stands to hug me. Like we're old friends who haven't seen each other in a while. The sound of a cuckoo clock goes off in my head. This one is a little on the crazy side. I hug her back so I don't seem rude, but I'm not really here to see her. I want to see Nick. "What are you doing here?" she asks, surprised. I can't say I blame her. I went from being here almost daily to not being here at all. And I'm sure Nick has bumped my ranking to the *Do Not Allow* side of the guest list.

"I'm here to see Nick," I inform her. She gives me a curious glance. "I know I don't have an appointment, but I really need to talk to him….If he's not busy that is," I say, hoping she isn't about to tell me he has Taylor bent over his desk.

Candace sits back down. Well this can't be good. I swallow hard and wait for her response.

"He didn't tell you?" she asks as if she can't believe I have been left out of the loop on whatever piece of information she has.

I take this as a good sign. It means I haven't been blacklisted. "I've been out of town and haven't spoken with him in a few days." Hey, it's not a lie. I can't tell her he hates me. Then she'd never tell me whatever it is she thinks he should have told me.

"Oh, okay." She looks like she's debating whether or not to fill me in. I have to think fast. I pretend I'm thinking of the absolute worst scenario I can so she feels obligated to tell me to keep me from becoming more upset.

"What is it? Is everything okay? Did something happen to him?" My words are breathy and I make her believe I am about to break down. It works. "No. Nothing bad. He's fine. Don't worry hun," she reassures me. "He's moving to DC. He called last night and had me get in touch with a realtor. He put his house on the market this morning."

No. No. No! I suddenly feel like a very large person in a very small room. My hands begin to shake and my breathing becomes irrational. I reach out and grab the edge of her desk to steady myself. The breakdown becomes real now. The last thing I wanted was to let Candace see how the news affects me, although I'm sure it's totally obvious I'm in shock. "Wow. That's news. Did he say why?"

She looks at me warily. "You know why."

What? No I don't. Surely not because of me? We had a miscommunication. I get taking some time to think about it but holy hell...this is taking "I need space" to a whole other level. There has to be more to it. And now I might never know.

Apparently Candace isn't as ignorant to our relationship happenings as I thought. She is watching me with sympathy as I process the information. I can only imagine what my face looks like. I've never had much of a poker face. "I'm sorry Heidi. I was really rooting for you two," she says.

I feel my eyes begin to burn and I know the tears will be next. It can't end like this. No goodbye. No explanations. He just came into my life like a wave crashing on the shore, stirring everything up and making sure nothing is the same when it rushes right back out. The whole process is beautiful and exhilarating from far away. But when you're standing waist deep in the water, it doesn't take much for that wave to knock you over, and then there you are: left struggling to find your balance.

My anger fights with my pain and I save my tears for someone worthy. So it's just that simple for him? He just walks out of the room and never looks back. I have spent the past nine days missing him until my mind tricks my body into thinking he's here. I spend every second wishing I could take it all back and he has already moved on. Literally. I feel so naïve right now. Just because what I had with Nick changed me doesn't mean it changed him. I am an idiot for thinking it had. Just another trophy. That's all I was. *Asshole.* And this is why I keep my distance. If I don't even give you my name, there's no way you'll ever get my heart.

"Is he coming back at all?" I question.

She inhales deeply before answering. "Honestly, I don't know. I don't think so. He's in session until next week and then....well I'm not sure exactly."

"What about you? What about your job?" Okay, so maybe her employment status isn't my main concern but I do care what happens to her. I do have a real, live, beating heart, you know.

She doesn't seem bothered by the question. As a matter of fact, her tone reverts back to its usual perkiness. "Oh. He's keeping the office here. He just won't be here as much. I'll be fine."

I see. So much for being invincible. It's only eleven-thirty and I'm ready for this day to be over.

75

I give Candace a hug goodbye and let her know I'll keep in touch. Then I take my boxes and spend the rest of the afternoon packing my office.

I'm three glasses of wine in and getting wrinkles from soaking in the bathtub for almost an hour when someone knocks on my door. There are only two people it could be. Shelly. Or Alex. No one else knows the gate code to get in the complex. Except Nick. But people don't knock from a thousand miles away. Another knock. Damn, they're persistent. I wrap a towel around my body without drying off, and go see what in the world the big emergency is.

I haven't talked to Alex since Saturday night so it surprised me to see him standing at my door with picnic basket in hand. He notices my attire and tilts a corner of his mouth and arches one eyebrow. "Do you greet all your guests this way? Or just the ones who bring wine?" His tone is amused but not condescending.

I open the door further for him, allowing him inside. "You brought wine?"

And there's the Cheshire cat grin. "I may have picked up a bottle on the way over," he says as he sets the basket on the dining table and begins emptying its contents. There is a small aluminum pan with an aluminum cover, two wine glasses, a bottle of Shiraz, and a loaf of fresh bread.

"What are you doing?" I ask as I watch him peel back the cover from the pan.

He ignores my question. "Do you have plates?"

I huff at him and shake my head. "Of course I have plates. What are you doing?"

He twists the cork on the wine and pours two glasses while I remain in place until he answers me. "Feeding you. The plates?"

I roll my eyes and grab two plates from a kitchen cabinet. "Already chilled?" I observe as I take a sip from one of the glasses.

"Isn't that how you like it?"

There's something different about Alex tonight. He is usually light and playful, but tonight he is dark, focused, and a little intimidating. I narrow my eyes at him, trying to read his mood better.

He grins again, making me feel more at ease. "Relax, love, it's just dinner." He scoops what appears to be lasagna onto one of the plates and tops it with a sliced tomato and fresh mozzarella. "Unless you plan on spending the evening in that towel. Then I can't be held responsible for my actions." His tone is mostly light but there's a hint of something more. I wonder if he knows about Nick. I really need to stop throwing his name in every thought I have. He's moving. He's over it. Now it's my turn.

"I could take the towel off if you prefer?" I tease. I'm treading on dangerous water and I know it. But I'm willing to own up to my decisions, to suffer the consequences.

He swallows hard and shifts in his seat. He looks over at me with an intensity in his eyes I've only seen once before: the night he asked for my number. The night he got jealous and broke up with my vagina. "Is that what you'd like, Heidi? To know what I prefer?"

Oh god. He's sat his fork down and is watching me. My chest is heaving and my breathing is becoming more rapid. I gulp down the rest of my wine, eyeing him over the glass. If I do this, there is no going back. It can't be undone. If I do this, I am telling all three of us that what I had with Nick is gone. I'm putting the final nail in the coffin. *Shit.* I need more wine.

I've lost my appetite. Alex must sense I'm nervous because he picks his fork back up and cuts into the lasagna. He cuts his eyes at me before taking a bite. "Keep it on," he says. Once he's finished chewing, I see the corners of his mouth turn up, revealing a perfectly adorable set of dimples. "For now," he adds.

I manage to relax enough to finish off half of the lasagna and another glass of wine. By now I am feeling pretty freaking good and not caring much about the fact that I'm practically naked with a man I used to have sex with. He looks so sexy in his jeans and dark red t-shirt. Alex is long and lean but very fit. His clothes don't cling to him the way Nick's do, but there is no question that what lies underneath is delicious. His jeans hang loose on his hips, revealing the waist band of his Under Armour underwear, where Nick's hug the tops of his thick thighs and wonderfully toned ass. Alex's t-shirt is tight across his chest but doesn't cling to his biceps the way Nick's do.

Once it's obvious we've both had enough to eat, I stand to collect our plates and set them on the counter. Alex meets me in the kitchen, standing directly in front of me so that I am trapped in between his body and the countertop. He looks down at me as he reaches for the hem of his shirt and pulls it over his head. Every crease and crevice of his perfectly sculpted abdomen beg for my hands to touch them. I reach out and place a hand on his chest, causing him to close his eyes briefly. Then he hands me the shirt and backs away. "You should put this on."

I nod. "Okay," I reply.

Alex sits on the sofa while I go to my room and make myself more appropriate. I put on a t-shirt of my own, along with panties and a pair of pajama shorts. I plop down on the sofa beside him and hand his shirt back. He chuckles and throws it on the coffee table. "Wasn't good enough for you?" He's smiling and I know I have my playful Alex back.

"You knew I was never really going to wear it. You just wanted to show off your abs," I say as I slap him on the stomach. "You should really think about going to the gym."

He laughs at the statement. "I'm not really into that sort of thing."

"It shows." I give his midsection a look of mock disgust.

He reaches for his shirt. "I should probably put this back on then?" he questions as he peeks at me from the corner of his eye.

I snatch the shirt and throw it across the room. "Don't even think about it," I warn. I laugh as I speak but as soon as the shirt hits the floor, my laughter fades and I am suddenly feeling anxious.

The room is quiet and we are sitting dangerously close to one another. The wine sends courage streaming through my veins so I climb onto his lap and run my fingers through his hair. He tilts his head back and closes his eyes and opens his mouth. I use my grip in his hair to pull his head back forward, forcing his eyes open. I lick my lips. He licks his. I grind down against his lap and look him in the eye. "Is this what you prefer?" I ask right as I lean in and take his mouth with mine.

He continues kissing me as he lifts us both off the couch and lays us on the floor. I am on my back and he is settled between my legs. His hips roll, pressing his rock hard crotch into my soaking wet flesh. I lift my hips and press into him harder. His hands are under my shirt, making their way up my sides to my heaving breasts. My nipples are so hard they hurt. His mouth moves from mine to my neck. He continues rocking into me as he traces his tongue from my collarbone to right below my ear. I wrap my legs around his waist, pushing him harder into me. God he feels so good. We need to get rid of these clothes so I can really feel him. His hands finally reach my breasts, where he squeezes and rolls my nipple between his fingertips. I tangle my fingers in the curls at the back of his neck and moan. "Fuck me," I plead.

"Heidi," he whispers as he nips the bottom of my ear.

"Nick," I moan back.

Alex slams on the brakes so hard I swear I can smell rubber in my living room. He backs off me as if I have just burnt him. He's kneeling in front of me, still between my legs. I open my eyes and sit up. "What?" I ask.

He doesn't answer. He just continues on with his heavy breathing and staring. I scoot forward and touch his cheek. He flinches. "Alex? Are you okay? Did I hurt you?"

He moves backwards and falls on his butt, stretching his legs out in front of him. I crawl onto his lap and wrap my arms around his neck, holding my face just inches from his so he has no choice but to look at me.

He still manages to avoid eye contact. Finally I yell, "Alex! Talk to me. What the fuck?"

When his eyes meet mine, they are full of fire and rage. "Who were you with just now?"

I give him a confused look. "Just now? As in....on the floor, just now?"

"Who were you begging? Me or him?"

"Alex, who are you talking about? What is going on with you?"

"You said his name goddammit. With my mouth on your skin. My hands on your breasts. With my fucking dick between your legs. You cried for Nick," he yells.

Oh shit.

He closes his eyes and exhales a long breath. "Who were you with just now?" he repeats, this time his tone is calm and his voice cracks on the last two words.

"I.....I don't know," I admit. "I thought I was with you. I wanted to be with you. . I don't know where he came from. You have to believe that," I explain.

He takes my hands and unwraps them from his neck, placing them at my sides. "How am I supposed to believe something when you can't even believe it yourself?"

"Alex," I start, but I don't know how to finish.

"I want you Heidi. Any way I can have you. Except for this. Not this way. I won't be a stand-in."

I take his hand in mine and intertwine our fingers. "You won't be. It was a mistake. I'm sorry." I pull our hands to my mouth and place a soft kiss on his knuckles. "Please, Alex. Give it another chance."

He lifts me from his lap and sets me on the floor. Then he stands and walks to where I threw his shirt. He pulls it over his head and starts toward the door.

I panic. I don't know why. Maybe it's because of the wine. Maybe it's the past week finally catching up to me. I'm not sure why, but I'm suddenly desperate. I don't want to be alone.

"He's leaving. Did you know that?"

Alex stops and turns to face me. I note the twitch in his jaw as he clenches his teeth. "You were right. He isn't coming back. And I'm not sure I can handle that alone." I have never been more truthful about my feelings in my life. "Please. Don't go. I know it's selfish and completely fucked up, but I don't want to lose you too."

I let myself cry this time. All the pain, all the fear, and all the loneliness falls down my cheeks with every tear drop. Alex sighs and brings me into his arms. We stand there like that, him holding me, me crying, for what seems like hours.

Finally he lets me go. I wipe my eyes with the back of my hand and my fingertips. He holds my face in his hands. "I'm not leaving you, love. I just need some time to think," he says.

I wrap my arms around his waist and pull myself close to him. "Would you stay for a minute? Just a minute. I just want someone to talk to. Just for a minute."

I can feel him swallow against the top of my head. "Okay," he says softly.

We sit on the sofa and I tell him about Hudson. The whole story, starting from when he was born and finishing with the way I felt when I left Dr. Collins' office this morning. "Fuck, Heidi, why didn't you tell me about this sooner?"

"It's my rock. I'll carry it. I just needed someone to listen. Thank you," I say.

He places an arm around my shoulder and pulls my head against his chest. He rubs my hair as he speaks. "I know you are a strong woman. But even the strongest person in the world sometimes needs someone to hold their hand and tell them things are going to be okay."

I smile against his chest. God it feels good to share this with someone. To not have to fake a smile and pretend like everything is fine.

"So you see, even though this whole ordeal with BKG seemed like a nightmare at first, it's actually not such a bad thing after all."

"And you feel Nick is responsible for that?" he questions. It's not accusatory. More like just asking.

"I guess, but I don't want to talk about Nick right now, okay?"

"Well then, what would you like to talk about, love?"

I grab the remote from the coffee table and switch on the television. "I'm done talking for now."

I search through my recorded movies until I find one I feel is appropriate, then I settle in Alex's arms while we watch *The Best of Me* until I fall asleep.

CHAPTER TWELVE
Nick

I dreamed of Heidi two more times Friday night and woke up with my dick hard enough to break glass. Saturday night, I had determined, wasn't ending up the same way. I ended up back at the club where I met Charla. Then we ended up in the back seat of the Denali. I sent the driver inside with some cash and told him to give me thirty minutes. A decent blow job shouldn't take longer than that. As it turned out, the blow job only lasted about ten, leaving me twenty to learn that Charla is a fan of back door entrances. I sat her on my lap and let her bounce her way into oblivion. She rode my cock while I teased her clit until she came with a scream loud enough to wake the fucking dead. She tried to give me her number again, but I politely informed her that wouldn't be necessary. If I want to fuck her again, I will come find her. It didn't make a difference how tight her ass was, Charla didn't help me cross the finish line. So I still went home needing a release that only one woman could give me. Correction: A release I was forced to give myself while thinking of her.

Sunday didn't turn out much better for me. Monica called twice and Elise called once. I have nothing to say to either one of them. As a matter of fact, I'm done with all the bullshit. I need to wrap up this whole screwed up situation with all of them. If Monica thinks she's going to continue cashing my checks after I found out she's a cheating, lying, little snake, she better think again.
And if Elise thinks this opens a door for her to slither back into my life, she's mistaken as well. I'm not a fan of reptiles. I have to be in Washington until next Thursday, then this session is over and I have the next seven months to decide what I want to do. Aside from the occasional open floor, that is. I decided to use that time to travel. I already have an apartment here and that's all I need. I can pop in the New Orleans office just enough to keep constituents happy, and spend the rest of my time doing whatever the hell I want. As long as

I keep a computer and a phone nearby for conferences and interviews. And just like that, it was settled. I called Candace and told her to put my house on the market. The last thing I need for the next seven months is to sit in a house surrounded by all the negative shit.

We don't convene on Mondays so today I went grocery shopping. I need to put something in my stomach besides alcohol or I'm going to be replacing a liver instead of traveling the world. I'm standing in my kitchen, completely sober, chopping onions for fajitas when I hear it again: Heidi's voice calling my name. I'm losing my goddamn mind. I turn up the television and finish my meal.

 I'm too tired to go out, but I also refuse to spend one more night all pussy whipped over some woman who hasn't even bothered to call and explain what the fuck it was I walked in on last Friday night. Although I do have a pretty good idea. It doesn't take much of an imagination when she actually admitted to fucking him. Even if she didn't have the guts to call me about what happened with Nate, I would have thought she'd at least have had the decency to call about the money. I know Graham gave it to her because he called to question the other fifty thousand. You see, I'm the one who purchased the cashier's check Heidi threw back in Graham's face. I can picture her tearing into him. He told me the whole ridiculous story. I couldn't help but laugh at Heidi's idea that we had some sort of conspiracy going. I can just imagine all the ways her creative little mind had turned me into the bad guy. I can also imagine her in the elevator when Graham came on to her. It fucking pisses me off the way he talked about having her hands all over his dick. I think the arrogant bastard actually liked it. I don't give a shit if she meant it to hurt him or not, the fact remains: she put her hands on another man's cock. Did she like touching him? Now that she believes he's not the asshole she thought he was, even though he absolutely *is* an asshole, will she see him again? I chuckle to myself. It's not like she has boundaries when it comes to not fucking your boyfriend's friends. It makes me wonder what she's doing. Right now. Where she has her hands. Right now. My imagination keeps fucking with me until I need a drink. So much for staying sober. I open a bottle of

Johnnie Walker, not caring that I have to be on the senate floor at seven a.m.

CHAPTER THIRTEEN
Heidi

Tuesday, July 15

I woke up in my bed, but I could have sworn I fell asleep on the sofa. Yep, on the sofa, in Alex's arms. Now that spot is vacant. Why does he keep doing that? He's like a ninja.

Our night got off to a rough start but it felt really nice to have someone to talk to. He didn't try to fix it or fix me. He just listened and sometimes that is the only thing a girl really needs. If I were him, I would have walked out that door and not looked back. Right now, I'm glad he's him. I never would have imagined the first night I was with Alex in the boxing ring that we'd turn out like this; him holding me while I cry over another man and then again while I dump all my problems in his lap. I wish I could make myself feel for him the things I feel for Nick. Life would be so much easier if I could. Don't get me wrong, Alex is the catch of a lifetime. And there is some serious physical attraction there. I just don't get goose bumps when he says my name. Or feel the rest of the world disappear when he walks into the room.

I tried. I tried really hard. I took myself to the one place where I thought I would be able to let him in, and I failed. Epically. And it ended up causing more damage to an already strained relationship. I can only hope that after talking to him and spending the night in his arms, he knows that in my own screwed up way, I care for him.

I send him a text while I'm getting ready.

Me: *What's with the disappearing act, Houdini?*

Alex: *I was afraid you'd wake up and put on another chick flick.*

Me: *Don't act like you didn't love it.*

Alex: *On the contrary, I had to cup check to make sure I still had my balls.*

Me: *Okay drama queen, you pick next time.*

Alex: *Next time?*

Me: *I hope so*

Alex: *Careful what you wish for….*

Talking to him like this almost makes me feel normal and I think maybe I could be okay with what we had. Who needs butterflies when you can have back to back orgasms? *Nick gave you both* screams the annoying voice in my head that just can't seem to let him go. *Yea? Well Nick ran like a little bitch the minute things got tough...so there,* I scream back.

I am at the store, packing up things from the supply closet and kitchen when I decide it's time to let him go. Surely he knows by now that I stopped by his office yesterday. Candace is a sucker for juicy gossip. I crossed the line he drew and he still hasn't bothered calling. It's been over a week. He's had plenty of time to think. Now he's just being a dick. But I still owe him a thank you so I stop at a Walgreen's and pick up a card. It's a basic card with a simple "Thank you" on the front and a blank inside. I spill my guts, as much as I am able, then I drop it by his office. Candace lets me place it on his desk instead of leaving it with her. "Just in case he stops in when I'm not here", she told me. I think the truth is that she'd be tempted to read it if it were right under her nose.

I've done all the packing I feel like doing for one day. Between Meghan, Shelly, and I, we have everything but the store inventory packed and ready for the movers to haul off to storage until I can find a new location. I used the money from Graham and my mysterious benefactor to pay my girls two month's salary while we worked on the move. I'm so thankful I don't have to stress about what they will do during the transition. I made sure to add that in the card.

I clean my apartment then take an afternoon nap before I meet Shelly and Meghan for kickboxing class. Ashton has taken advantage of our involuntary time off and gone to spend some time with her family in Texas.
I walk in and get a few suspicious looks from the other two instructors, who usually spend most of our class sitting on the sidelines talking about our body parts. Perverts.

I take my spot at my usual bag, right in front of our instructor, who happens to be Alex. He walks out from the locker area in his athletic shorts and no shirt. He has his sweat towel draped over his left shoulder and a water bottle in his hand. As soon as he spots me he grins. I shrug and smile back.

He approaches my bag, holding it steady with his hands as he leans against it. "Pleasant surprise seeing you here," he says.

"I didn't want to let myself go. I'm not fond of cats and game shows," I reply with a wink.

"Lucky for me," he says.

The music gets softer in the background, indicating it's time for Alex to begin class.

"It's been a while...so go easy on me, okay?" I add before he walks away.

He turns and walks back to my bag, stopping right behind me. His hands take my arms and raise them above my head, encouraging me to grab hold of the top of the punching bag. "You think because you show up, bat your eyelashes, and flirt with me, I'm going to take it easy on you? Because it's been a while?" He slowly runs his hands back down the underside of my outstretched arms as he speaks. Everyone is watching us but he doesn't seem to care. I can hear the smile in his voice but I am also smart enough to understand the double meaning behind his words. I lick my lips and carefully try not to look at him. I need to play the role of obedient student right now and one look at his boyish grin will unravel my composure.

Alex chuckles then leans in closer, speaking more quietly this time. "What you need to understand, love, is that up until this moment, I have been taking it easy on you."

He walks around to the front of my bag and speaks slightly louder now. "Everything you have done with your body, until now, has been your call. Not anymore. Here, under this roof, this," he guides his hand along one side of my body, "is mine." He gives me one final glance before he turns to address the rest of the class. "That goes for all of you. We're taking it to the next level, ladies. I'm ready to get serious," he flirts. Alex is hot as hell and he knows it. All he has to do is flash his superstar grin and women practically rip their panties off. Not to mention having a body that says "I live at the gym."

He wasn't exaggerating. That class almost killed me. By the time it's over, I am huffing and puffing, and barely able to walk to my Jeep. I ease back in to my former Tuesday night ritual of showering after class then waiting for Alex to stop by. He shows up thirty minutes later smelling like soap and aftershave.

"This is familiar," I say as I open the door and invite him in.

The adorable grin spreads across his face as he walks through the dining area into the living room. "So it is."

"Can I get you a drink?" I offer.

He shakes his head and pulls a small blue and white bottle from one of the pockets of his athletic shorts. "How 'bout a blanket?"

"What's that?" I ask, nodding my head at the bottle in his hand.

"This," he says as he holds the bottle so I can see it, "is the reason you are going to love me tomorrow."

"Promises, promises."

Alex shrugs. "You'll see. Blanket?"

I reach into a basket by the sofa and pull out a throw. "Now what?" I ask, exaggerating my frustration at his secrecy.

"On the floor will be fine," he replies nonchalantly.

I spread the blanket on the floor and have a seat on it. "Are we having a picnic?"

He simply shakes his head and kneels beside me. "Lie down," he orders.

I lay on my side and continue to eye him curiously.

He grins. "Uh uh. On your stomach, love."

"Is this some kind of British knock-off of Simon Says?"

He laughs out loud at the idea. "Not quite. I worked you pretty hard tonight. You're going to be quite sore tomorrow. I'm just going to rub some oil on your muscles. Trust me."

A massage? Heck yea, I'm all in. I get comfortable on my belly and let his hands work their magic.

He sprays the magnesium on my calves and the backs of my thighs then begins to rub and knead my already aching muscles. He moves from one calf to the next, first working the back then moving to the front. His fingers work the soreness out of the bottom of my thighs and slowly inch their way upward. He is massaging the backs of my legs, just below my butt, with most of his fingers, but his thumbs are kneading circles on the insides of my thighs. Heat starts to spread through my core at the nearness of his touch. I fight back the urge to roll my hips, causing his thumbs to graze my most sensitive parts. The spray stings a bit but the satisfaction of the massage outweighs the sting of the oil. His hands move to my sides and begin to slide my t-shirt up to bare my back. He scoots up so he has better access to my upper half, one knee on either side of my hips, and his crotch resting on my behind. He leans forward and unfastens my bra, then sprays my back. As he rocks back and forth, rubbing from my shoulder blades down to the base of my spine, I feel him getting hard against me. "Alex," I say, not sure whether it's a plea to keep going, or a plea to stop.

He lifts himself up off me and moves to my side. "Heidi," he says hesitantly. "There's something I need to tell you."

Life lesson: "There's something I need to tell you" is not a woman's idea of pillow talk when she's ready and willing and lying on the floor between your legs.

"I'm listening," I humor him.

I move to flip myself over but he places a hand on my back to keep me still. "Not yet. It will be easier to say if I can't see your face."

Alright, now he's starting to make me nervous. "Alex?" I probe.

He sighs and runs his fingers through his hair, which I have learned is a nervous habit for him.

"I have been offered a partnership at a highly prestigious and well recognized law firm."

I ignore his request not to look at him and aim a beaming smile in his direction. "Ohmigod, Alex. That's great!"

He remains dispassionate.

"Right? Don't you think that's great?" I say as I sit up next to him.

"I do," he says finally.

"But?"

"It's in Miami," he concedes.

"Oh." *Could he run any* further *away from me?*

I pull my shirt down and fasten my bra. The moment is gone. Instead of hot and bothered, now I'm just lukewarm and deflated.

Now is not the time to be selfish. I don't know much about Alex's professional accomplishments but I can only assume he deserves this. I should be happy for him. I *will* be happy for him. "When do you leave?" I ask after what seems like an eternity of silence.

"If I take the partnership, they want me there as soon as possible." His eyes reluctantly find mine and he gazes at me regretfully.

This is what I do not want. I do not want him thinking this has anything to do with me. I don't want him feeling bad for me nor obligated to stay because of me. I shouldn't have told him about Nick leaving. I shouldn't have opened my soul to him about not wanting to be alone, or about what I'm going through with Hudson. He needs to make this decision with an open mind.

"If you take it? Alex, you have to take it. This is amazing news. Be proud." I take his hand in mine and give him an encouraging smile. "Don't worry about me. I'll be fine. You'll meet some supermodel look-alike, who also happens to be a surgeon of some sort. The two of you will get married, have 2.5 beautiful kids, and live in a house on the beach. I'll see the whole thing transpire on Facebook and be insanely jealous, all the while telling my friends that could have been me."

Alex graces me with his ridiculously sexy grin and pulls my head into his lap. He runs his fingers through my still damp hair. "You could always come with me," he says.

I don't respond right away. I'm not quite sure how. I mean, I'm not a hundred percent against the idea and I can think of a million worse ways to spend my life than on the beach with a gorgeous, successful attorney who also happens to have a beautiful soul.

"You're starting fresh anyway. And the Miami Children's Hospital is ranked one of the best in the nation for pediatric cardiology."

Wow, he's done his research, which makes me wonder. "How long have you known about this?"

His smile disappears and I know the answer can't be good. "They first approached me about two weeks ago."

Aka: Right about the time shit went down for real.

"Why did you wait until now to tell me?"

"Truthfully?"

"Of course," I reply.

He swallows hard before answering. "Until now....you coming with me was never an option."

What he's really saying is *"Now that Nick is out of the picture, we might have a chance."*

This isn't something I can decide right now and it's certainly not something I can decide on my own. "I can't just leave, Alex. I have Shelly, Meghan, and Ashton to think of. Even though I'm starting over, I'm starting over with them. We're a team. They've been with me from the beginning. I can't just leave them hanging," I explain. I'm not feeding him a line of bull. It's the honest to goodness truth. We are girls and you always have your girls' back. It's rule number one in the best friend's handbook.

He smiles reassuringly, "I understand, love. The offer has no deadline. It's an open invitation." He looks into my eyes and I know he is sincere.

"Why can't everything just have a simple answer? Why does it always have to be complicated?"

"Says the woman who has rules against complicating things," he replies with a laugh.

I gasp, like he has just said something brilliant. "You're right!" I exclaim. "Enough with the serious talk. I believe we were in the middle of a massage," I say as I lie flat on my stomach next to him. No sooner has he lifted my shirt again and re-sprayed my back, than my phone buzzes against the wood of the coffee table. "Alex, can you hurry and grab that? It might be Hudson." He's closer and by the time I get him off me and sit up, I may miss it.

Silence.

"Alex?"

Silence.

"What does it say? Who is it?"

He holds the phone in front of me, allowing me to read the name on the screen. *Nick Knight.* My heart races and my stomach flutters. Did Candace tell him I came by? Did he get my card? Why else would he be calling? I can't answer. Not right now. Not with Alex here. That's not fair to either one of them. Crap. This sucks.

"What was that you were saying about complicated?" Alex quips.

Wednesday, July 16

Alex ended up finishing my massage. Under the pretense that he didn't want me to be sore today. My head wasn't completely in it, but my body was loving every minute.
With the new revelation from Alex, and Nick calling last night, I feel like Alice. Like I've fallen down a hole and landed in some alternate, completely screwed up universe, and everywhere I look there's some crazy, fucked up situation testing my sanity. And people wonder why I drink. It's either that or prescription medication.

Alex and I ordered pizza and talked about the phone call that quickly became the elephant in the room. I told him about the card. Well, the cliff's notes version. I felt like the gory details would have been hard to swallow. He understood and respected my courage, which I thought spoke volumes for his character. He encouraged me to call Nick back, but I declined, claiming I wasn't sure I had anything else to say.
Whether he knows it or not, Alex has been a sanity saver the past week. Things aren't black and white between us. In fact, they are very, very gray. But it works. For now. He has given me a shoulder to cry on, a friend to laugh with, and an ear to listen, all while making me feel like a beautiful, desirable woman. No matter where the future takes us, or doesn't take us, I will always care for him because of it. I wish I had let myself see him, really see him, before the whole thing turned into the shit storm of the century. Me and my stupid rules.

Today, Shelly and I are packing up the store. Then we'll be done. Ready for step two.
It takes fifteen boxes, four hours, and a vast array of Chinese take-out, but we finally finish. I seal the last box then take in a deep breath as I look around the now empty space. I remember all the work we put into this place. All the dreams I had while I was

sketching out the floor plan. The excitement of opening day. The way I would smell the cookies all the way into my office.

"We need to make sure the new place has cookies too," I tell Shelly, who is currently staring at the empty spot where her desk used to be.

She walks over and wraps me in a big hug. "It will lil momma. Don't you worry that pretty little head of yours."

"You're not official if you don't have cookies," I say, holding back a tear.

She rubs my back and continues to hold me. "We'll be bigger and better than ever. I can think of all sorts of things to do with Daddy Warbucks," she says with a wink. I give her a disgusted look and she adds, "And his money, of course."

"You're gross. He's a douche."

"He's a sexy douche," she says.

"This conversation is over," I tell her.

"What? I have to hear all about you and Senator Heartbreaker. It's my turn."

"Because a front row seat to the make out session on the balcony wasn't enough?"

She laughs. "I forgot about that."

I mimic her tone, only in a higher pitch, "I forgot about that."

"Speaking of our friendly neighborhood politician, have you called him?"

"Yes. I have," I say proudly.

"And?"

I sigh. "He didn't answer. I tried."

She gives me a look that says *that's lame, try again.* "So you left a voicemail then?"

I pull my lips into my mouth as if I'm too ashamed to speak.

"Heidi Renee Lemaire."

She did not just bust out with my full name! "Lisa Meshell Broussard," I spit back.

She glares at me for using her given name. "Yea. That's right. You have a name too."

93

"You're impossible," she tells me. "You'd rather walk around miserable for the rest of your life than admit you were wrong and ask for forgiveness?"

"I left him a card," I admit.

She bursts out laughing. Hey, I thought it was a good idea. "A card. Like Hallmark?"

"No asshole, a business card. He might need a decorator when he moves into his new place. Yes, a Hallmark card."

"Wait. Rewind. When he moves?"

I nod.

"Explain," she demands.

I sigh again. This is all very draining and I didn't want to talk about it. If you haven't noticed, I don't like talking about things often. "Nick is selling his home here and moving to Washington DC. Alex is moving to Miami to be a partner in some huge corporate law firm. And Hudson is having open heart surgery next Tuesday. Anything else you'd like to know?"

Shelly takes me into another hug. I feel like she may be overdoing the affection a bit, but she isn't touchy-feely often so I run with it. "Oh Heidi, I'm sorry. Dang you've had a rough week. Want to go for a drink?" She's trying to make light of the situation, but a drink doesn't sound like a bad idea.

"Maybe tomorrow. I'm really tired and I just want hot water and lots of bubbles."

She nods in agreement. "Look, I'm here to do whatever you need with Hudson. You know that. And I know you are upset about Alex. I know you were hoping he would be a good substitute."

I open my mouth to correct her. That's not how it was with Alex. *Was it?* She holds up a finger to stop me before I start. "Eh eh. Hear me out."

She puts her finger down and gives me the serious face. "Alex is a great guy. But he's someone else's great guy. You belong with Nick. I see it in your face when you talk about him. I saw it in his eyes the first night I ever met him. At Jackson Street. Remember? I saw how he looked at you. And again here at the office. Watching you two together is like eating ice cream and not gaining weight. It's completely satisfying and at the same time, absolutely unbelievable. It's rare. Don't let that go."

I hate when she's right. "Okay. I will try. But if he doesn't try back, then I....*we*..have to just let it go." I start singing the song from *Frozen* to lighten the mood. Shelly rolls her eyes and walks away. "Hopeless," she mumbles.

I take one last look at the place I once called my very own miracle. Once a cozy, comfortable, welcoming environment; now a sterile, open, and empty space. Nothing is left but bare walls lined with the now empty built-in shelving units I had installed. I make sure all the lights are turned off then I say goodbye to one dream, hoping the next one is everything that this one has been, and maybe even more.

Thursday, July 17

I didn't talk to Alex much at all yesterday. A text or two about summed it up. He wanted to come over last night but I didn't think that was a good idea. I told him I was tired and mentally drained from packing. Tonight he has kickboxing class so avoiding him shouldn't be too difficult. It's not that I don't want to see him because I do. I'm just worried my mind will cross wires with my body and I'll end up trying to persuade him to stay. One way or the other. I have become too dependent on Alex to fill the void. I'm afraid I'm doing it for the wrong reasons and that can't turn out well for either one of us. I need to disconnect with him before one of us...or both of us..ends up hurt.

The best way I can figure to do that is to take some "me time." Get my life back the way it was before either Nick or Alex were a part of it. Back when things were simple and *feelings* were for fairy tales.

I call Shelly and take her up on her offer. Girls' night is in full effect. I vote against going to Jackson Street Pub just in case one of the two whom shall not be named end up being there. We venture in to a new place on Bourbon. We usually try to stick to Jackson Square or Frenchman Street, and stay away from Bourbon. But tonight I wanted something new. Some*one* new. I didn't say I was taking anyone home. But a little flirting never hurt anyone, right?

I slip on a pair of my tightest jeans and a turquoise sleeveless top with a jeweled neckline that criss-crosses right at the crest of my breasts. The top is cut high on the sides, and the jeans sit low, revealing just the right amount of flesh at my hips. I leave my hair down and wavy, slide on a pair of sandals, and hop in the Jeep. I feel good. Confident. In control. Things I haven't felt in a long time. Tonight I take back my life. Close the door on all the negativity and start over. Tonight, we celebrate new beginnings.

CHAPTER FOURTEEN
Nick

I ignored the call from Candace on Monday, but the text I got on Tuesday was pretty hard to ignore. *Please call the office. You had a visitor you should know about.*

My first thought was Elise again. Then Nate. Surely he's not stupid enough to come by my office. Then I thought about Heidi and my response was immediate.

Sure as shit, Heidi Lemaire had stopped by my office, not once, but twice, in the past two days. Candace informed me that the second visit involved her leaving an envelope on my desk. I can think of a dozen different things that could be inside that envelope, some of them good, some of them not so much. Regardless of what my imagination dreams up, the fact remains that whatever it is, it must be important for her to have come by twice. I consider asking Candace to open the envelope and tell me the contents, but quickly change my mind. I'd rather keep my personal stuff personal. So on that note, it will just have to wait.

I couldn't concentrate on shit Wednesday and today I flew out of the blue room like my ass was on fire. Why do I let this woman do this to me? What is it about her that drives me insane the way she does?

I go straight from the airport to my office. Candace has already gone for the day. Good. I'm alone. I open the double doors and switch on the light. As I walk up to my desk, I see it. A white square envelope with my name neatly written in cursive across the front. I take a seat and lean back in my chair, just holding the envelope in my hands and staring at the name. It feels too heavy to be a check, so I can scratch off the thought that she returned the money. It feels more like a card. I open the back flap and remove the contents. A fucking card. "Thank you," is all it says. Very simply and elegantly written in black on the front of a bright yellow card. She brought me a thank you card. I can honestly say that wasn't one of the options floating around in my head for the past two days. I open it up and realize what it actually is: a letter. The inside of the card is filled with her words. I get the sinking feeling in my gut again as I start to read:

Nick,
Let me start this off by saying I hope you are well and kicking some serious ass up there at the Capitol, Senator. What I have to say next isn't going to be easy. I have never been the type to be overly affectionate or share my feelings. Maybe that comes from having a shrew for a mother and a non-existent father, I can't be sure. Whatever the reason, the fact remains, I am not a talker. But there are a couple of things I need to tell you. So, listen up. Please ☺

First, I would like to thank you. I won't bore you with the details, but the money you negotiated, and most likely even contributed, has done more for my son (and my sanity) than you could ever imagine. Without you in my corner fighting for me, I would be in a completely different place right now, so, thank you. I can assure you, the other women who depend on my business for their livelihood would also like to thank you for saving it. For saving us. I owe you more than just those two words, but for now, that's all I can give.

I don't know the details of your demons. But I do know you have been brave. You have allowed yourself to love. And because of that you have allowed yourself to get hurt. This may mean your heart is beaten and bruised, but it hasn't left you. It's still there. Still beating….still capable of loving. The only way to stop a heart from ever breaking is to stop it from ever loving…to let it grow hard. I know this. I live this. We always have a choice Nick: either a hard heart or a beautifully broken heart. With you, I know which I'd choose.

That being said- I am sorry. Let me say that again- I. Am. Sorry.
I need you to know that whatever thoughts you have spinning in your head about Alex and I couldn't be further from the truth. I am guilty. That is true. But not of what you think. One day, when you're ready to listen, I will explain everything. You told me once, before you kissed me, I would be yours. At the time I had no idea what that even

meant. Now I know. I am ruined. No one, I repeat- no one, so much as laid a finger on me after the moment you said "Mine." From that night until I take my last breath, I will always be yours. Should I ever be touched again, it will be your hands that I feel. Should I ever be kissed again, it will be you that I taste. And should I ever make love again, it will be your face that I see. You are the fire in my soul that cannot be put out.

A reply is not necessary, or even expected. I just hope you can understand my need to tell you these things and that one day you will be able to forgive me.

Yours,
Heidi

I've read it twice and still don't know what the fuck to think. What is it that she isn't telling me about her son? Why would she have kept something so obviously personal from me?
Nate must have told her about Elise. Asshole. It's not his place to tell my story. Now Heidi sees me as broken and weak.
And what is this shit about me having the wrong idea? I saw him touching her. I heard them talking. She told me she fucked him. The evidence has been presented. The jury has decided. I blew her case wide open. Guilty as charged. What could I possibly be confused about?
What is all this talk about someone touching her? Is she taunting me? Rubbing it in my face that she is moving on? Is it supposed to make me feel better that even though she's getting fucked, she'll be thinking of me? Fuck that.

I need to talk to her. I need to hear her explanation. Growing up, I used to listen to my mother practice what she was going to tell my father, how she was going to explain a sudden out of town trip with the girls, or coming home late when she didn't even have a job, or where all the money from the savings account went. She would rehearse in the car on the way home, in the kitchen while she was preparing dinner, and in my room while she was putting away laundry. Explanations have never meant much to me. I've always viewed them as well thought-out lies. I need Heidi to prove me wrong.

It's just after six o'clock and I'm sure she's not at work, but I stop by her store anyway. All I see through the large glass windows are empty white shelves and a row of boxes lined up against a brick wall. It's such a contrast to what was here the last time I came. Time suddenly seems like an enemy. It feels like so much of it has passed. I drive around for a while, ultimately making a pit stop at Pour, an exclusive wine bar in the Warehouse district. I order my usual and think about the past two weeks and everything that has changed. I think about the card and everything Heidi said. I wonder what she meant about a broken heart and knowing which one she'd choose. I know exactly what she means about a fire in her soul that can't be put out because she is the same for me. I finish up my second scotch and go home to face my next set of demons, as Heidi likes to call them.

The house is completely dark with the exception of one lamp in the living room and the light above the stove. I don't bother turning anything else on. Honestly, I'd rather the solitude the darkness brings. I pour myself a drink and have a seat out by the pool. It's a cool night for mid-July. I'm mentally re-reading Heidi's card, trying to make sense of it, when Monica joins me. *Great.* An imaginary bell rings, signaling the start of round two.

"I didn't know you were coming home today. You haven't returned any of my calls or texts," she says. Her tone is agitated and I'm not in the mood for her shit.

"I wasn't aware I had to check in with you." I don't look at her when I speak.

She seems flustered. I have never been rude to Monica. I will tell her when to back off, and even let her know when something is none of her business, but I've never been an asshole about it. Except for that day in my office. But I was drunk so that's a technicality, right?

"You don't. It's just....you normally do. And I saw the sign in the yard. I wasn't sure if you would even come back." She laughs nervously, obviously trying to lighten my mood.

I don't answer. I just drink and look straight ahead. I know if I say anything, I might regret it, so I choose to tend to my scotch.

"You wanna explain that to me?"

She's talking about the for sale sign I'm sure. I finally glance over at her with an amused grin. "You mean like you explained that Matthew was Olivia's father when you knew he wasn't?"

She glares at me. "That's not fair."

"Letting me pay for a stranger's mistake is fair? Letting me live with the guilt of Olivia being fatherless for the past four years is fucking fair?" I hear my voice getting louder with every word I speak. My blood is boiling. She opened the gates and now all my anger and disappointment in her is finally set free. "You knew, Monica. You knew there was someone else. But you let me feel sorry for you. You took advantage of me. Of my kindness and of my guilt."

She is crying now but I don't care. The truth is, I'm not angry because I've taken care of them. I probably would have done that regardless, had she simply asked. I am angry because she made a fool of me. She saw an opportunity and she took advantage of it, of me. I'm angry because after four years, I see her for what she is. A woman just like all the rest. A liar and a cheater. A schemer. Just like my mother. And here I thought she was different. Better.

"I can explain, Nick. Please let me explain," she pleads through her tears.

My phone rings and I debate for a second whether or not to answer it. Then I see it's Heidi calling. Monica's excuses will have to wait. "You can explain later. I need to go," I say as I get up and start back inside.

"Please tell me you're in New Orleans," the desperate voice on the other line says as soon as I say 'hello.'

"I'm in New Orleans." I check my caller ID again. *Heidi Lemaire.* But the voice on the other end of the line is not Heidi.

The caller breathes a sigh of relief. "Nick, this is Shelly, Heidi's friend."

"I know who you are." *That still doesn't explain why you're calling.*

"I need your help. Heidi needs your help. You're the only one she'll listen to," she begs. Damn, she sounds really upset.

"Fine. Put her on." I humor her but I swear if this is some kind of game….

"I can't." This chick really sounds like she's freaking the fuck out. "I don't know where she is. Nick, can you just come? Please? I don't know who else to call."

Alright now she has *me* freaking the fuck out. "Slow the fuck down and explain." I've already grabbed my keys and am heading to my car. "How do you have her phone?"

"I asked her for it," she answers, like I should have known that already.

"Why are you calling me?"

"This guy. He was buying us drinks. It seemed harmless. Heidi was being Heidi," she says and I feel my blood pressure rising. *She was flirting.* It shouldn't make me mad. That doesn't mean it doesn't. The friend continues, "after a couple of drinks, I see the guy buy her a beer. I didn't think anything of it. Guys buy her beers all the time." I'm really not in the mood to hear this shit right now. "I get the picture. Get to the point."

"Sorry," she says. "He put something in the beer."

"What did he put in the beer Shelly?"

She begins to speak louder and I can tell she's becoming more frustrated. "I don't know," she exclaims. "Something small. A pill maybe. And now they took her. And I don't know where they went."

"They?"

"Yea, three guys. They were dancing and now they're gone."

I find out where they are and get there as fast as I can. A thousand different things go through my head as I drive. After two weeks, she has finally reached out to me. And now, if something happens to her….I stop my thoughts from going any further. Shelly greets me at the door and we start looking for Heidi. She apologizes at least a hundred times and I let her know I'm glad she called. I send her upstairs while I continue looking down here.

I spot something in a hallway that leads to a restroom. There are only two men, not three, and a woman. One guy has his hands on the woman's ass while another is standing off to the side. "You're an eager one aren't you baby?" the guy in front of her sneers. I can't tell if it's Heidi because her face is hidden by her hair. Her head is hanging forward. What is she doing? I squint to get a better look. She's unfastening the first guy's pants. Something happens and she laughs. When she does, her head tilts back and I finally see her face. Heidi. My heart stops. Guy number two grabs her by the hair and forces her to look at him. He leans in like he's going to kiss her but the first guy shoves him back. "Wait your turn asshole," he yells. What the fuck. Watching this makes me sick to my stomach. These men know nothing about the beautiful sexy woman in front of them. They have no idea how amazing she is. And tomorrow, she'll be just another woman they took advantage of. Yet here they are, slipping her pills so they can have their way with her just because she made their dick hard. I've been clenching my jaw so hard it's starting to hurt. Heidi is giggling at the fighting friends. God she's fucking gorgeous. She's got no idea what they have planned. But I do. I used to put assholes like them in jail for shit like this. Adrenaline and rage rush through my veins as I walk up to the man in front of her.

"It's time to leave the lady alone," I say as calmly as I can, given the situation.

The man looks at me and then back at Heidi. "This lady?"

"She's with me," I warn.

He laughs a cocky laugh. "Didn't look like she was with anyone to me."

Heidi realizes something is going on and looks up. The moment her eyes meet mine, her face lights up. She reaches forward with one arm. "Nick!" she exclaims.

I move beside her and wrap my arm around her waist. She places a hand on my stomach, clenching my shirt in her fist. I haven't changed clothes since leaving Washington, so I am still in my gray button up and black trousers. Her touch sends tiny shockwaves through my body. "Unless you and your friend both want to walk out of here with your own balls down your throat, you will leave now," I threaten. I pull Heidi closer to me to emphasize my point that she is not going anywhere. The creep acts like he's about to step in and pull her away from me so I quickly take two fingers and jab him in the throat, taking his breath away. He's holding the bottom of his throat and slowly falling to his knees while I am leading Heidi through the crowd and out the door. Before we leave, I stop to let security know what happened. I may not stop them from taking advantage of women altogether, but I can guarantee they won't be doing it at this club anymore.

Once we're outside, I call Heidi's phone to let Shelly know to meet us out front.

She takes Heidi in a big hug as soon as she finds us.

"I should kick your ass right here," she says.

Heidi looks confused. "What did I do?"

"You, are going to self-destruct. And put me in the crazy house while you do it," her friend scolds.

Heidi laughs. "Oh Shelly, you so silly."

Shelly looks at me with eyes that beg me to let her make good on her threat. I shake my head in disapproval. I understand her concern, but this is not Heidi's fault. She accepted a drink. She didn't ask for this. But sadly, it happens every day. "I'm taking her home," I inform her.

"Good idea," Shelly says as she hands me Heidi's phone. "Take this. She'll want it tomorrow."

I tuck the phone in my pocket and wave bye.

Shelly looks back over her shoulder as she walks away. "Thank you Nick. Seriously."

I reply with a genuine smile.

I can't stand nosey friends. Typically it's a pet peeve of mine, but I could kiss Shelly's ass for calling me tonight. I don't even want to think about where those guys would have taken Heidi if I hadn't shown up, or how many of them there were, and what all they would have made her do.

On the way to my house, I steal glances at the woman sitting beside me. She can't keep her hands still. She is licking her lips while she traces her fingers on the glass of the window, then runs them along the wood grain of the dash. She traces shapes and patterns all over the passenger side of my vehicle. After about five minutes of silence, she looks at me suddenly, as if she's just realized I'm here. "Candace told me you were leaving. But you're here. Why would she tell me that? Why would she be so mean?" There is genuine pain in her expression and I immediately feel like an asshole.

Fuck. Candace and her big mouth. I'll deal with her later. Now is not the time to talk to Heidi about my decision. "We'll talk about it tomorrow, okay? Let's just listen to some music. We're almost there."

She smiles appreciatively. "Okay," she agrees.

I turn the volume on the radio up and pray she doesn't want to talk any more. Every now and then I glance over at her and notice her body writhing to the beat of the music. I catch myself watching her a bit longer than I should. I don't think she even realizes how sexy she is right now. Her hips are moving and her hands are all over the place. In her hair, running down the sides of her body, and she lightly grazes past her breasts as she comes back up to her neck. This is going to be a long night.

We make it into the kitchen before she realizes where we are. "You didn't take me home," she states, half questioning and half observing.

"That's a matter of perspective," I tell her with a sly smile.

"You stop that right now!" she exclaims, pointing an accusatory finger my direction. "Don't you smile at me like that."

I do it again purposefully and she growls.

"Can I get you something to drink?" I ask with a chuckle.

She doesn't answer right away. Probably because she's preoccupied with the island top. She is running her hand back and forth across the smooth granite surface. Her mind seems a million miles away and I wonder what she's thinking of. "Nope," she finally replies as she hops up on the counter. She doesn't quite make it all the way so I hurry over and grab her hips to steady her.

Our eyes meet and I feel a familiar currant in the air between us. I clench my jaw and fight the urge to fuck her right here. "Time to get down Heidi. Let's get you to bed." Probably a bad choice of words, considering the rapidly growing erection in my pants.

She grins at me. "I thought you liked me up here," she teases. Does she even know how difficult this is? Of course not. She's high as a fucking kite right now. And shitfaced drunk on top of that.

"I do. But you need to get down now," I say, coaxing her off the island.

She lets out a frustrated huff, but complies.

I feel a hard tap on my butt as she walks past. *Did she seriously just smack my ass?* I chuckle to myself and shake my head. This woman. So full of surprises.

She makes it up three stairs and trips, banging her elbow on the hard stone. That's gonna leave a bruise. I help her to her feet then lift her into my arms and carry her the rest of the way upstairs. She twists her fingers in the hair at the nape of my neck then nuzzles her face in the crook there. She inhales deeply then exhales slowly, her hot breath causing the hair on the back of my neck to stand up. "You smell so good. You always smell so good," she says. After she speaks, she runs her mouth along the side of my throat. I can feel her breath on my neck, though she never actually kisses me. She's just teasing me with her lips. I'm beginning to sympathize with the pill pushers. Heidi makes it very difficult to *not* want to fuck her.

We finally make it to my room before my balls explode. "Stand still," I tell her as I fold down the comforter on my bed. I don't know if I can take her touching me again without doing something about it. She settles under the covers and into the pillow. I see her wiggling underneath the comforter and give her a questioning look as I reach to turn off the bedside lamp. It is then that I see her toss her jeans from under the blanket onto the floor. I wonder if her top will be next. She doesn't give me much time to ponder the thought because the next second she is grabbing me by the shirt and pulling me toward her. She stops when our faces are just inches apart. "Let me touch you Nick. Let me kiss you. So I know it's you. So I know you're real." She has moved her hand to my cheek now. Her thumb slides across my bottom lip. Her eyes are desperate. Her lips part as she moves her eyes to my mouth. I can see her hips rolling in anticipation underneath the covers.

That's it. Fuck chivalry. This is too much. I have to do something. I take a handful of her hair and pull her closer, closing the gap between us. My mouth finds hers and I don't hold anything back. I can't get enough of her taste. Once my tongue is inside, it explores every inch of hers. I tighten my grip in her hair as she moans in my mouth. When we are both out of breath and our lips are tingling and bruised, I finally let her go. Her eyes remain closed for a moment and when she re-opens them, they are dark and full of want. Her lips are red and swollen. An insane sense of accomplishment washes over me at the sight, and I smile. *I did that.*

"Is that real enough for you baby?"

She licks her lips and smiles back. "I want more," she says. "You want more." Her eyes move to my crotch. "I can see it." She guides a hand over my hard dick. "I can feel it."

She's still fucked up and we still have a lot to talk about before we go there. She's right though, I definitely want more. But not like this. Not while she's in a different world and I'm stuck here sober and confused about what the fuck to do. Now more than ever. Being with her now, having her here, kissing her like that, it's like we're right back where we were before it all went to shit. It feels so natural. We don't even have to try. But we do have to talk.

"That's all for tonight, okay?"

She sighs and slides her hand beneath the covers, giving me a mischievous grin. She arches her back and closes her eyes. Holy fuck. Is she doing what I think she's doing? She moans and licks her lips. Her eyes open and meet mine and I swallow hard. I can see her hips moving against her hand. Even though she is covered up from the waist down, my imagination has no trouble filling in the blanks. Her back arches again as she lets out a louder moan this time. "Fine, I'll start without you," she says. Then she closes her eyes again and I watch as she picks up the pace. I want to look away. I need to look away. But I am hypnotized by this woman. I can't fucking move. All I can do is watch. I watch as she bites her lip and thrusts her hips while she rubs her clit. She's kicked the comforter off now and I have a front row seat to her private show. Her hand is inside her white lacy panties and she is fucking herself into a frenzy. She brings the other hand underneath her top and squeezes her breast. Then with one final cry, she opens her eyes and looks straight fucking into mine and moans my name when she comes. *Fuck. me.*

I stand frozen as she catches her breath. No woman has ever caught me off guard the way Heidi just did. I have seen and done some pretty spontaneous shit, but that....that was a curve ball I never saw coming. It takes every ounce of willpower I possess not to fuck the shit out of her right now.

Heidi moves her eyes to my hard-as-a-rock dick then back up to mine. "Your turn," she says. Then she giggles. Like it's fucking funny. Utterly clueless as to what she is doing to me.

I reach down and sweep her hair from her forehead. "Go to sleep baby. I said that's enough for tonight."

I spend the next fifteen minutes stroking my cock beneath the therapeutic mist of my shower. Once I'm satisfied I can control myself from taking advantage of someone who is totaled, I climb in bed next her. She's sound asleep. I can even hear her snoring softly and I smile. *Finally.* I watch her sleep until my eyes grow heavy. Just as I am drifting off, Heidi lays her arm across my chest and I place one arm beneath her head. Suddenly I wish I were the one high on pills and tequila. It would make tonight a whole hell of a lot easier to forget.

CHAPTER FIFTEEN
Heidi

Friday, July 18

I wake up slowly. My bed is so comfortable, the comforter so soft. I pull it up to my chin and snuggle down deeper inside. Wait. I open my eyes again and take a look at the space around me. This is not my bed. This is not my room. I flip the covers down and sit up to look around. This is Nick's room. How in the world?

I look over my body and sure enough, I'm pantless. Oh god. I feel the space next to me. It's cold. Maybe I slept alone?

I don't even remember seeing Nick last night, much less coming home with him. Did I really have that much to drink? I mean, there were the two drinks that guy bought, then maybe one beer. Not enough to wake up lost. I try to remember the moment I could have ended up in this bed. I got nothing. I remember Tequila Guy. I remember standing outside the club talking to Shelly. I remember music. I was in a car listening and dancing to music. Was I with Nick then? Why can't I remember anything?

Well it could be worse. I could be waking up in a strange place with a strange man. Always a silver lining. I have no idea where Nick is but I know I feel gross and desperately need a shower, so I help myself. I squeeze some toothpaste on my finger and scrub my teeth the best I can while the water heats up. Nick has water sprays on all sides of his shower in addition to the one above my head. The water is hot and it feels like heaven beating against my skin. I'm sore. And my elbow really hurts. Holy crap it's bruised. Badly. What the hell happened with that?

I'm lathering shampoo in my hair and I could almost swear I see someone out of the corner of my eye. I rinse the soap out and look again but no one is there. Surely if it were Nick, he would have just joined me. Or maybe last night didn't go the way I'm imagining. I really wish I knew. This is very frustrating. I know I asked for it. It was bound to happen. Sooner or later I was going to drink too much, take it too far. But I honestly don't remember getting *that* tanked. When I get out of the shower, I notice a white v-neck t-shirt lying on the bed. *So he was in the room.* I put the shirt on, along with my panties from the night before, and venture downstairs to find a sexy senator.

He's sitting on the L-shaped sofa. I pause just a moment to take him in. His legs are outstretched and resting on a large square ottoman. He has one arm draped across the back of the sectional and his head leaned back resting against the plush cushions. He's wearing black athletic pants and a white t-shirt like the one he left for me. His eyes are closed and I wonder for a second if he's sleeping. I hear him breathe in a deep breath through his nose and exhale back out slowly. My eyes soak in every feature of his perfect face. The fullness of his lips, the way his long dark eyelashes are a direct contrast against his tan skin, the ruggedness of his five o'clock shadow along his sculpted jawline. My hands itch to reach out and touch him. My daydream comes to an abrupt end when he opens his eyes and catches me staring. A familiar fire races through my veins the second our eyes lock. My breath hitches and my lips part. A dark intensity replaces the usual golden hue in his eyes as they examine my body from head to toe. I feel very much on display for him, but the truth is, I love it. I *want* Nick to look at me the way he is looking at me now. I have been here in my dreams more times than I can count. I stand completely still until his eyes finally make it back to meet mine.

He clears his throat and stands. Suddenly I'm nervous. Not a nervous that makes you want to run away, but the nervous that you feel when you know something big is about to happen. He stops directly in front of me and my heart pounds heavily in my chest. He licks his lips and I part mine in anticipation. "Are you hungry?" he asks. *Not for food.*
My stomach growls at the mere suggestion. *Okay, so maybe I am.* "Apparently so," I joke.

He doesn't laugh with me. He just continues to look at me with that same intense expression. "Come with me," he says firmly.

I do, of course, follow him.

He leads me into the kitchen and pulls a plate from the cabinet. "Have a seat," he suggests, aiming his head toward a stool on the opposite side of the kitchen island. He opens the warming drawer and takes out a pan holding a stack of pancakes and a pile of bacon. He sets the pan on the counter, evoking my senses. My mouth waters at the delectable scent of butter and maple syrup. He stacks two of the pancakes and a generous portion of the bacon onto my plate.

"It smells delicious," I tell him.

I witness one corner of his mouth turn up at the compliment. Why is he trying so hard to shy away from me? Did I do something wrong last night? I'll ask later. Right now these pancakes are screaming my name.

Nick begins to leave the kitchen. "You're not eating?"

He looks over his shoulder at me. "I hadn't planned on it," he replies. My eyes scan the fourteen other pancakes and half pound of bacon on the pan. "There are starving children in Africa that would kill for this kind of meal," I call out as he starts walking back into the living room. He can be a dick all he wants. It doesn't mean I have to retaliate. I, for one, am pleased with where I woke up this morning. Let him pout. I'm hopeful.

He stops walking and turns around. He allows the rest of his mouth to join the first half in a full on smile. "You sound like my mother."

I chuckle at his comment. "I sound like *my* mother."

Nick prepares himself a plate and sits next to me. "Keep cooking like this and I might have to stay for dinner," I tease.

He is silent for a moment as he pokes at the food on his plate. "I'm not sure yet if that's a threat or a promise," he says finally.

Ouch. "What is that supposed to mean?" I'm trying to figure out if he's really upset with me or if he's just playing hard to get.

He puts his fork down and turns his whole body in my direction. "Do you have any idea what you put me through? Do you remember last night at all?"

Crap. So I did *do something wrong.* Here we go. "No. Well, yes. Some of it. Why?"

He scoots the plate out of his way and places his elbows on the counter. "Tell me what you do remember."

Not much unfortunately. "I went out with Shelly. We had a couple of drinks. I remember dancing one minute and standing outside talking to Shelly the next. There was music. I was in a car. I know this sounds crazy, but I remember the way the music made me feel. I remember it making me *feel* good. It's the weirdest thing. But I don't remember you. In the car, was it you? The driver."

"Yes," he says simply.

I move my plate now. "Did I call you?"

He shakes his head but still isn't looking at me. "No."

Okay, we're not getting very far with the one word answers, Senator. "Then how…" I begin, but he interrupts.

"Shelly called me."

Oh god. "Tell me I didn't get arrested." Because that would be humiliating.

He laughs and it lights up his face. Thank goodness. I was worried for a sec. "No, Heidi, you didn't get arrested." He stands and turns to go towards the living room. "We have so much to talk about and this is not the way I had it planned," he tells me. I can't read his expression, but I know he's right. Regardless of what happened last night, we do have a lot to talk about.

I take his hint and act accordingly, following him into the living room. He resumes his former position at one end of the sectional while I sit on the same side, just not immediately beside him. I tuck one leg under my butt and cross the other over the top of it. I can feel the cool air against the skin of my thighs and become suddenly aware of the amount of flesh that is exposed there. I tug on the t-shirt, trying to cover what I can and Nick smirks. God, that smirk. That sexy, delicious, tilted smirk that triggers a carnal awareness of his presence. "I think we're a little past that point, don't you?" he says.

So, we *did* have sex last night. I'm suddenly more frustrated than ever that I can't remember. I let go of the hem and hold on to the edge of the sofa, not sure what to do with hands that are aching to touch him right now.

He doesn't wait for me to answer his obviously rhetorical question. "To answer your question, no. I didn't fuck you. I should have. But I didn't."

How did he know...Nevermind. He always knows. "Someone put something in your drink." He looks up and to the right and licks his lips as if he's remembering something. "You were," he pauses then looks at me, "entertaining."

"*Something?*" I narrow my eyes, trying to grasp what he is saying. "Like drugs?"

"Yes," he says shortly.

"No way. People really do that?"

I see his jaw twitch and get the picture, he's not kidding. "They do and they did."

"So that's why I can't remember anything." It's more of a statement than a question. "Oh god. Shelly. If she called you, I bet I scared the shit out of her."

He looks away when he answers. "She's not the only one."

Now I feel like an asshole. I'm officially the friend who has to be babysat. Great. "I'm sorry Nick." It's the only thing I can think of to say.

"What the fuck were you thinking? At a strange place. Taking drinks from a man you don't know. Goddammit Heidi."

Is he really scolding me right now? We haven't spoken in two weeks and he's putting me in time out? "I needed to run. I needed to hide," I explain.

"From what?" He looks taken aback.

"From you," I reply. He wants answers, well there's no time like the present. I take a deep breath and begin to unload on him. "You walked out of the room that night and I knew you weren't coming back. I *hoped* you would, but I knew you weren't. Nick Knight is not a 'benefit of the doubt' kind of man." I wait a second before continuing. Nick doesn't interrupt. I think he knows he needs to hear this every bit as much as I need to say it. "I thought about you every minute of every day. I tried everything to distract myself. I threw myself into my work. I even lashed out at Graham because of some ridiculous image of you I had created in my head. I had to villainize you, to make myself the victim. That was the only way I could let myself be okay with you leaving. To make it your fault."

I can hear my voice shaking as I speak. "But when I talked to Graham, he told me the truth, even though deep down, I already knew. I knew what happened was my fault. I had just never accepted the blame because it made me feel…..less than. So I did what I do best to make me feel more than." Nick takes that moment to look away from me. I know what he's thinking so I continue. "But it didn't happen, and I was left trying to find another way." He blows out a breath of relief and once again meets my gaze. "During all this, I had been putting off a decision. A decision that will ultimately affect the rest of my life, and Hudson's. A decision that would have been made for me if it weren't for you." I can feel a lump begin to form in my throat at the thought of what Nick has done for my son, but I choke it back. I will not cry. "So I wanted to tell you how much I appreciated that. And I wanted to tell you how much I missed you. But you weren't there." I have to stop for a minute. I can't look at him through this. I will lose it. I look out the window as I continue. "When Candace told me you had left, I lost it. All of the courage, all of the strength, all of the hope. Gone. My lungs started to contract and I felt like I was suffocating. Trapped. I didn't know what to do." I feel my chest tighten as I remember that day and the way it felt. "I thought I was never going to see you again." I finally look back over at him and find him watching me intently. "It didn't matter who I was with or what I was doing, that's all I could think about. So I decided to get lost. For just one night, I didn't want to think. I didn't want to feel. I didn't want to be found."

Nick waits before responding, making sure I've said everything I need to say. "Heidi," he starts, then pauses. "I know how that feels. Believe me. I *know* how that feels. The past two weeks have been hell. When Candace told me you came by the office that was it. I was done. The truth didn't matter. The past didn't matter. The only thing that did matter was me getting home to see you. To be with you." He swallows hard and closes his eyes briefly. "But the truth is, it does matter. I need to know what happened. Before this goes any further, I need you to tell me about Nate."

I knew this was coming. I just wish I had had time to rehearse. Who knows what's liable to come out of my mouth now. "Do we have to start with that? Isn't there anything else you want to know?" He shoots me a warning with his eyes. I huff. "Fine. Where would you like me to start?"

"How about with, did you fuck him?"

"It's not that simple," I say.

"It's a yes or no question, Heidi. That's pretty fucking simple."

I guess there really is no easy way to do this, is there? "Yes," I say. "But…"

I don't get to finish because Nick pounds his fist into the arm of the sofa as he stands up. "Fuck. Fuck! FUUUUUCK!" His voice gets louder with every 'fuck' he spits. He runs his fingers through his hair and looks up to the ceiling. "You know, I was hoping I had misunderstood. That somehow, somewhere, the wires got crossed and the whole thing was some big cosmic misunderstanding."

I stand and move toward him but he takes a step back. "It is a misunderstanding. Let me explain."

He looks back down and stares right through me, his eyes full of fury. "What is left to understand? What I want to know is why? Was I not good enough for you? Did I make you wait too long? You couldn't find someone other than my best friend?"

"I didn't know he was your best friend," I explain.

He laughs. Not a *haha that's funny* laugh, but a *I'm about to lose my shit* laugh. "Did you miss the part where I introduced you?"

"You didn't introduce us."

He leans against a built in bookcase and scans the room as if the explanation is hidden somewhere in here. "I knew Alex long before I ever stepped foot in your office. When I met you, it had already happened. It was already happening." Nick remains completely still and completely silent, though I can see his chest moving faster as his breathing picks up speed. "That day, when I saw him in your office. I thought it was a game you were playing. I thought you knew about Alex and were trying to throw it in my face somehow. I panicked."

116

Now my chest is heaving. God this is hard. "Then you introduced him as your best friend. I didn't know what to do. So I followed his lead. I figured he's your best friend. He knows you better than I do. If he thought you'd be okay with it, then I would tell you. When he didn't say anything, I decided I shouldn't either. It was wrong. I know that now. But Alex was afraid you'd look at me differently if you knew. Like I would be," I stop to think of the word, "damaged goods."

Nick still doesn't speak so I creep up until I am standing right in front of him. He is looking out the window. He hasn't looked at me since I began my explanation.

"Nick? Say something."

When he turns his head and his eyes finally meet mine, my heart stops beating. His lids are heavy and his eyes are bloodshot and full of water. His face bears the most terribly pained expression I've ever seen. "What's left to say?" He closes his eyes tightly and brings his head down. When he brings it up again, traces of unshed tears line his long eyelashes. Then he moves aside and starts toward the stairs.

"Don't. Nick, don't do this," I call to him. "You want to be mad at me, be mad. You want to yell at me, yell. You want to call me names and curse me out, then do it. But don't you dare fucking walk away from me. Not again," I yell.

He turns around to face me, the sadness gone, replaced by the mutant love child of pain and anger. "You're damn right I'm mad. But I don't need to yell for you to know that." He moves closer to me and I can feel he's about to unleash his wrath so I dig in my heels and get ready. "All your reasons and excuses don't mean a damn thing to me anymore. You are a liar. What am I supposed to do now, Heidi? Every time I look at you, I see his hands on you. Every time I touch you, I will wonder if he's touched you the same way. He's right. I can't do this."

No. I will not let this happen. "No one could ever touch me the way you do. Don't you get it? I'm yours. Body and soul." I reach out to touch him but he backs away.

"Tell me, Heidi. In all your efforts to *heal*, did any of them include him?" He says the word *heal* like it's a dirty word. His eyes bore into me as he waits for an answer.

"It's not the same thing," I tell him.

He clenches his teeth and I can see him getting angry again. "I should have known."

"You mean to tell me you sat in an empty apartment for two weeks? You never once found an eager volunteer to hop on your dick and fuck the pain right out of you?"

"You're goddamn right I did," he yells. "You want a play by play or just the part where she…."

I hold a hand in front of his face, tears finally falling from my eyes. "Stop! Just….stop. I want to go home."

"Shoe's not so pretty when it's on the other foot, is it?"

I glare at him as I fight back any more tears from escaping. "Take me the fuck home," I demand.

CHAPTER SIXTEEN
Nick

Never in my life have I shed a tear over a woman. Then again, never in my life have I lost something I knew I couldn't replace.

The drive bringing Heidi home turns out to be the longest forty-five minutes of my life. She doesn't say a word as she leans her head against the glass and stares out the window. I open my mouth a dozen times to apologize, but nothing ever seems to come out. The angel on my shoulder keeps telling me to do something, to say something. But it's the mother fucking devil in my head that wins every time.

The minute Heidi told me the truth about Nate, I knew any hope of having a future with her was crushed. I knew it because I felt it crash to the ground and crumble to a million pieces, right there along with my heart. I know what she meant when she said it felt like she was suffocating. My chest hurts. My head hurts. I never thought it could get any worse than the past two weeks but today showed me the past two weeks haven't been shit.

I can't pretend it never happened. Nate was right. She is damaged now. And because of that I had to become someone Heidi could hate. She told me herself she needed me to be the villain if she was ever going to move on, so that's what I did. And it is fucking killing me.

I want to turn around and take her back to my house, tell her I'm sorry, tell her I'm an asshole, then spend the next three days making it up to her in orgasms. But I'm not wired that way. I spent too many years watching my father waste time making up for shit he didn't do. My father taught me to hate apologies. Apologies are for the weak. Even though a huge part of me knows this is wrong, I just can't bring myself to do it. The demons of the past will always find a way in and that's not fair to Heidi. So we just continue to ride in silence until we reach her apartment.

Once we're there, she doesn't even look at me when she gets out of my vehicle. Damn, I wish she would. I wish she would take one look at me and just *know* all the things I wish I had the balls to say. But she doesn't. She simply steps out and says, "Goodbye Senator" in her sultry little voice. I remember hating when she would call me that, until I realized it was a game to her, that it turned her on. Now I fucking love it. I sit here like a stalker watching her door long after she's gone inside. I guess I think she's going to just come running out back into my arms. *Think again asshole. She's done with you. And that's what you wanted. Isn't it?*

I'm barely home fifteen minutes when I hear the beep that signals someone entering through one of the back doors. I don't go to see who it is. There's only two people it could be.
I haven't even become properly reacquainted with Johnnie when Monica meets me in the kitchen. "It's already been a shitty day, might as well make it a productive one," I say.
Her forehead crinkles in confusion. "Let me have it baby. I'm all ears," I continue.
She slams a stack of papers down on the granite in front of me. "I figure actions speak louder than words, wouldn't you agree, Nick?"
What the fuck? Surely she isn't crazy enough to sue me. The top paper is a form or an application of some sort and the bottom is a street map with printed directions on the bottom. Maybe she wants me to help her find someone? Or a job? Or if I'm really lucky, a place to live. I examine the top paper more carefully. *Universal Genetics.* What the hell is this? "You need me to help you get a job?" I question. "Just make sure you don't lie on your application."
She rolls her eyes in frustration. "Don't patronize me Nikolas. Fill out the form. Show up for the appointment. Then we'll finish this conversation." And on that note, she leaves just as quickly as she came.

A fucking paternity test. Universal Genetics is a lab and Monica wants me to take a fucking paternity test. Is she that desperate? There's no way I'm Olivia's father. Sure, I fucked her. But that wasn't until after....
Holy shit. What are the chances she was with Matthew right before the bottom fell out and that's when she thinks she got pregnant? I

never asked. Guys don't pay attention to shit like dates and countdowns. Less than a week after she left Matthew, Monica was crying on my doorstep. A bottle of tequila and a good hard dick will do wonders for a broken heart. I'm pretty fucking sure we used a condom. *Yeah, and those things are fool proof, right?*

I don't know how all that shit works, but if she had the guts to give me the paper, then I better find the balls to fill it out before she has me on Maury. After all, this isn't about me, or Monica for that matter. This is about making things right for Olivia.

The lady at the lab said the results from the blood test should take anywhere between three to five days. Now would be a good time for me to go on a bender until then. I let Monica know I took the test and she lets me know she appreciates me not giving her any shit about it. "Thank you. This is difficult enough already," she tells me. I can only imagine how difficult it must be. She never had a doubt in her mind that Matthew was the father of her child. And then one day, here she is, dealing with the harsh truth that he isn't and having people like me judge her for it. In a single moment her world was turned upside down. I know exactly how that feels. It seems I was wrong about Monica. It seems I have been wrong about a lot of things lately.

I head upstairs to lose myself in the relaxing torrent of a steaming hot shower. What should have started out as a normal Friday has ended up being an overextended stay in the Twilight Zone. I may have lost Heidi, but at the same time, may have gained a daughter. *My daughter.* Damn, that's a mouthful. That beautiful curly-haired child already has me completely wrapped around her little finger. I suppose in a way, I always have been her father. Her entire life, I have taken care of her and loved her the way a father should. And in three to five days we'll all find out exactly how much weight that title really holds. I'm excited. I'm nervous. I'm anxious. I'm hungry. I realize I haven't eaten anything since the bite of pancake this morning so I bring my therapy session to an end and think of something to cook.

Just as I'm popping the waistband of my boxer briefs, I hear a faint buzzing sound. Listening closely to find out where the noise is coming from, I realize its Heidi's phone. Shit. I forgot I even had it. She probably doesn't even know it's missing.

I see Nate's name on her screen, or Alex rather, as everyone but me, likes to call him. Why is he calling her? I wait for it to stop ringing then pick it up. Curiosity gets the best of me and I can't help but to scroll through her notifications. That's when I discover she has no password protection so I have a seat on my bed and debate how far to actually take this.

It's wrong on so many levels, but I can't help myself. He's called three times since yesterday and text twice. Damn, he's a persistent little fucker.

Staring at an empty bag where a beautiful body is supposed to be. You wouldn't be standing me up would you love?

That was last night a little after six. He must be talking about his kickboxing class. So she's taking his classes now, too?

She returned that text with *Cat lady is taking the night off to have drinks with Shelly. Movie tomorrow?* Cat lady? What the fuck?

To which he replied: *I suppose I can suffer through it.*

There were no more texts until this morning when he said: *I was thinking we could watch The Hangover.*

I find myself laughing at the insinuation and I have to admit, that was clever. Like it or not, I can see why she's drawn to him. He's not a bad guy. He wouldn't be my best friend if he were an asshole. There are worse men I can think of for her to be with. Like Graham, for example. Thank god she didn't fall in that trap.

Of course she never replied so at four o'clock he sent another text. Although he had called once before then. *You win. You pick the movie.*

I wonder if watching movies is something they together do often. The way Heidi and I used to read. Does he hold her? Do they share popcorn and laugh at the same time? The thought makes me sick to my stomach. Any temptation I may have had of wanting a peek into their private world is gone now. I don't want to know any more. Fuck dinner. I need a drink.

Saturday, July 19

I fell asleep on the couch with my dick in one hand and my drink in the other. I was hoping to wake up to find yesterday was April Fools' Day and I was the unsuspecting victim of some seriously screwed up pranks. Not so lucky.

I shower, get dressed, and get ready to face another day. Heidi's phone buzzes again. This time it's Shelly. I consider answering and having her meet me somewhere so I can hand it off, but I don't feel like explaining why I can't do it myself so I let it ring. Nate called again. Then it hits me, he and I have unfinished business. Hey it seems a shame to stop when I'm on such a roll, right?

Might as well get *all* the skeletons out of the closet. I grab Heidi's phone and take the familiar road to Nate's loft.

I have no trouble getting in since previous experience has given me the privilege of knowing all the codes. Nate answers on the second buzz and I'm not sure if I'm relieved or disappointed that he's home. We have been friends for a long time. We've been through some serious shit together.

Neither one of us says anything when he answers the door. He just steps aside to let me in.

I'm sure he's trying to figure out if I'm here to kick his ass or not. I'm not. Not yet anyway. I pull the phone from my pocket and hand it to him. "She left this at my house. I thought you should be the one to return it."

Nate scrunches his eyebrows together and tilts his head to the side. "Which part confuses you more? The part where I want you to return it? Or the part where she was at my house last night?" I know my tone is cocky but I'm well past giving a shit.

He clears his throat and turns away in an obvious attempt to mask his feelings. "It doesn't surprise me that she was with you. It also doesn't surprise me that you've already found a way to get rid of her."

*This mother fucker here….*I clench my fists hard enough to cause even my short fingernails to dig into my flesh.

"You want to hit me?" His eyebrows raise as he squares his shoulders and smiles slightly at the hint of an oncoming fight.

You're fucking right I want to hit you. "I'm not some little bitch you spar with at the gym, Nate," I warn.

He takes a step forward, daring me. "Believe me, I haven't forgotten," he says, rubbing his jaw.

"And yet you're still standing here, asking for more." My observation is brazen and unapologetic.

The air in the room is growing thicker as we speak. I stand my ground. Nate pushes his boundaries with each step he takes. "If that's what helps you sleep at night," he taunts.

It's my turn to take a step forward. We are less than a foot away from each other now and it wouldn't take more than one wrong word for me to knock his ass on the ground.

"You know what I want?"

Nate cocks his head to the side as he waits for me to answer my own question. I close the remaining gap between us. "I want you to stay the fuck away from my girlfriend," I spit through clenched teeth.

He laughs to himself and shakes his head in amusement. "So now she's your girlfriend?" His eyes lift to meet mine and he scrunches his forehead, narrowing his eyes. "Is that why you've asked me to return her phone?"

Cocky bastard. I open my mouth to explain, then close it again, realizing I have no explanation. Shit. All I know is that Nate is my best friend and I didn't come here to do this. I came to let him know he's won. That I know the truth. I also know that I have really fucked things up with Heidi and for the first time in my life, I feel lost and didn't know where else to go.

Nate steps aside, walks to his kitchen, and pours us both a drink. Even if I feel like ripping his fucking head off and shoving it up his ass, he's a good enough friend to know the way to my heart is through a bottle. He takes a seat on a stool at the bar, sliding the stool next to him back far enough for me to sit.

I sit Heidi's phone on the counter in the middle of our glasses. The pink and blue striped case sticks out against the black granite. Like some sick physical reminder of what, or who, is coming between us. Nate finishes his whiskey with a single swig and slams the glass back down in front of him. He glances at the phone, then over at me. "I'm not returning this to her," he tells me.

This guy must have balls of steel. "Don't be an asshole. She doesn't want to see me," I say as I finish off my drink and slide the empty glass in his direction.

"Maybe not. But my guess is she's been looking for that," he says, nodding his head toward her cell phone.

"Which is exactly why she won't care who returns it."

Nate stands to pour both of us another drink. He shoots back a hefty portion then pours some more. "Why can't you get it through your thick skull?"

I take a sip from the glass he's just placed in front of me and look off into the kitchen like it wasn't me he was speaking to.

He lowers his voice and speaks into the whiskey as he empties his second glass. This son of a bitch is worse with the liquor than I am. "She's made her choice. It's over."

For the first time since we've been friends, I see pain in his eyes. Here I am, acting like a tit because Heidi ran from me. When all along, she ran from Nate too, right into my arms. The difference is, he begged her to stay still while I fired the starting pistol. I remember the way he used to talk about a woman he was fucking and how pussy whipped I thought he was. I gave him so much grief over her. I never knew anything about the woman he was falling for, but now it all makes sense. It had to have been Heidi the whole time. I took her from him. And I'm the one wanting to beat his ass, while he's pushing me to go see her. That's the kind of man Heidi deserves. Not someone like me.

I polish off my drink as we both sit in silence for what seems like hours. We manage to knock back one more before either one of us speaks. "Tell me about her. About you and her," I finally find the courage to say.

"Are you fucking nuts?"

"Maybe." Maybe I am. But something inside me needs to know. I need to know how it was with them so I can know it was different with us. I need to know *I* was different.

Nate lets out an exasperated sigh and moves to the couch. "Since you're obviously into masochism, I'll summarize. But you're not getting details." He chuckles at the last remark, bringing a slight grin to my face as well.

"We met in my kickboxing class a few months ago. She's hot. I'm a guy. So we made an agreement. Nothing personal. First names only. No *mushy shit*, as she called it. All her idea. She claimed she wanted to keep things simple. I played along for a bit. But after a while I started thinking of her during the day. Missing her. Wanting to see her more than thirty minutes on Tuesday nights. Stuff like that. I wanted to share things with her. When I told her this, she went cold. Things slacked off a bit. I guess it scared her. I don't know. Then she met you." He doesn't elaborate on any of it and I can't tell if he's sparing me the details or if the details are too painful for him to talk about.

I continue to stare at him long after he's finished, still playing the arrangement over in my head. "So you never dated?"

"No."

"And going to the movies isn't considered dating?"

He laughs as if he's stumbled upon a fond memory. "You mean chick flicks on her sofa? That started the night she found out you were leaving."

I lean back in my chair letting him know I'm still listening. "We never went out. We never left her apartment. That's when I really got to know Heidi. She opened up to me in ways that I had spent the past two months wishing she would." Okay he can stop now.

"You fucked her while I was gone," I state flatly, not sure if I'm asking him to confirm or letting him know I know.

"No," he says. He stands and makes his way to another drink. "But not because I didn't want to." He breaks out an embarrassed laugh. "I'm not *that* good of a friend."

Neither am I. Because after all he's just shared with me, heart on his sleeve and all that shit, I still want Heidi. Maybe now even more than ever. I still want to her to want me. Only me. She *was* different with me. They were fuck buddies. So what? She never wanted anything more from him. Like me and Taylor Montgomery I suppose. I've heard all I can stand to hear for one night. "So what happens now? I knock on her door, she forgives me, and I just go on like she never fucked my best friend? Love is blind. Right?"

Nate sets his glass on the counter and looks at me solemnly. "No, Nick. Love isn't blind. Love is the only way you ever truly see. Look at Heidi. See her for who she is, not as some stereotype you built based on Elise and all the shallow little Mardi Gras queens you normally wake up next to. This one is different. Tell me you see that. Because if you don't, you never deserved her."

We spend the rest of the afternoon finishing the bottle of whiskey and taking it back to where we left it before my world went to shit. I tell him about Olivia. He says he's surprised it took this long.

He tells me about Miami, and I wish him the best. Until he tells me he's asked Heidi to go with him. I feel my jaw clench at the thought she would actually consider it. Hell, it's not like I asked her to come to Washington with me. *Would* I ask her to come to Washington with me? Would she come? Can I even go now that I may be leaving a child behind?

Heidi's phone buzzes against the counter, disrupting my thought process. That's the second time in less than an hour. Who the fuck is Cole and why can't he take the hint? She's not answering, asshole. Maybe it's the whiskey, but I've decided I'm taking her phone back. I'm taking *her* back. Doesn't matter what it takes. Heidi belongs with me. I think back on Thursday night. The way she was moving to the music in my truck, plopping her sweet ass on the counter, then in my bed. The way she touched herself while I watched. My dick gets hard just thinking of her.

I've had enough. Playtime is for children. I'm taking back what's mine.

CHAPTER SEVENTEEN
Heidi

Saturday, July 19

I've always wondered how a man like Nick Knight has managed to
      stay single all this time. Well,
now I know. He's an ass. Don't look at me that way. I am always
      completely honest and
straight forward with the men I bring home. I never tell them "I'm
      not going anywhere," or
"You're mine," and then wave my other sexual exploits around in
      their face. And to top it all
off, I'm pretty sure I left my phone at his house after my temper
      tantrum yesterday.
As soon as I realized it was missing, I went to Shelly's, hoping she
      had it. I couldn't be so lucky.
Of course she told me she gave it to Nick. I don't have it. Shelly
      doesn't have it. So that leaves me
phoneless until I get the patience to deal with him again.

Honestly, I think I'm more upset with myself than with Nick. I put too
much faith in him. I just expected him to take my explanation about
Alex and go back to the way things were. Pretty naïve huh? I try to
put myself in his shoes. If he had slept with Shelly, no matter when it
happened, I would definitely not be okay with it. And Nick doesn't
seem nearly as willing to compromise as I am. I guess I was asking
for too much.

I'm folding my second load of laundry when it hits me. *Crap!* I was
supposed to meet Alex last night. What if he called? What if Nick
answered? Well now that would certainly put the icing on the big fat
slice of awkward cake, wouldn't it? What if Nick didn't answer? And
Alex thinks I'm ignoring him on purpose. There is way too much

thinking going on in my life lately. I'm ready to get back to simple. See what dating does to you, ladies? It makes you think you're crazy. I finish putting the clothes away and decide to pay Alex a visit. I may be confused about what will become of us in the future, but one thing I am sure of is that he has been a constant in my life the past couple of weeks and I could use some stability before I become a total train wreck.

I don't get dressed up. I don't have to with Alex. I do stop by the store and pick up a bottle of wine and a Redbox movie, though. A short while later, here I am, buzzing his loft, in my black capri leggings and black tank top. Yep, I'm a prize.

"Hey handsome, want some company?" I sing as he answers the intercom.

Mute and pause. *Okay, maybe not.*

"Hello, love. I'll be right down."

Why wouldn't he just let me come up? "Should I be flattered or worried?" I ask.

"Why would you be worried?"

"Am I interrupting something?"

Another mute and pause.

"6129. Type that on the keypad when you enter the elevator. There are only two doors on the 18th floor. You want the one on the right."

I smile like a happy child who just got ice cream for dessert.

The door is cracked when I arrive, so I knock once then push it further. "I brought wine," I yell around the now slightly open door. Then I push it the rest of the way and go inside. Alex is walking toward me with a nervous smile on his face.

"And a movie. Action for you and some man candy for me. So it's a win-win," I say as I wave the plastic case in the air.

His eyes glance behind me and to the side, like he's waiting for me to be attacked by ninjas or something.

"Are you sure I'm not interrupting anything?" I narrow my eyes at him and then look around the room. My eyes land immediately on the familiar pink and blue stripes on the island counter. "Is that my....How did you..." I stutter as I approach the counter.

That's when I notice movement out of the corner of my eye. I look away from my phone into the living room. My breath hitches and I almost drop the bottle of wine. You'd think I'd just seen a ghost. Only I'm not feeling a chill right now. In fact, my body reacts in the complete opposite way when I see him. "Nick," I say once I'm finally able to catch my breath.

There he stands: messy hair, tilted smile, one hand in his pocket, and that sexy glimmer in his eye. His tan skin glows against the color palette of his outfit. He's wearing white shorts and a light blue button up that's untucked, sleeves rolled up to his elbows, and unbuttoned just enough for me to want to unbutton the rest of it. He looks as if he's just come home from a weekend at the Hamptons. He slowly runs his tongue over his bottom lip, never moving his eyes from mine. "Heidi," he says, and I melt. Literally. I can feel my body actually dripping, starting in my panties.

I look back at Alex, realizing what he was so nervous about. He is walking slowly from where I stand toward the living room, while Nick is walking slowly from the living room to where I stand.

I set the wine on the counter and grab my phone. "This is a bad time," I ramble, trying to form a coherent thought. "I should go." My eyes have yet to leave Nick's intense gaze as he moves closer to me. "Thanks," I tell him, holding my phone in the air, "for returning this." I can feel my heart racing in my chest and I know it's obvious in the way I'm breathing when I speak.

Nick hasn't said more than one word and I am falling apart right here in front of him. In front of Alex. I have to go. He has that look in his eyes. This can only end badly. I pull my eyes away from his long enough to look around the room for Alex, but I don't see him anymore. Nick has a way of doing that to me though, making the rest of the world disappear when he's near. It doesn't matter how mad I am. He still affects me. Like poison in my veins. But this is not the time or the place. Fight or flight instincts kick in and I bolt toward the front door. *Sorry Alex, no time for goodbyes. Enjoy the wine.*

Next thing I know, a strong hand lands on top of the one I have on the doorknob. A second hand takes my other hand and brings it to rest on the door above my head. I feel his hard body against the back of mine. He rests his forehead on the back of my head and inhales my scent. "So it's man candy you want?"

Oh god. I can't speak. I can't think. I can't breathe. I lean my forehead against the door in front of me.

He brings his head to the side of mine, placing his mouth immediately behind my ear. "Or maybe it's action," he breathes. I can smell the alcohol on his breath and my mouth waters. I have never loved the taste of whiskey as much as I love it when it's on his tongue. He presses himself against me, making me acutely aware of his erection. "Do you see what you do to me Heidi?"

His voice is like velvet and I pick up the slightest hint of an accent he normally tries to mask. He shouldn't. It's sexy as hell. I close my eyes and tilt my head back, leaning it against his chest. Instinctively, it rolls to the side, presenting my bare neck to him for the taking. His hand slides down the arm that rests on the door. His fingers graze underneath my arm, then the side of my breast, before coming to rest on my waist. He pulls my body backwards into his, digging his erection harder into my backside. Holy shit.

Holy shit. Alex! Ohmigod. I am a horrible human being. I spin around quickly and move away from the door. I search the entire open downstairs area but still don't see him. Nick is standing with his back leaned against the door, his legs crossed at the ankle as he watches me.

"Alex," I call out.

Nick folds his arms and clenches his jaw. "Yes, love?" Alex answers from a room at the end of a short hall off the kitchen.

"Are you okay?" Do I even want to know the answer?

He emerges from the hall, smiling. "Just having a pee. But I'm finished now. Unless you wanted to shake it?"

I roll my eyes at him, saying a silent 'thank you' that he missed the show. "I'll pass," I tell him. "I do need to go though."

He spots Nick at the door and looks back at me, understanding in his eyes. *If he only knew.* "Another time, then," he says and I smell the alcohol on his breath as well.

"Good grief, what did you two do, raid the liquor cabinet?"

Alex grins and I hear Nick let out a huff from across the room. He's watching my interaction with Alex quietly through narrowed eyes and I can't help but wonder what he's thinking. I hope he's jealous.

I wrap my arms around Alex's neck and he pulls me close. "Take it easy on him. He's not used to feeling shit," he whispers loudly in my ear. He lets his hands fall a little too close to my butt and I see Nick stand up straight. *Okay, I get it. No games.*

"Got it coach," I reply with a wink. "Drink some coffee. Take a nap. I'll call you later," I say as I make my way to the door where Nick is still waiting.

"I'll be leaving with her," Nick says boldly as he opens the door for me.

I stop in front of him and look up at him defiantly. I don't remember him asking to come with me.

Amusement dances in his eyes as he lifts one corner of his mouth. "Unless you'd prefer not to finish our," he pulls his plump bottom lip under his teeth and his eyes darken, "conversation."

My mind brings back the feel of his erection against my back, the smell of his breath, the softness of his touch.

Alex is now standing next to Nick, ready to defend whatever decision I make. I look from Alex, to Nick, and back to Alex. "It's fine," I tell him. "But I'm driving," I say, bringing my attention back to Nick, who grins victoriously.

I watch as Alex stands in the doorway and watches us wait for the elevator and I see concession cover him. Like an invisible cloak. He knows. Nick knows. And I know. Although it wasn't spoken as such, I have just made my choice. It may have seemed as innocent as driving a drunk man home, but we all know it's so much more. Two of the most amazing, yet completely unique, men I have ever known were standing side by side and I chose. The finality of it is almost crippling. Part of me wants a do-over. I want time to think. I don't want to lose Alex. I know what I've just given up with him. And at the same time I have absolutely no idea what I'm getting into with Nick. With Alex, I have security, happiness, and really good sex. Alex is the sensible choice. But with Nick, I am alive. Every part of me is more alive than it's ever been. And it's not about security or happiness anymore. Because with life comes those things. I need him. As much I need the air I breathe. And as much as it hurts me to walk into this elevator with Nick, it would have absolutely killed me to walk into it without him.

I'm beginning to become familiar with this kitchen. It's not quite dark out yet so the view of the lake from the windows that line the southern wall of Nick's home is stunning. Since I have no pockets, I place my phone on his counter and stand in front of the closest window to take it all in. It's dusk so the water appears to be various shades of blue and purple with a hint of oranges and reds. The last rays of sunlight peek through the billowy blue clouds, forming a beautiful orange and yellow backdrop. It's breathtaking. I can't imagine him wanting to leave this behind.

I hear the popping of a cork so I turn to see what Nick is doing. "You haven't had enough yet?"
He stares into me with dark eyes. "I'll never have enough."
He pours the red wine then extends the glass in my direction. "This is for you," he offers.
I join him by the island. Just as I reach for the glass, my phone buzzes. We both stare at the screen for a moment. "I'm sorry. I have to get that," I tell him. His eyes move from my face back to the name on the screen, then back to my face. He tilts his head in mock approval and I answer. I was going to answer anyway. I was just giving him a courtesy.

"Hello handsome," I say to Hudson when he greets me with an excited "MOM!" after I answer.
"I miss you," he tells me.
"I miss you too baby," I reply.
Nick is watching me carefully.
"I called you three times mom. You never answer your phone!" he exclaims, feigning frustration.
I chuckle at his pretend adult behavior. "I'm sorry. I forgot my phone at a friend's house and I just got it back today."

Nick's eyes widen at my explanation, but he continues to watch in silence.

"That's okay. I got your note. I can't wait to see you," he says.

I went by Cole's after I left Shelly's last night. Just to let him know how to reach me if there were an emergency with Hudson. Michelle informed me he had taken Hudson to the zoo and aquarium so I ended up leaving a note for each of them. "I can't wait to see you too. Soon, okay?"

He sighs. "Okay."

"I have to go now, but I have my phone so call me any time you want, okay?"

"How about in five minutes?" he jokes.

"How about not in five minutes," I reply with a smile.

I hear his little giggle on the other end. "I love you," I tell him.

"I love you too mom."

Nick stands up straight and lifts his chin at my last statement.

Hudson hangs up and I place my phone back on the counter.

"Left your phone at a *friend's* house huh?" I hear Nick scorn.

As soon as I look up, he has his hands tangled in my hair, pulling my head back as he kisses me with a fierceness like I've never known. The intoxicating taste of cinnamon and whiskey engulfs my taste buds and I am suddenly drunk on him. I wrap my arms around his neck, twisting my fingers in the back of his hair and pulling him closer.

He releases me from the kiss but doesn't let go of my hair. "Well, friend," he says as he keeps my head tilted back, bringing his mouth to my neck. One of his hands move to cup my cheek, his thumb slowly sliding down and skimming over my lips. "This," he says, indicating my mouth, "is mine." He is staring into my eyes with a fervent desire. I can't look away. I don't want to. I want to touch him. Badly. But he has a point to make so I let him make it.

His hand moves down my throat to my collarbone, then slides inside the top of my shirt, pulling it down as he moves. He cups my breast through my bra and moves his eyes to his discovery. "This," he says again, "is mine." I arch my back in hopes he'll give me more.

He brings his hand out of my top and slides it down the front of my body until he reaches the one place that has been longing for his touch for weeks. He cups my mound through my thin pants. "This," he says as he licks his lips, "is mine."

A moan escapes my lips as he applies more pressure to his hold, letting his middle finger penetrate the thin material.

His mouth finds my neck as his grip in my hair tightens. "Tell me you understand, baby. Tell me what I need to hear."

"It's yours. I'm yours," I say, breathless.

I feel him smile against my skin right before he kisses my neck, all the way up to the sensitive spot right behind my ear.

Nick lets go of my hair and looks me in the eyes. "Who is Cole?"

His tone is not angry or accusatory. More like curiosity with a hint of jealousy. I knew it was only a matter of time before he asked. Hudson said he'd called three times. I'm sure that didn't sit well with the senator. I'm not sure if I should keep playing with him or tell him the truth. I'm kind of liking jealous Nick a little. My body likes him a lot. "My ex-husband," I say simply.

He grabs a handful of ass and lifts me up until I'm on my tip-toes and my body is pressed firmly against his. He's hard as a rock and I am about to lose my shit, although I proudly maintain my charade of calm and collected. "I think it's time for a vocabulary lesson. Don't you?"

His other hand grabs butt cheek number two and he lifts me up and sits me on his pelvis. He carries me into the living room and sets me on the back of the sofa. He stands between my legs, close enough for me to feel his arousal teasing me through the barrier of material between us.

I wrap my legs around his waist and pull him even closer. He dips his head until we are eye to eye. His expression is determined with a slight trace of wickedness. "Mine," he asserts. "A possessive pronoun, indicating something that belongs to me," Nick says as he takes the bottom of my tank top and pulls it slowly over my head.

He runs his tongue over his bottom lip in that sexy way that he always does. "I don't know how *Cole* feels about things, but I don't like to share what's mine."

I place a hand on either side of his face and give him a reassuring smile. "I guess you'd have to ask his wife, Michelle." I place heavy emphasis on the word *wife*, for his benefit.

Nick takes a step backward and pulls me down from the back of the sofa, but continues to stand in front of me as he runs a single finger across the waistband of my pants. "And Michelle, does she know her husband is calling you?" He slips the finger inside, just barely, and keeps tracing over my nervous stomach.

I reach for one of the buttons on his shirt. When he doesn't object, I begin unbuttoning my way down. His flawless golden skin and perfectly sculpted torso are screaming to be touched. I slip my hands inside his now open shirt and run them over his chest and back down across his chiseled stomach. "He doesn't call me," I admit.

He removes his hand from the waistband of my pants and I swear I whimper at its absence. He grabs me by the wrist, stopping me from touching him. Then he spins me around so that my front is against the backside of the sofa and his front is against my backside. He takes my hands and places them on the back of the sofa, locking them in place by holding his own hands on top. "No more games Heidi."

I'm half naked and I can't move. I'm completely at his mercy. And it has me excited as hell. I wiggle my butt against him just to see how he will react. He moves one of his hands and uses it to quickly maneuver my pants down around my ankles. I assist by slipping off my shoes then stepping out of the pants. The sooner they're off, the sooner he's in. And I am dripping wet and ready.

I feel a strong hand smack my backside and I gasp. He just slapped my ass. And I liked it. What the fuck? "Don't move," he commands. *Slap it again. Please.*

I struggle between obeying him and pushing my limits. I decide to be still, to assure him that he is the one in control. Because that is what he needs. And deep down, I need it too. "He doesn't call you?" he questions.

I shake my head fervently.

Nick unfastens my bra then reaches around to caress my breast. His thumb lightly skims over my nipple, sending tiny waves of pleasure straight to my core. I moan and throw my head back. His hand glides

136

down my stomach, past my belly button, to the top of my panties. He slides his fingers in just far enough to brush the top of my sensitive mound. *Yes, there. Keep going. Please.* Then he stops. "Tell me, who were you talking to? Who do you miss? Who do you love? Who are you trying to convince I'm just a *friend*?"

Why has he suddenly turned into Chatty Cathy? Good grief, just fuck me already. "Hudson!" I say, a little louder than I meant to. Hey, can you blame a girl? He has me right on the edge and my child is the last thing I want to talk about right now. "My son called me. From his father's phone," I explain breathlessly. "Now please, Nick, no more questions. I'm sorry for making you jealous."

In hindsight, he has been drinking and making him think I was talking to another man may not have been the best idea.

He is silent for a moment so I turn my head to peek over my shoulder at him. He cocks his head to one side and I see the corners of his mouth twitch, indicating the beginnings of my favorite smile. "Hudson?" he repeats.

I close my eyes and sigh. "Yes."

My eyes re-open just in time to catch the sexy tilted grin spread slowly over his face. "Say it again," he requests.

"I'm sorry."

The grin widens across his entire beautiful mouth as he looks away briefly then brings his eyes back to mine. "Not that," he says. Amusement quickly turns to lust and he runs his hand slowly but firmly up my spine, pushing my body forward as he goes, so that by the time he reaches the spot between my shoulder blades, I am completely bent over the sofa. My head is down now so I can't see him anymore, but I can feel him lean over on top of me as he hooks a finger in each side of my panties. "I meant the part where you beg, baby."

Without even thinking, I respond, "Please, Nick." Even if my mouth didn't say it, my body is screaming it. I am soaking wet between my thighs and I am breathing so hard, my mouth is dry. My bra fell off my shoulders when he bent me over the sofa and the cold leather feels like heaven against my hot skin.

He moves to slide my panties down my body, leaving a trail of tender kisses along the way. My body quivers as his soft lips touch every inch of me from my ass to my ankles. I feel him take a step back in order to get out of his shorts, I assume. I know it's probably just the alcohol encouraging him to be like this with me, but I can't make him stop. I want Nick. Anyway I can get him. And if that means taking advantage of his drunkenness then so be it. He can be mad at me tomorrow. Tonight, I'm a woman in need.

I hear the sound of his clothes hitting the floor and my core tingles in anticipation. Nick runs his hand up the side of my thigh then back down again. I close my eyes and wait for his touch to reach the one place I am dying for. His hand moves to the inside of my thigh as he works his way back up. "Please what? What do you want Heidi?"

His hand is inching slowly up the inside of my leg. I'm positive I'm dripping on his fingers. I lick my lips and find my voice. "I want you inside me."

He brings his hand all the way up my leg and runs a long finger along my opening. I can't help but gasp at his touch. He guides the finger back and forth, coating the entire area with my arousal, then he slips it inside of me, knuckle deep. "Like this?"

Yes. I moan. *No.* More. I want more. I need more. But at the same time, I don't want him to stop touching me. I push myself down further onto his finger, but shake my head uncertainly, my body arguing with my mind.

He hovers over me again, placing his other hand at the bottom of my jaw, right above my throat. He lifts my head so his mouth can reach my ear. "I love you like this. So fucking wet. So ready."

He withdraws his finger, moving it a few inches back, spreading my wetness over uncharted territory. I open my mouth to object but nothing comes out. I know he feels me tense up at his exploration because he kisses my neck and brings a finger to my mouth. "Relax baby. I promise I won't hurt you"

Nick brings his other finger back to my front and dips it inside again. Then he moves it to my rear, lubricating it. He repeats this process until I am soaked and sticky from front to back. He kisses and nips at my neck the whole time, distracting me, then he slowly guides the tip of his finger inside the tight little hole.

Oh. mygod. I gasp at the sudden hint of pressure there. Soon, I feel the hand that was on my mouth, now moving deliciously over my

138

swollen clit. I close my eyes and let myself get lost in the sensations that are quickly overpowering me. As one finger continues to send fierce waves of pleasure over my entire body, the other slides further and further inside of forbidden places. I begin to move my hips in sync with the perfect rhythm he has created. His mouth has moved from my neck to the top of my shoulder. His warm, wet mouth on my skin. The heady scent of cinnamon and whiskey on his breath. The bewildering combination of intense pleasure and pain initiated by his touch. It's all too much.

Nick knows. He knows my body better than I do. "Let me hear you," he tells me.

And just like that, as if my body was waiting on his permission, I come. Loudly. Just like he asked.

I have barely caught my breath when I feel him inside of me. He isn't easing his way in by any means. He is fucking me. With a vengeance. His thick cock stretches me to the hilt as he pumps in and out. He's forgotten about the tender kisses on my shoulder, his hands now on my hips as he pulls me into him with every thrust. I will probably have bruises from his fingers digging so deeply into my flesh but I don't care because it feels so good. So fucking good. I hear him suck in air through clenched teeth then release it in a sexy masculine grunt as he finishes.

He doesn't pull out right away. Then again, he never does. I love the way it feels to have him inside of me. Whether it's like this or while he's relentlessly pounding me.

He runs his hands down my arms, locking his fingers with mine when he reaches my hands. I stand up straight, breaking our connection, and he groans.

He turns me around to face him. "Damn I've missed you," he says with a smirk.

CHAPTER EIGHTEEN
Heidi

I may regret this tomorrow. Nick may wake up and realize he's made a mistake. But tonight he can't say no, and I'm not about to retrieve my halo just yet.

Nick handed me his shirt so I wouldn't get cold, but politely requested that I wear nothing else, for now. I left it unbuttoned for his viewing pleasure. And for mine, he's made himself comfortable in nothing but his boxer briefs and we've moved from behind the sofa to sitting in the corner of it. He's got his legs stretched out along one side of the sectional while I sit next to him with my legs draped across his lap. He's tracing his fingertips along the outside of my thigh and watching me as I admire his magnificence. I could stare at him all day. This man is perfection.

"I hope you don't hate me in the morning," I say. My tone is playful but there's a small corner in the back of my mind where the statement rings true.

He stops his movement and looks at me questionably. "And why would I do something like that?"

I intertwine my fingers with his, preoccupying myself with his hands in hopes he doesn't read the hint of truth in my words. "For taking advantage of your clearly impaired judgment." I'm smiling but still nervous of his reaction. Every moment longer I stay with him, I become more anxious about what tomorrow may bring. As badly as I want him like this, I don't want him like *this*. It all happened so quickly. The thing at Alex's, then the thing with the phone call, then the sex. *Oh god, the sex.* Our bodies just kind of took control. But now that it's over, I want to know it's him wanting me, not just his mini-me wanting me.

He takes his free hand and strokes my cheek. "I'm not the kind of man to get half shot after three glasses of whiskey," he says with a grin. "I am light years away from hating you," he adds. "And I happen to know exactly what I'm doing." As he says the last part, his hand moves from my cheek to my collar bone, then between my breasts, spreading the unbuttoned shirt open as he goes. He licks his lips at my newly exposed body.

One look and I've forgotten all of my insecurities. He's right. I suppose I'm the only one around here who gets sloppy after a few shots of the hard stuff. Sex with Nick isn't conditional. There is no: give me this so I don't go somewhere else, or give me that so I'll pay attention to you. Its two people who can't seem to stay away from each other. Plain and simple. I need to stop thinking so much. Unless it's about the way he is looking at me right now. Holy shit those eyes. Normally they're light brown with flecks of gold. Not now. Now they are an intense deep shade of brown with dilated pupils. I bite my lip and return his gaze. "Yes, you do," I confirm.

I climb onto his lap, greeted immediately by his hard on. I rock my wet slit back and forth against him to relieve some of the pressure building there. The shirt I'm wearing falls the rest of the way open with my movement and he rakes his teeth over his bottom lip. "If you keep at it, I'm going to end up inside you again."

"That's kind of the point," I tell him, rocking once more.

"There's something I need to talk to you about first."

Really? Now? We need to talk about it now? I sigh and stop moving. He blesses me with a crooked smile then his face transforms into something more serious. His eyes follow his hands as they brush over my hard nipples. "Did he touch you like this?" He pauses a second before continuing. "After I left, I mean," he clarifies.

I know he's talking about Alex and I knew this would come up sooner or later. I was just really hoping for later. Maybe when we're both fully clothed and I'm not hot and bothered. His eyes make their way back to mine.

"No," I answer simply. There. May we continue?

"Did you want him to?"

You have got to be kidding me! "Do we seriously have to talk about this now? Why is it even important?"

His eyebrows bunch together and he stops touching me. "Because it just fucking is," he says firmly. His eyes narrow and he cocks his head to one side, like he's examining me for something. "Are you in love with him Heidi?" His lips part and his eyes widen as if he's just realized something he thought he'd forgotten.

141

"Are you high?" I huff in disbelief that he would even go there. "No, I'm not in love with him." I make very sure to be specific with my answer so there is no room for confusion.

He seems satisfied with my answer and I smile inside. "Did he kiss you?"

Seriously? This is painful. Like dragging nails on a chalkboard. "Yes." I figure there's no use in lying. The two of them spent an entire afternoon, or longer, and a bottle of whiskey together. They were bound to talk about me sooner or later. Besides that, it went no further than that kiss, which is more than he can say for himself. "Are you done now?"

Nick just stares at me in silence for an uncomfortably long time. I'm sure he's picturing me with Alex. Kissing Alex. The same way I've pictured him a dozen times screwing some girl senseless. Most of the time that girl is Taylor Montgomery. Sometimes it's a stranger. But every time, it hurts. I don't even want to imagine how it would feel if that person were my best friend.

"He wasn't you. No matter how badly I wanted him to be. Kissing him didn't make him you. Touching him didn't make him you. Even calling him by your name didn't make him you." I place my hands, palms down, on his stomach and guide them up his chest and across his broad shoulders. Then I cup his cheeks and look into his eyes. "This is what I want. You. Just you."

I feel his jaw clench underneath my hands. "You touched him?"

Really? That entire speech and that's what you choose to reflect on? *Men.*

"You're being a bit hypocritical don't you think? Considering."

"Considering?" he questions.

I shrug and look at him like the explanation is stamped on my forehead. "Yes. Considering you had your dick shoved up some greedy little hole at some point in the not-so-distant past."

"It's not the same."

"Isn't it? Who was the lucky lady? Was it Taylor? Or were there more than one?" I didn't want to fight with him. I swear that wasn't my intent. I guess my mouth overloaded my brain and all my thoughts from the past day and a half just came tumbling out. I have taken my hands away from his face now and am getting ready to move off his lap, but he grabs my hips and holds me in place.

"I will not apologize for how I chose to repair what you broke," he says.

"I don't want an apology. I want an answer. Come on Senator, you weren't so tight lipped yesterday." I'm antagonizing him. Showing him I can be just as aggressive as he can. This is a battle of wills now.

"I know what you're doing Heidi," he says as he holds back a smirk. "Okay, you win. We won't talk about it anymore." He takes a deep breath and looks at me seriously. "I just need to know your feelings, or infatuation, or whatever you want to call it, with him is over, and we can consider this conversation done."

"Alex has done a lot for me, and I will always be grateful for him. I won't lie about that. Maybe you call that infatuation. I don't know. I still have a lot to figure out about how your mind works." I smile at him, attempting to lighten the mood.

Nick looks away but I touch his cheek and guide his face back toward mine. "But it's nothing like the way I feel about you. I don't need him like I need you. I don't want him like I want you."

He contemplates my words for just a moment then I feel his hands on my shoulders, sliding the shirt off slowly. "Don't tell me you need me. Show me," he says as his fingertips trace an imaginary line down the front and center of my body. He stops just below my belly button, moving his eyes to meet mine. "Don't tell me you want me." He shifts so I can feel his erection between my thighs. "Prove it."

I lift myself just enough to ease him out of his underwear then I slide back down on him. If I thought he was big before...holy hell. He is filling me in places I didn't even know were empty, and I'm not even all the way down yet. This is the first time he's let me take control, so I take my time and ease my way onto him. He places his hands on my hips to assist, but I quickly put mine on top to halt him. I shake my head slowly and bite my lip as I smile at him. He concedes and lets me have my way. I settle myself on his hard thickness, allowing my body to adjust to his fullness. My body sets its own pace, slow and steady at first. Nick lays his head back against the cushion of the sofa and I watch as he closes his eyes and lets me please him. His fingers dig into the flesh on my hips and he begins to thrust his hips. I can't keep control this way. I need more of him. I feel the sensation building and know it won't be long before I'm right where I want to be. My pace quickens and I'm right on the edge. He opens his eyes and licks his lips as he slows his movements. His hands take a firmer grip on my hips and he slows my motions as well. "I'm not finished," I tell him, breathless and throbbing around him.

He lifts one corner of his mouth in a twisted grin. "We're far from finished, baby." He lifts me off him then stands and picks me up. What the hell? I was right. there. I think I may have even growled at him because he chuckles and leans his forehead against mine as he carries me towards the stairs. "Trust me," he says.

Once we reach his bedroom, Nick lays me on the bed face down then kneels above me. He takes his time rubbing my back, placing soft kisses across my shoulder blades then down my spine. His hands run over my bottom then slip between my thighs. He lies on top of me and kisses and nips at the back of my neck while his fingers work me from behind. Just as I am about to let myself go again, he flips me over and kisses me. Softly, sensuously, like I'm his favorite flavor. Every inch of my body is a ticking time bomb, waiting to explode at the slightest touch. I moan in his mouth, letting him know how deeply he's affecting me. I feel his hard body on top of mine and I wrap one leg around one of his and grind myself against him. "Soon, baby," he whispers in my ear. I feel his warm wet mouth on my breast. He teases my nipple with his tongue before taking more in his mouth, then backing off and teasing it again. I tremble and tangle my fingers in his thick hair when his teeth graze the hard peak. My other leg is wrapped around his now, locking our bodies together and urging him into position.

He brings himself back up so we're once again face to face. He balances himself on one elbow while he uses his other hand to move a stray piece of hair from my forehead. He is positioned perfectly between my legs, taunting me. He's looking intently into my eyes, studying me. God he's beautiful. His lips plump and full from kissing and teasing me, his eyes dark with want, his tan skin flawless in every way. I stroke his cheek just to make sure he's real and he grins shyly. "I could look at you all day," I confess.

"I love the way you look at me," he says. He adjusts his position, creating friction between his hard flesh and my swollen clit. I could almost come from the sensation.

"You see me in a way I've never been seen. You have taken me places I never knew existed." He moves his hips, once more sending shockwaves of pleasure through my core. He is barely moving against me as he speaks, bringing me to the brink of insanity. My body is one giant electric current with every inch of flesh, every cell, quivering and tingling with his every move. "You drive me completely mad yet keep me grounded at the same time." I open my legs wider, prompting him to slide easily inside. My hands have moved to the back of his neck, twisting his hair in my fingers, urging him to let me finish. "No one has ever wanted anything as much as I want you." With his final statement he fills me, completely. Finally giving me what I need.

CHAPTER NINETEEN
Heidi

Sunday, July 20

I would swear last night was just a dream if my vagina didn't feel like a freight train drove through it. Well, that and the fact that I woke up in Nick's bed. He isn't here but I can still smell him all around me. On me. In me.

When he finally let me come last night, it was the most amazing and intense feeling my body has ever experienced. I remember his satisfied smile as I caught my breath. He does it to me every time. No matter how much I may believe I'm in control, he is always the one with the power. He knew exactly what he was doing the whole time. From the way he graced my body with a seemingly random touch to the way he got my adrenaline pumping through my emotions, Nick had me right where he wanted me. He is a skilled conductor and my body is his orchestra.

My gorgeous maestro walks into the room carrying tray full of fruit, oatmeal, juice, coffee, and almond croissants. I guess he thought I might be hungry. His smile immediately lights a fire between my thighs. Or maybe it's the sight of him barefoot and shirtless with the top button of his jeans unfastened. Either way, I'm suddenly hungry for more than strawberries and cantaloupe.

"Good morning sleepy head," he says as he sits next to me, placing the tray in front of him. "Hungry?"

I sweep my eyes over his body, stopping to admire the important parts, then look back at him. "Starving," I reply.

He chuckles and takes a strawberry from a white porcelain bowl, holding it in front of my mouth. "Open."

He watches intently as I slowly part my lips and accept his offering. Holy crap, it's so sweet. And juicy. Even his fruit is perfect. As I'm chewing, he reaches for the oversized coffee mug and hands it to me. "Just the way you like it," he says with a sly grin.

I'm skeptical. There's no way he remembers little things like how I take my coffee after this long. I take a sip and sure enough, it's just right.

Nick notices the pleasant surprise in my expression and arches a brow. He lightly traces the outline of my jaw with his fingertip. "You haven't figured out by now that I know exactly what you like?" His finger falls to my neck, where he trails it to just behind my ear.

The sheet is pulled up and tucked under my arms but I am completely naked under here and his words awaken every single part of me, making me completely aware of his closeness. Just then, my stomach growls, alerting me that other parts of my body need attention too.

Nick smiles and scoots the tray in my direction. "Eat, baby. You're going to need your energy," he says with a wink as he stands.

"What about your energy?" I ask as he moves toward the door.

"Doesn't seem to be a problem," he says with a smirk when I notice the ever-growing bulge in his pants. "I have a few phone calls to make. Meet me downstairs. There's a dark gray t-shirt in the second drawer. You know what to do."

I finish the strawberries and oatmeal, along with the much needed cup of coffee, then take a shower and freshen up. I pull my hair back into a French braid and go hunting for this t-shirt. When I open the drawer, there it is, right on top. A dark gray shirt with the words "Pleasure Seeker" written in black cursive across the front. Isn't he just full of surprises this morning? I smile to myself as I remember the conversation at my apartment not long after Nick first started coming over. I had called him a pervert and he argued a better term. I suggested he put that on a t-shirt and he said only if I promised to wear it. Only it. I slip the shirt on and wonder when he had it made.

I skip down the stairs like a love-struck teenager and find he isn't in the living room, or the kitchen. He said he had phone calls to make so he must be in his office. I don't want to bother him, and it is a beautiful morning so I make my way onto his patio. The last time I saw it, it was lit up and decorated like a California vineyard on warm summer night. That seems like forever ago. Now there are a few chairs overlooking the pool, a barbecue pit encased in brick, a sink, a rattan sofa facing a wall-mounted television, and a mini fridge which, knowing Nick, I would assume contains alcohol.

I walk over to the pool and dip my toes in the water. It's warm, but it's too early in the morning for the sun to have affected the temperature so I guess it's heated. I remember the window to Nick's office being on this side of the house so I walk until I find it. There he is, sitting at his desk, in heavy conversation with the person on the other end of the phone line. I stand in front of the window for a few seconds, watching him express himself vehemently. When he finally notices me, he greets me with a smile that's a stark contrast to his apparent conversation.

I splay my arms out at my sides, showcasing my obedience for his choice of wardrobe. He stands and walks to the front of his desk. I lift the hem of the shirt just enough to reveal that I am not wearing anything underneath. He leans his butt against the desk and drags his tongue over his bottom lip. He spins his pointer finger in circles in the air, commanding me to turn around. So I do. I lift my arms over my head, pretending to stretch, but in reality I just want him to check out my bare butt. When I turn back around, he shamelessly adjusts himself in his jeans. For my benefit, no doubt. I know what's waiting for me in those jeans and it excites me just thinking about it. Even though I actually want nothing more than to run in there and suck him dry, I contain myself and decide to play hard to get. I shrug and smile half-heartedly, then saunter off back toward the pool, letting him finish his phone call.

I leave the t-shirt on as I walk into the water. His pool has a beach entrance so the water level rises gradually as I walk further in. Once I'm deep enough, I dip under the water, letting it consume me. It is so soothing. I contemplate taking the shirt off because the water makes it heavy as the material clings to my body. I'm about waist deep and relaxing against the edge when Nick runs and cuts a front flip into the deep end.

He comes to the surface, treading water and looking like the cat who ate the canary. "What? You're not impressed by my talent?" he teases as he swims my way. I love seeing the playful side of him. I also love when he's relaxed and in control. I think I'm beginning to "more than like" him...period.

I eye him cautiously. "I'm very impressed by your talents, Senator. I just can't decide which one impresses me most."

He's standing in front of me now, wiping the water off his face and smoothing back his damp hair. I reach up and tousle the top of his head. I like it better messy. His hands find my waist and he wraps his arms around me. Playful Nick is quickly being replaced by lustful Nick. He might just be my favorite. "It could be the way your touch makes the rest of the world disappear." His hands slide down and cup my bottom, lifting me up so I can wrap my legs around his waist. I bring my face beside his so that our cheeks are barely touching as I speak softly in his ear. "Or maybe it's the way your kiss satisfies my deepest cravings." I move back around to face him, letting my lips skim his jaw line as I back up. The short unshaved hair is rough against my mouth but I don't mind because it reminds me that there's an undeniable rough side to this otherwise perfect gentleman. We are now face to face, our mouths just inches from each other. I see his lips twitch as he concentrates on my lips. "It could be the way you already have me wet with that sexy one-sided smile of yours." He looks at me and purposefully grins my favorite grin. I roll my eyes and squeeze my legs tight around him. "But I'm still undecided about the whole orgasm torture thing you pulled last night," I say with a smile.

Nick glides his hands up my sides, easing my shirt up as he goes and reminding me that I'm fully exposed from the waist down. He's managed to change into a pair of dark blue swimming trunks. So his attempt at removing my top makes the playing field a little uneven, wouldn't you agree? He stops just below the sides of my breasts and looks me in the eye. "Torture?" he questions as his hands move to the front of my body. His hands cup my breasts and he skims a thumb over my nipples. "You didn't enjoy it, then?"

He removes his hands while he waits for my answer. "I enjoyed it very much," I reply, hoping he'll touch me again.

He grins and leans in to kiss me. Even in his kisses, he is powerful. The way his hands hold my head steady while his tongue skillfully dances with mine. He leaves me moaning and breathless every time.

"Orgasm *control*," he says once he's tasted enough of me. "Edging. And it's strictly for your pleasure. It keeps me from blowing my load the first round, and keeps you satisfied longer."

"Well, you're very good at it Senator. That must have taken lots of practice." My words are more playful than accusatory.

He shakes his head and smiles shyly, the way you would when someone compliments you for something you don't feel warrants a compliment. "I know your body, Heidi. I know what it wants. What it needs." His hands run along the backside of my thighs and up to my bare bottom. "That's not something you practice. It's just something that was meant to be."

His mouth finds mine again, but not with the intensity from before. This time he places a simple gentle kiss on my lips. "It would be far more interesting if I had you tied up, completely at my mercy, and begging for it, though," he says with a smirk.

Holy shit. Count me in. Where do I sign up for *that*? "I thought you weren't into that kind of thing."

"I don't want to *dominate* you, Heidi. I don't need you to obey me. I don't want to be the master of your mind, because I happen to fucking love your mind. Or of your soul, because it's beautiful just the way it is. But I *will* be the master of your body. Just as you are master of mine."

Oh god. I think I just orgasmed. This man could tie me up, cover my eyes, whip my ass, and fuck me like he hates me...and I would love every minute of it.

I reach between our bodies and stroke his erection through his shorts. "Let me have you then," I plead.

"Not here. Let's go inside," he says flatly.

"You have something against the water?" I joke. From the feel of things, the temperature isn't affecting his....ability to perform, so I don't see what the big deal is.

His expression remains stern. "Bad memories. I don't fuck in the water."

Ouch. That was clinical. *I don't fuck in the water.* Like he was explaining to the waitress he doesn't want tomatoes on his salad. *I don't eat tomatoes.* I shake it off and try not to take it personally. "I understand bad memories, Nick. I know all about them. Don't do that. Don't put up the wall." I see his jaw clench and place my hand on his face there. "We'll make new memories. Good ones. Give me your monsters. Let me chase them away."

"You already are."

CHAPTER TWENTY
Nick

Weakness is never something I wanted to show Heidi. I prefer to keep my monsters under the bed. I never should have jumped in the pool. I knew she was naked under the t-shirt. And I know I can't keep my fucking hands off her. It was bound to come up.

I'm no psychologist so I can't tell you why, but I do know I don't want anything I have with Heidi tainted by the vision of my mother and her secret lover out there, hiding their sin beneath the water. Like that somehow makes it okay, because it was unseen. That day forever altered the way I see women, and I can't bring Heidi into that world. I'd rather fuck her right here on the side of the pool than take her under the water. Let her and the rest of the world know I have nothing to hide with her.

I hold her around my waist and carry her inside. The wet t-shirt clings to her body. I want to peel it off and make her scream. Like she did last night. She has no idea how sexy she is when she comes. Her eyes closed, mouth open, hands clenched in the sheets. The way she licks her lips right afterwards while she catches her breath. And it drives me fucking nuts when she moans my name like it's some kind of prayer.

She's shivering so I grab a towel from the half bath off the kitchen and wrap it around her. I stand behind her and pull her close. "I'm sorry baby. That wasn't meant for you."

She leans her head back against my chest and gives me an encouraging smile. "I'll take my apologies in the form of an orgasm from now on Senator."

Have I mentioned I love her sassy fucking mouth? "I'm pretty sure I can handle that." I grab Heidi and throw her over my shoulder. Then I take her to my shower and let my tongue apologize for twenty minutes under the hot water.

I throw on my jeans from earlier. I don't worry about underwear or a shirt. I'm sure I won't need either one today. Or tomorrow if I'm lucky. Monica took Olivia and went to her parents' for the weekend so we shouldn't have any interruptions.

I lean in the doorway and watch the water kiss her skin as she lathers the shampoo in her hair. She's lost in her thoughts and I am lost in her. I've wasted too many days thinking I'd never be able to look at her this way again. Just when you think you've got shit all figured out. You think you can outsmart life. Keep your distance and play it safe. That bitch flips her hand and shows you a royal flush, knocking you completely out of the game.

It doesn't matter what Heidi did with Nate. Not anymore. Yea, the thought of another man's hands anywhere near her, makes me sick to my stomach, but she has given herself to me in a way she never gave herself to him. The fact that she's here right now proves that. I didn't have *that* much to drink yesterday. I knew she could have chosen to stay with him. Or to turn around and go back home without either one of us for that matter. But she didn't. She left with me. Because just like me, she knows. We opened Pandora's Box. There's no going back. She is mine. And I am undeniably hers.

I lay out a pair of baggy boxer shorts and a white t-shirt for her to wear. It's more for her comfort than anything else. If I had my way, she'd be perfectly fine with nothing on. She doesn't have panties either, but she won't be needing them.

I have a phone call to make while she's occupied. The deputy who booked the pill pusher creep from the club called this morning with an update. He informed me they were investigating him for multiple crimes related to what he tried to pull on Heidi. Apparently there were some pretty fucked up videos on his cell phone. He is part of a group of at least four other men who get off on taking drugged up women to abandoned buildings, taking turns fucking them with whatever happens to be handy, and leaving them there. Some of the more uncooperative women were beaten and violently raped. And the sick bastards actually film this shit. Like trophies. To make matters worse, there's a website that sells memberships to people who like to watch those videos. It's all one big royally fucked up operation. Twisted sons of bitches.

To even think what would have happened if Shelly wouldn't have called me, or if I had still been in Washington, makes me want to kill a motherfucker. Which brings me to my phone call. I am a man in a position of power. I know people who use this same position to manipulate life. They use favors unnecessarily, take money from people who earn it illegally, and talk their way out of *trouble*. I choose to keep my favor count to simple things like box seats at a Saints game. Every single one of my financial contributors make their living the honest way. And I have never paid for pussy.

Just because I'm not crooked, doesn't mean I don't know people. I live in New Orleans for crying out loud. It's like the New York City of the south. There is so much diversity here. You're bound to know all kinds.

I happen to know Carlo Suppato. Carlo Suppato has guys. Guys who can make you disappear, or at least sincerely wish you had. I'm not on his payroll, but you don't have to be to know not to fuck with Carlo. There are families in this city that have been here a lot longer than the politics and his is one of them. I played college ball with his oldest son, Cal, and we became pretty good friends. Carlo assures me if this asshole is lucky enough to get out of jail, before he so much as looks at another woman, his knees will be shattered. I'm good with that. What's having to ride around in a wheelchair for a couple of months compared to the trauma these women will have to suffer the rest of their lives?

I'd do it myself if it didn't mean risking Heidi's safety and my career. Carlo's guys are like shadows. Fucking ninjas. They'll break your nose while you're taking a piss and you'll never even know they were in the room.

I finish my phone call before Heidi finds me in my office. I'm in my chair. Her hair is damp and hanging loosely over her shoulders. She looks like heaven in my clothes. The boxers swallow her up and do absolutely nothing for her ass, but the v neck t-shirt does nothing to hide her beautiful braless breasts. She walks over and plops her ass on my desk in front of me. "Why so serious, Senator?" she asks with a familiar gleam in her eyes.

I choose not to fill her in on the mornings' events. No need to add that to her list of things to feel like she needs to handle. I've handled it for her. I wish she'd let go and me handle whatever else she worries about when she's alone. Which reminds me...

"Tell me about Hudson," I say.

She immediately looks away and slides off the desk. I watch as she swallows a lump in her throat then looks back at me. "Why?" she asks, moving from in front of me to look out the window.

I move to lean on the front of my desk, closer to her but giving her space at the same time. "Because it's important to you. And you're important to me."

I hear her sniffle and know she's crying. She doesn't turn around. I assume because she doesn't want to appear weak. My Heidi. If she only knew how badly I want to be her strength. I don't push her though. She brings her hand to wipe underneath her eyes before she speaks. "Hudson was born sick. He has a heart defect."

Fuck. I swipe my hand over my face to regroup, but she continues. "Initially they believed it would self-correct, but it's gotten worse."

She turns to face me but stays where she is. Her eyes move from one corner of the room to another, never meeting mine. "He has to have surgery. Or he could die. Something about blood clots in his lungs..." she tells me.

I see the pain in her face. Pain I am helpless against. I knew her son wasn't well, but I never expected this. All this time, she's been carrying this around alone. And I have been acting like an asshole. Way to go Nick.

"Are you ready for the punch line?" she says, sarcastically laughing to herself. I just wait, letting her finish when she's ready. "Not long ago they discovered he also has a blood disorder. Mild, but present. So the surgery, could either save him, or kill him. Depending on how his body reacts to it." She pauses a moment then starts speaking again. "Not the surgery itself. He should handle that fine. But the recovery process will be critical."

Fuck. What do you say to that? Her eyes finally meet mine and I know she's said all she's going to say for now. I walk over to the window where she stands and wrap my arms around her. "I'm so fucking sorry, baby. Tell me what to do and I'll do it. Whatever you need, it's done."

She tilts her head back and looks up at me with a meek smile and tears in her eyes. "You've already done it."

I don't understand. If she means by making her forget about it for a night, then as grateful as I am for that, it's not enough. I want to help her. To take care of this. I know doctors. I just need to make a few calls and....

Heidi interrupts my internal planning. "The check you sent. The money from Graham," she pauses to smile at me, "and his mystery partner, paid for the surgery. It wouldn't have even been an option without it. So, thank you Senator," she says coyly. I can tell she's trying to distract herself from thinking about it too heavily.

"So you've scheduled it, then?"

"Yes. It's Tuesday," she replies.

What the fuck? "As in, the day after tomorrow?"

"Yes."

I back away from her and stare at her blankly. "Were you going to tell me about it?"

"Yes....No....Maybe. I don't know." She takes my hands and pulls me back to her. "You weren't here. Then you *were* here. And I wasn't sure you were going to *stay* here...It was a lot to deal with and I didn't want to complicate things."

She didn't trust me. I back her up against the window, placing a hand on the glass on either side of her head, my face less than a foot from hers. "I am here. And I'm staying right fucking here."

I see her breath hitch as I move in closer. I need to taste her. Her lips are so full and soft. I bring one hand down hook it under her knee, pulling her leg up onto my waist. She moans in my mouth. I use my other hand to hold both of hers above her head. I let go of her leg, letting it slip off my hips, then I unzip my jeans and let them fall to the floor. "Time for these to come off, baby," I tell her as I pull down the boxers she's wearing. I lift her back up by both legs this time. She's locked around my hips, her back pushed against the glass, wet as fuck. I adjust myself underneath her and slide inside. Goddamn she's hot. "So fucking hot." I close my eyes and savor the warmth of her for a moment. She struggles against my hand, wanting to touch me. I hold her still and open my eyes. I use my other hand to brace myself on the window then I slowly begin to move, easing myself all the way in. She takes in a deep breath when I fill her. It's so tight. So warm. I don't ever want to leave this place. I nuzzle my face in her neck, inhaling her sweet clean scent. My mouth matches the rhythm of my hips, licking and kissing her while I rock into her slow and steady. She moans my name and squeezes her thighs and I lose my shit. I let go of her hands so I can steady myself and really fuck her. Hard. Her hands immediately find the hair at the back of my neck. I love how she pulls on it when she gets excited. I feel my balls start to tighten up and know I won't last long. "Let go baby. Come for me." Heidi slams her body into mine then throws her head forward and bites down on my shoulder as her insides clench around my throbbing cock. "Fuuuck." The pain shocks me but the feeling of her intense orgasm around me has me about to blow. God it hurts but feels so fucking good at the same time. I grab her hips, digging my fingers into her flesh as I thrust myself deeper. And then I come.

Heidi is in the kitchen making sandwiches with grilled chicken breast and roasted red peppers on French bread while I sit quietly on a barstool and watch. She left the boxers on the floor so she's prancing around in nothing more than a white t-shirt and licking her fingers as she attempts to create a sauce for the chicken. It's been established I have a constant hard on when she's near. I didn't think that was even possible. The woman is a fucking magician. She brings her sauce covered finger to my mouth. "Taste," she commands. *Gladly.*
I open my mouth and allow her to tempt me. Damn. "Not bad."
Her mouth falls open and she looks at me wide-eyed. "You had doubts?"
"Not a single one," I lie.
She glares at me then spins back around to face the stove. "So," she begins, "tell me about this mystery woman."
Godammit Heidi. "There is nothing to tell." And there isn't. I regret ever bringing it up. Women are like elephants. They never forget.

She turns to me with a smile. "I promise not to get mad. I just want to know. The same way you wanted to know."

Good move. Way to throw my own words back in my face. I might as well give up. And she could probably use the reassurance that it wasn't Taylor. So I nut up and tell her the truth, running with the hunch that she means what she says about not getting mad. "It was once. It was nothing. And it wasn't Taylor. May the witness step down your Honor?"

She laughs and it lights up her face. She sticks the stuffed French bread in the oven and walks over to me, settling between my legs. Her hands run along the tops of my thighs and she bats her eyelashes at me while she bites her bottom lip. She has definitely got seduction down to a science. "Then tell me who she was."

Why do women do this? She doesn't really want to know like she thinks she wants to know. But if I don't tell her, then she thinks I'm hiding something and gets upset and it makes everything worse. Shit. "No one. A dancer. I don't even remember her name." I do. But she doesn't need to know that.

She looks like I just slapped her. "A stripper?! You fucked a stripper?! Are you kidding me?"

I told you she didn't really want to know. I just stare at her in amusement while she processes.

"Nick!" she says, disgusted. "Did you at least use a condom? You don't appear to be a fan of latex," she says sarcastically.

"For the record, I'm a huge supporter of latex. *Except* when I'm with you." No need to elaborate on the details with Charla. It won't do either of us any good. So I divert, as usual.

She's standing with her hands on her hips and a pout on her face. I grab her ass and pull her back between my legs. "And that's because you make it impossible not to want to fuck you every time you open your smart mouth. Or look at me with those beautiful green eyes. Or brush against me with this sexy little ass." With my last comment, I pull my hand back and smack her bare butt. She yelps but doesn't move away. She just cocks her head and eyes me curiously. I narrow my eyes and study her reaction. I can't hold back a satisfied grin. "I think you liked that."

She shrugs nonchalantly. "Maybe I did. Maybe I didn't."

"I think you did. And I think you want me to do it again."

She licks her lips and confidently squares her shoulders. "I think you liked it. And I think you want to do it again," she says with a hint of mischief. She narrows her eyes and suppresses a grin. "I think you like my ass. Don't you Senator?"

I think if she opens her mouth one more time, I'm going to bend that ass over and fuck her seven ways til Sunday.

Heidi backs up and turns around, then starts swaying her hips from side to side, dropping lower each time. She looks back at me over her shoulder. "Or maybe you like it when I do this?" she teases.

Goddamn she's sexy. The bottom of her ass peeks out from underneath the shirt when she moves. I know she's just trying to take a jab at me but between her sassy mouth and current ass-wiggling, my dick is about to bust through my zipper. "Heidi," I warn.

She straightens up and turns to face me. "Sorry, I forgot. You prefer your dancers to come with a pole."

It takes all my effort not to laugh. She's fucking adorable. But she doesn't want to be laughed at. She wants to be fucked. I can play her game. "Heidi," I say again with a straight face as I stand.

She rolls her eyes at me. "Okay, okay. I'll check the food," she groans.

"Fuck the food. Come here."

CHAPTER TWENTY-ONE
Heidi

I wasn't provoking Nick on purpose. Honestly, I was just giving him shit about the stripper so he would know I wasn't upset about it. I was there. I know what it feels like to need to forget. If things had gone differently with Umbrella Guy, he would have been another notch on my belt. So I get it. I really do.
But I have to admit, it was seriously arousing having Nick go all cave man on me. And the sex. Holy hotness, the sex.

After he banged my brains out on the kitchen counter, we ate our sandwiches, and now I'm settled between his legs while we watch a movie. Originally, I had rented it to watch with Alex, but I'm good with the way it worked out. "So this is what you call man candy?" Nick asks after the first action scene. I can't speak for everyone, but I say Channing Tatum is the kind of man candy that comes all wrapped up in a pretty box with a nice silky ribbon.
"If you're into the whole tall, dark, and handsome with zero percent body fat and an irresistible smile-type….then yeah," I reply with a shrug. It immediately dawns on me that I have just described the man lying beneath me at this very moment and I mentally fangirl at the thought.
"So this is my competition?"
I flip onto my stomach to face him and give his gloriously toned bicep a squeeze. "Eh, I think you could take him."
He thrusts his hips upward and grins. "I'd rather just take you."
I scatter kisses across the top of his stomach, peeking up at him seductively. The man is a freaking robot. "Or," I say as I unzip his jeans, "I could take you." I lick my lips anxiously at the sight of the hard cock that awaits me. Nick lifts his hips off the sofa, making it easy for me to slide his jeans down. He knows what I want and he wants it too. He takes my chin and lifts it so I'm looking up at him. His eyes are dark and full of desire. "There you go with that beautiful fucking mouth."

He sucks the air through his teeth the second my lips wrap around his girth. I have to work to fit all of him in, but my own spit combined with the drops of built up arousal on his thick head, makes it easier. Nick grunts and starts thrusting his hips. I have to place one hand flat on his stomach to hold myself steady while he urgently fucks my mouth. My other hand is busy pumping his length while I suck harder as he thrusts faster. I can't help but moan at the thought of knowing how good I'm making him feel. My hand moves to his balls while my tongue licks his tip. Nick's thrusts become more urgent and his grunts louder and more frequent. He bends his knees, pulling his legs up, and grabs a handful of my hair and lets me know he's coming. And I relish every delicious drop of him. God he's so sexy right now. Eyes closed, head tilted back, and out of breath. Because of me. I want to live my life pleasing him like this.

So much for watching a movie.

I get up to make us both a drink then lay back down, this time in front of him, as we try to finish a movie that neither one of us are into anymore. I end up falling asleep only to wake later to Nick watching a Braves game on ESPN.

He's mindlessly running his fingers through my hair. Suddenly it feels like I'm watching someone else's life. It's too perfect. He's too perfect. I keep waiting for the ball to drop. The dream to end. The carriage to turn back into a pumpkin. But it hasn't yet, so for now I'll just keep letting Nick Knight make me happier than I've ever been. And hope I'm able to make him happy too. Who knows, maybe all the crap is behind us now. We've dealt with the bad stuff and might actually be able to enjoy a future together.

Reality check Cinderella. He's leaving. Remember?

Well shit. There's that.

I sigh a little too loudly. Nick notices and turns down the television. "Did I wake you?"

How can one man be so utterly thoughtful and compassionate yet so completely masculine and powerful at the same time? I'm starting to think Shelly was right and he *was* scientifically created in a lab somewhere. "Not at all," I state simply.

"Tell me what you're thinking," he says.

Why would he think I'm thinking anything? "Nothing important," I lie.

"People who sigh like that usually do so because they're bored or frustrated. Am I boring you baby?" I hear the smile in his voice as he moves his hand from my hair to make a trail down my arm.

Might as well rip off all the band aids in one trip, right? No use in dragging it out. "When were you planning on leaving?" I ask boldly.

He is silent for a moment. Then I hear him exhale a long deep breath. "Tomorrow."

And there it is. I automatically sit up but try not to react in any way that would set off alarm bells that let him know what's really going on inside my head. *Keep it cool Heidi. This is his decision. Don't make him feel bad about it.* I stare silently straight ahead, trying to think of something positive to say even though I am internally having a mini melt down. He could have said next month. Next week even. But tomorrow? All I get is two freaking days with him? I mentally backtrack to see if I can figure out at what point in my life I seriously pissed karma off. Hudson will be coming home tomorrow so at least I won't have time to think about it. And there are still a few hours between now and tomorrow and I'm not going to spend it being a drama queen. "In that case, you might want to think about packing," I say with a painted on smile. *Please don't see through it.*

Nick sits up beside me and takes my hand in his. He leans over, his mouth just inches from my neck. I can feel him breathing me in and when he speaks, the heat of his breath sends chills over my whole body. "Four days ago, I knew exactly what I wanted." His voice is calm and smooth. His other hand snakes around my waist and rests on my stomach. It's like he's using his body to shield me from his words. "Then I show up at my office and there's this card on my desk." *I almost forgot about the card.* "And then I get a phone call. And then there you are, in my bed. And then, you're gone again. Then Monica throws me a fucking curve ball." *Monica? What does she have to do with any of this?* He stops speaking for a second, then kisses me softly on the neck before continuing. "Then I find myself at Nate's trying to regain what little bit of sanity I have left.....and there you are again." His hand slips under my shirt, making my breath hitch. "Looking hot as fuck in those tight ass pants and little tank top." He swallows hard at the memory then his hand falls between my thighs. I take a deep breath as his fingertips skim my mound. Instinctively, my legs part, allowing him room to explore. He takes full advantage and finds my throbbing clit and begins to rub slow steady circles around it. "Damn baby, you're so wet. Always so ready for me." His finger dips deep inside of me and I moan. He slides it back out and goes back to work on my clit. Fuck me, it feels good. I forget what we were talking about. All I know is his presence. His breath on my skin. The way he lets me squeeze his hand as I arch my back and roll into his touch. He whispers into my ear, "I can't leave you alone." I don't know if he's talking about touching me or the reality of actually leaving me, but it's all semantics right now. I just want him to keep doing what he's doing.

"Then don't," I say back, breathless.

He increases in pressure and speed and I am rolling right along with him until the next thing we hear is the sound of his name spill from my lips as the orgasm rocks my body.

Nick and I are out on the dock next to his boat. He's sitting next to me with his arm around my shoulders as we watch the sunset over the water and have a drink. He's got his scotch and I've got my wine. There's a slight breeze coming off the water, taking the heat out of a normally hot July evening. It's so peaceful and beautiful and I can't think of anywhere I'd rather be. I lay my head on his shoulder and finish off my wine. It's starting to get dark and I probably need to go home so I can get ready for my baby boy's return home tomorrow afternoon. I probably need to, but I really don't want to. I wonder what he meant about Monica throwing him a curve ball, but I don't ask. Nick is a very private person and I respect that. I'm surprised at how much he's opened up to me already. And even though there's so much more I want to know about this man, I don't want to push it.

"I should go," I say, even though there isn't a whole lot of enthusiasm behind it.

"You should stay."

I want to stay.

"I really have to go."

He sits up straight and sets his glass on the end table. "Then let me go with you."

It's impossible to say no to him. No man has ever come home with me with the intention of staying. Okay there was that night with Alex but those were different circumstances entirely.

It doesn't take more than a kiss to persuade me, and we're on our way to pick up Nick's car from Alex's loft.

I'm glad Nick offered up the idea of going by Alex's. It gives me time to shower and pull myself together before he gets here. I can't imagine wanting to be without him but I'm scared to death of what that means. It feels almost criminal to wash him off of me. At the same time, the hot water that surrounds me feels like paradise. My body is so sore. Nick is not an average man, in any form, and I am feeling the consequences. It doesn't keep me from wanting more, however. I am already missing him. I have time to get out, put on a pair of white lace panties and a white cami, (I figure there's really no point in dressing up) and straighten up a bit before my phone pings.

Knock, Knock.

God, I've missed seeing that text.

Nick walks in and sweeps his eyes over my body. "I'm about to get you very dirty baby," he says with a smirk. My eyes widen as the corners of my mouth turn up slightly in anticipation. He chuckles as he walks past me, setting a bag on the dining table. "Now who's the pervert?" he teases. He wraps an arm around my waist then lets it fall to caress my bottom. I raise up on my tip-toes and plant a swift kiss on his cheek. He smiles and empties the contents, Thai ribs and corn grits for two from Zea's. I'm not sure how he knew what to order, but it's heaven in my mouth right now.

After dinner, we end up in the sunroom on my swing bed. "So this is where the magic happens?" Nick asks, noticing all the boxes from my office stacked against the wall by my desk.

I lick my lips and run my foot up his calf. "It could be."

"You haven't had enough of me yet?"

"Not even close," I answer.

He smiles his crooked smile and squeezes me tight. "Patience, baby. We have all night."

I let out a huff and he chuckles then kisses my forehead. I look up at him, resting my chin on his chest. "Okay then. I want to know more about you."

He arches a brow, "Oh?"

"Yep. Let's start with: Why are you a senator?" We'll start slow.

A wide grin spreads across his flawless face. "That's an easy one. Because my father was. Next," he says.

Okay. Simple enough. "And your mother?"

The smile fades and his jaw tightens. Maybe this was a bad question. "She's a senator's wife," he says flatly.

I will probably regret my next question because the answer is pretty obvious, and trying to get Nick to open up is like stealing a pearl from an oyster. "Are you close?"

He looks off to the side as if trying to pull memories out of the air. "As close as we need to be. If you're asking about Sunday afternoon family dinners and chats by the fire, no. We're not an AT&T commercial. But I talk to my father often and visit when I have time."

Nothing about his mother.

"Your turn," he says. "Tell me about your family."

I should have known this was coming. He likes to divert when he's doesn't want to dig deep. I know this tactic because it's one of my own. I exhale and prepare to give him the Cliff's Notes version. "My father was an officer in the military. My mother was an officer's wife," I say, mimicking his unenthusiastic description of his mother. I guess we have that in common. "Dad had wandering eyes. Mom found out, which then lead to her mid-life crisis in which she decided being a parent was no longer a priority. I was sixteen. Dad was preoccupied with a woman half his age and mom couldn't stay out of the bars long enough to care. I left the day after I graduated high school and can't say I've ever regretted a day of my life since."

Nick takes my hand and brings it to his lips. "Not all men are like your father," he tells me as he kisses the back of my hand.

I give his hand a light squeeze. "And not all women are like my mother," I pause and decide to be bold and continue, "or yours."

"I'm starting to figure that out," he says before he pulls me up so that we're face to face and he brings his mouth to mine.

We move to my bed and talk for almost an hour more. Nick has ditched his jeans and is lying next to me completely naked, making it difficult to concentrate on our conversation. Luckily, we keep it light for the most part. He tells me about his love for baseball and I share Hudson's mutual love of the game with him. We talk about college and things we'd probably rather forget. He tells me how he learned to cook and I talk about my passion for dance. Then he tells me about Elise. It's the most personal thing about himself he's ever shared with me.

"She was everything I thought I wanted but turned out to be the very thing I'd lived my whole life despising."

I nestle closer against him. "And what about now? Do you know what you want now?"

"Now?" he repeats. "Right now?" His arm under my shoulders curls upward, pulling my body into his. His other hand touches my cheek and his eyes peer into my very soul. "I want you."

I feel his hardness press into my belly as I climb on top of him the rest of the way. I straddle him, placing a hand on his abdomen to steady myself, and rock against him. He hooks a finger in each side of my panties and tugs. I lift my hips and with one hard pull, he rips the thin material at the seams until there's nothing left on my body. He pushes up into me, teasing me with his erection. "I want to taste you," he says.

I lean forward and bring my mouth down slowly, my lips just barely touching his. Our eyes are locked and we're sharing the same air as we breathe each other in. He runs his tongue over his bottom lip, letting it brush against mine when he does. "Sit. On my fucking face, Heidi."

Oh. That kind of taste. Oh god. I can't speak. I can't find my voice. All I can do is follow his lead as he takes me by the hips and guides my body up his until I am perfectly positioned right above his face. His hot breath is ecstasy on my core. The tip of his tongue runs along the wet slit above his mouth and I moan. He pulls my hips down and I grab onto the headboard for leverage. His fingers have me open and ready for his mouth. His hands move to my ass while his tongue goes from licking my throbbing clit to teasing my opening. I throw my head back and cry out, "God, Nick, please." I don't know what I'm begging for. I just know I need *something*. I want this feeling to last forever, but I also want to come. I don't want him to stop, but I also want to feel him inside of me. So many feelings at once. All building up to the moment when it becomes too much to take. I'm holding the headboard while I grind his face as his skilled tongue fucks me crazy. Holy shit, that's it. I'm going to come.

I taste myself when I kiss him. "Delicious, isn't it?" Nick says with a smirk.

"You. Are delicious." His hard dick presses against my thigh as I lie on top of him, so I reach between us and begin to stroke him.

He flips us over, so that he is now on top, and holds my hands above my head. "Now, do *you* know what you want?" *Yes.*

I look into his dark brown eyes and nod.

"Tell me," he says, tracing the tip of his nose along my jaw and breathing softly against my neck.

I can't touch him. I can't move. His body has me pinned and his hands have mine locked above my head. I move my hips as much as possible. "You. I want you inside me."

He adjusts his hips until the tip of his cock is at my entrance. Then he slips in slowly and smiles arrogantly. "Like this?"

I rock my body, trying to feel more of him. He slides in deeper. And deeper. *God, yes. Just like that.*

I moan as he maneuvers himself all the way inside, then slowly slips back out. So agonizingly slowly. He does this several times until I can't take any more. I pull my legs from under his and wrap them around his waist, pushing his butt into me with my feet. "Fuck me Nick."

"Gladly," he replies as he lets go of my hands and braces himself by holding the headboard above my head. My legs are still wrapped around his body as he pounds into me with a fury. He's fucking me so hard, I feel my body inching further and further up the bed with each thrust. It's like he can't get deep enough. One hand lets go and grabs one of my legs and brings it to his shoulder. Shit, he's so deep it hurts. He turns his head and kisses my ankle as he slows his pace. I see his head tilt back and hear his deep throaty grunt and I know he's coming soon. A few more urgent thrusts and he's there and I am right there with him. He's so damn sexy with his sweat glistening on his chest and his hair damp. He keeps his eyes closed as he struggles to control his heavy breathing.

I don't know if tonight is the last night I will have with him or not. He never specifically said whether or not he truly is leaving tomorrow. But I know this is how I want to remember it: Me smiling like an idiot because I have never been more satisfied in my life, and Nick sweaty and breathless from fucking the hell out of me.

CHAPTER TWENTY-TWO
Heidi

Monday, July 21

I wake up to Nick's fingertips making gentle invisible trails across my back. He's staring at me with a smile as my eyes adjust to the sunlight. I'm not sure when exactly I fell asleep last night. I remember being completely sated and hearing Nick's voice tell me I am beautiful as my eyelids got heavy. I bet he's not thinking I'm beautiful right now. With my bed head and jungle breath.

"Good morning baby," he says, tucking a piece of stray hair behind my ear.

I can't help but smile when he looks at me this way. If I woke up to this every morning, I'd never get out of bed. Oh crap. Hudson. "What time is it?" I ask, frantically sitting up to check the clock.

Nick watches me curiously but remains calm. "Seven o'clock," he answers.

"Shit," I exclaim. "You have to go." Oh lord, I can't believe I just said that. I don't want him to go. But I don't want Hudson to meet Nick like *this*. I scramble nervously for my words while the naked man in my bed watches in amusement. "Well, you don't *really* have to go….just grab some coffee and come back. Fully dressed. Okay?" I climb out of bed and search the room for my clothes. I smile when I see what's left of my panties lying on the floor.

Nick gets out of bed and walks over behind me. Either he has to pee or…..god he's not making it easy to tell him to leave. He nuzzles his face in my neck and places his hands on my hips. "Not exactly the *good morning* I was hoping for," he says in his smooth silky voice. *Me either.* I'd much rather have yesterday's activities on repeat….every day for the rest of my life…but I have responsibilities and I have missed my son terribly.

"Cole is bringing Hudson home on his way to work. They should be here any minute," I explain.

His expression tightens but he lets go of me and reaches for his jeans and t-shirt.

I take his hand as he's working on his zipper. I finish zipping his pants then button them for him, taking my time to be careful since he decided to go commando. I wrap my arms around him, pressing my bare breasts against his bare chest. "I want you to meet him," I say sincerely. "He's a smart kid. He'll know you spent the night. And I want to do this the right way. Please?" I want him to know this has everything to do with Hudson and nothing to do with Cole.

He kisses the top of my head and runs his hands up my back. He's still hard. I can feel it through his jeans. My body wants him to throw me on the bed and make me scream. But my mind knows better. I place a row of kisses across his chest and he chuckles.

"You can't ask me to leave then start kissing me."

Oops. "Well maybe if you weren't so kissable…." I say.

I let go of his waist and step away so he can put on his shirt. He's looking as tempting as sin in his jeans and solid black tee, while I am satisfied throwing on a pair of black running shorts and hot pink t-shirt. I pull my hair up into a bun and brush my teeth then kiss Nick goodbye, but not before he promises to come right back.

While I wait for Hudson, I decide to do what I can with some makeup. Nick is bound to get tired of *I woke up like this* Heidi sooner or later. I'm still alone so I grab a coral chiffon sundress with spaghetti straps to replace my running gear. I leave the hair though. I'm going for cute but effortless here.

Just as I slip into the dress, I hear a knock on the door.

"Monkey butt!" I exclaim as Hudson runs into my arms.

"Mom!" he says. He wraps his little arms around my neck. "I missed you so big."

I laugh and give him about twenty kisses. "I missed you so big too."

I put him down and move aside so Cole can bring Hudson's bag to his room.

"Wow. You look really pretty today," Hudson says with wide eyes and an even wider smile.

His compliment makes my heart melt. He's always been so generous with his words.

"You're right. She looks beautiful," Cole says as he re-enters the room.

It must be that glow you get after being freshly and skillfully fucked. I take the compliment with a smile and give Hudson one more hug.

"Good morning," a voice says from behind us and I realize I left the front door open. *Nick.*

Just the sound of his voice sends tiny waves of pleasure straight through to my core.

I turn around and there he is, standing in the doorway holding a carrier with two cups of coffee and a juice box in his hands.

"Nick. Come in," I say nervously. My heart is pounding. This is huge. Hudson has never as much as seen me talk to another man in over two years. And while I'm sure Cole knows I haven't been celibate all this time, he's never seen me with anyone either. Then there's Nick. I'm inviting him into a very delicate and precious part of my life.

"Am I interrupting?" he questions as he comes inside.

I take the coffee from his hands and give him a knowing look. "Not at all. You're just in time," I assure him.

"In that case, I have to agree. You look beautiful," he says, looking me in the eye. For a moment, I nearly forget there are other people in the room. I snap back into it and take him by the hand, leading him into the dining room where Hudson stands next to his father.

"Hudson, I'd like you to meet Nick Knight," I say as I look back and forth between the two of them. "Nick, this is my son, Hudson."

Hudson stretches out his hand and smiles at Nick. "I remember you. You're the guy with the boat," he says as he shakes Nick's hand. My little gentleman. And my sexy man. Does it get any better than this?

Nick smiles and nods. "You have a very good memory."

"Are you still helping my mom?"

Cole is curiously watching the entire interaction without saying a word. Not surprising. He's never been the outspoken type.

"Well that's up to her, I suppose," Nick answers as he looks at me out of the corner of his eye.

Okay. Here goes nothing. I'm diving into the deep end. Head first. Go hard or go home, right?

"Nick keeps me company when you're not here. And he makes me smile when I'm sad because I miss you," I explain as best as I can. It's not like I can say *"Hey, this is Nick, the guy I screw."*

Hudson bunches his eyebrows together and studies Nick for a second. "So, he's your boyfriend?"

Nick smiles and squeezes my hand. "Something like that," I reply.

Hudson rolls his eyes and lets out a sigh. "It's about time," he says as he walks to the living room and plops down in his comfy chair.

"Hudson!" I look at Cole, half expecting him to say something, but knowing he never would.

Then Hudson looks at him too. "It's true. Tell her, dad."

Nick turns his attention to Cole, who is currently giving me an apologetic shrug.

"Nick Knight," he says as he extends his hand to Cole. "Boyfriend," he continues, identifying himself according to Hudson's observation.

Cole takes his hand and matches his gaze. "Cole Lemaire," he says. "Ex-husband."

The two men size each other up a minute longer than I'm comfortable with. I witness Nick's jaw do that twitching thing it does when he's clenching his teeth. Maybe this wasn't such a good idea.

"You should go, Cole. You don't want to be late for work," I say, interrupting their staring competition.

"You're right," Cole answers. Then he leans down and gives Hudson a hug and kiss as he tells him goodbye. "I'll see you tomorrow Heidi," he adds deliberately just before he walks out the door and closes it behind him.

I go into the dining room to retrieve our coffee and what I assume to be Hudson's juice box. I hold it up and wave it around and Nick just smiles. "You are a very thoughtful man," I say as I walk past him.

"Would you like to know what I'm thinking right now?" he asks as his eyes land on my legs.

I shoot him a glare then hand Hudson his juice.

Hudson informs me he's hungry so Nick offers to take us to breakfast. All morning, I watch in awe as my two favorite people in the world interact like they've known each other all their lives. They swap food, and tell jokes. They laugh and even talk about me a bit.

Of course Hudson had a million questions about Nick's job. You'd think being a US Senator was the equivalent of being a superhero to him. Nick answered every single one with patience and humility though. He even offered to bring Hudson to the White House someday. Now *that* really got him excited.

I'm not sure how I feel about Nick making promises about the future to my son. In one sense, I'm hopeful, but in another, I'm skeptical. I guess only time will tell. After three full size pancakes and a plateful of bacon, we leave IHOP and head back home.

Nick doesn't stay after breakfast, informing us he has business to take care of. I automatically fear that *business* involves him packing, but I don't bring it up. Partly because I am afraid of the answer. I'll find out soon enough. Until then, I'll just hope the past two days have been enough to make him want to stay, instead of some sordid way of him saying goodbye.

I spend the rest of the day hearing about Hudson's time with his dad and Michelle, along with getting packed and ready for our hospital visit in the morning. I make sure and fix him his favorite dinner and we relax on the sofa watching recorded episodes of Star Wars Rebels until time for his bath. It's been a full twenty-four hours since my last glass of wine, so I indulge while Hudson splashes around in the tub.

I haven't heard from Nick since he left this morning so when my phone rings, naturally I get butterflies. But it isn't Nick calling me. It's Alex. Suddenly I get a very different kind of butterflies. I haven't spoken to Alex since I left his loft with Nick. I take a deep breath, put on my big girl panties, and answer the phone.

"Hey handsome," I say.

"Hello, love," he replies. He pauses a beat then continues, "I noticed Nick's Cruiser finally gone from the parking garage so I imagined it would be an appropriate time to call."

Leave it to the attorney to gather evidence before making a decision. I feel a twinge of guilt at the thought of him sitting over there knowing I've spent the past two nights with Nick. I shouldn't. I don't owe him an explanation. So why do I feel like I do? I don't even know if he's asking for details or if he'd rather I just leave it alone. I go with the option B. "How was your weekend?" I ask, changing the subject.

"Long and uneventful. I spent it packing, mostly."

Crap. That's right. He's leaving too. I let out a defeated sigh.

"Look, I mainly just called to tell you if you happen to need anything tomorrow. With Hudson. I'll be here," he adds. His words are drawn out as if he's thinking about exactly how to say each one before he says it.

It amazes me that he remembered. Although, I guess it shouldn't. Alex is a pretty amazing man.

"Thank you Alex. That means more than you know."

Neither one of us say anything for several seconds until finally Alex clears his throat. "I should be going. I still have a lot to do."

"Let me know if you need me to help," I offer.

He laughs and I picture his gorgeous grin. "You've already got your hands full. But thank you anyway," he says before he lets me go.

I wonder if there was a deeper meaning behind his statement or if he just meant with Hudson and his surgery.

I get Hudson out of the tub and we lie in bed and read in our pajamas until he falls asleep. I know tomorrow will be a long day and I should be sleeping too, but I can't get rid of the million and one things swirling around in my head.

What if something goes wrong tomorrow? What if I don't know how to take care of him so he can heal properly afterwards? Why does it bother me so much that Alex is leaving? And why the hell haven't I heard from Nick all day?

CHAPTER TWENTY-THREE

Heidi

I finally fell asleep a little before midnight, only to have my phone wake me up two hours later.

Nick: *Are you still awake Ms. Lemaire?*

Me: *Still? No. Awake? Yes.*

Nick: *Would you like me to apologize for waking you?*

I remember the last time he apologized. And yes, I would love for him to do it again.

Me: *Let's just say you owe me one.*

Nick: *Just one? I don't remember just one ever being enough, Ms. Lemaire.*

Good god, just the thought has me soaking wet. Why does he do this to me? And why does he keep repeating my name?

Me: *Exactly how many are you good for?*

Nick: *Open your door and I'll show you.*

Ohmigod he's here. That means he didn't leave today. My stomach flips and my heart flutters. I carefully climb out of bed, making sure not to wake Hudson, and open the front door. Sure enough, there he stands. Sexy as hell in black baggy sweatpants and a black v-neck tee. His hair is a mess and he smells like scotch. But that crooked freaking smile….damn. He stuffs his phone in his pocket and walks toward me. He grabs my hands and pulls my body against his. His head ducks down as he speaks softly into my ear. "I know I shouldn't be here, but I had to see you."

I move my head to one side and let his teeth graze my neck. "What took you so long?" I quip.

He uses his body to force mine backward until I am up against the wall. Then he places a hand on either side of my head and leans forward, our faces just inches apart. "I have a secret," he whispers. "And when I tell you what it is, I'm going to lose you."

<Insert panic attack here> My mind races. What kind of secret could he have that would make me run? He's married? His being with me was a joke? A bet of some sort? He slept with Shelly? I watch too many movies.

"You're drunk," I state.

A lazy grin spreads across his face. "I am," he admits.

Well at least he's admitting it. "You shouldn't be driving."

"I'm not."

He moves his body closer to mine, pinning me against the wall. I am in my usual t-shirt and pajama bottoms and his pants don't do much to hide the fact that he wants to take this further.

I just remain silent and wait for him to make his next move. "I fucked Monica," he blurts out.

Monica. Holy crap. Of course. It makes so much sense. The way she acts around him. The way he paraded her around at the cocktail party. Him mentioning something about her throwing him a curve ball. He's been screwing her.

My chest tightens and I struggle to breathe. My vision begins to get blurry and I realize my eyes are filled with water. *Don't you dare freaking cry.* I can't deal with this right now. Why is he telling me this tonight? After two of the most perfect days of my life. Why now? Why couldn't it just wait until Hudson was well? Why can't life let me deal with one heartbreak at a time? *Because she's a bitch, that's why.*

I push him off of me and move to open the front door, but he immediately shuts it again, leaving me trapped between it and him. "It was four years ago, Heidi. It happened once and it hasn't happened since."

"Then why are you telling me this now? Did something else happen? Is that where you've been all day?"

"What? God, no. Hell no. Baby, no," Nick says as he moves loose strands of hair from my forehead. "Tell me why you have his last name," he says.

Are you kidding me? He's really going to change the subject right now? "Nick," I say as I take his face in my hands and make him focus. Not this time Senator. "What happened with Monica?"

"Nothing happened with Monica," he tells me.

Okay I know he's drunk but damn. He really isn't making any sense.

"I'm a father, Heidi. Olivia is my daughter," he says finally.

Oh. Wow.

Why would he think he would lose me over something like that? I mean, I need a minute to process the whole thing, but I would never leave him because he has a child. Anyone who would use that as an excuse is a coward. And I may be a lot of things, but a coward isn't one of them. Why didn't he tell me before? I thought Olivia's father was a douchebag. Why would he keep that from me? Unless that's the curve ball he was talking about. *Maybe he didn't know?* "How long have you known this?" I ask.

He looks down at his watch. "Twelve hours. Give or take."

Oh. Wow.

I seem to be thinking that a lot. What do you tell someone who just found out they've unknowingly been raising their own child? Damn. No wonder he's drunk.

I wrap my arms around his waist and hold him tight, letting him know I'm not going anywhere.

"You're going to be a great father," I assure him. And I believe it. I've seen him with Olivia. I've seen him with Hudson. He's a natural.

"I don't know the first fucking thing about being a father."

"You'll figure it out. Just love her. The rest will follow."

He tangles his fingers in my hair and tugs gently, tilting my head back. "And you're okay with that?"

"Of course I am," I say as I smile up at him. "But don't get any ideas Senator. She is the *only* female I plan on sharing you with."

"Have I ever told you you're absolutely fucking amazing?"

"I'm pretty sure that's Johnnie talking," I tease, taking a jab at the fact he's had too much scotch.

"No. That was all me. Johnnie wants me to tell you how bad I want to fuck you right now."

Not nearly as bad as I want it, I'm sure. Oddly enough, the fact that he's a father suddenly makes him more attractive, if that's even possible.

His mouth finds mine and he kisses me with a fierce intensity that sets my body on fire.

It is so incredibly hard to make him go home. "I guess we'll call this lesson one of my parenting skills...hands off when the kids are home," he says as he is walking out the door.

I have a feeling this is going to be a very difficult lesson for the both of us.

Tuesday, July 22

This is it. Today is the day. I don't think it mattered that Nick interrupted my sleep last night. It wasn't working well for me anyway. I'm too nervous about Hudson's surgery. I'll rest when it's over and he is okay.

They run Hudson's vitals and get him comfortable in a room. Cole met us here and so did Shelly. Dr. Collins runs through the procedure and approximate time frames with us once again. She could go over it enough times for me to practically be able to perform it myself and I still wouldn't feel comfortable.

I know it shouldn't take more than a few hours. I know they will hook him up to a machine that controls his heart and lungs so they can cut his heart open to place the patch. I know Dr. Collins is one of the best in her field. But none of that keeps me from fighting back tears as I sit next to him, singing his favorite song as the medicine drips from the IV into his veins. It's just meant to put him to sleep, but seeing his little body lying in this big hospital bed with the needle in his little arm breaks my heart into pieces.

"Will I be a better baseball player with my new heart?" he asks.

"How can you get better when you're already the best?" I reply as I squeeze his tiny hand.

"You're silly mom. Everybody knows Jeter is the best."

His eyes are getting heavy and his speech is more deliberate and drawn out. Cole kisses him on the forehead and I kiss his cheek. "I love you so big," I tell him.

He smiles a weak smile and tells me, "I love you big, big."

Then he falls asleep.

It's been two hours since they wheeled him back and there isn't enough floor in this waiting room for me to finish pacing. Finally, Shelly brings me a second macchiato from the Starbucks downstairs so I sit and try to make myself relax. I find myself wishing I had gone to nursing school. Then I could be back there with him. Making sure everything is okay.

Cole sits on my left, his arm around my shoulder, while Shelly sits on my right, holding my hand. I'm just about to get up and start pacing again when Nick walks into the room. I hear Shelly murmur a quiet *"Damn"* to herself at his presence. I have to agree with her. The sight of him makes me lose my breath. Maybe it's because I've become accustomed to seeing him in unbuttoned jeans or baggy sweats, or nothing at all for that matter, but seeing him walk in wearing black trousers with a white oxford, black jacket, and navy blue tie has my hormones doing backflips.

Nick is the last person I would have expected to see here. I told him about the surgery, but I never told him exactly when…or where. I'm not a hundred percent sure on this but I don't think its proper bedroom etiquette to invite the man you're sleeping with to a life altering event. Honestly, I am surprised at myself for even sharing this with him at all.

Smart girl Heidi steps out from the shadows with her pencil skirt and black rimmed glasses and stares down dumb girl Heidi who is just sitting here chewing gum and twirling her hair while she stares blankly at Nick. *That's because he* isn't *just some man you're sleeping with. Now step outside of your little box and admit you have serious feelings for this man.*

She's right. I can't just brush off what we have as "great sex" anymore. Because even though I didn't ask Nick to be here right now, there isn't a single other person in this world I want to be here more. He is my shelter from the storm, the peace that calms me, and the strength that guides me when I can't seem to find my way on my own. The mere sight of him standing there, so strong and in control, makes me feel like even though inside I am a twisted jumbled up mess right now, everything is going to be alright. So yes, Smart Heidi, he is so much more than just the guy I'm sleeping with. And the fact that he just walked through that door tells me that whatever I'm feeling, I'm not feeling it alone.

"Hey." When I finally find my voice, it is weak. He cocks his head and studies me for a moment. I wonder what he's thinking then I see his

179

eyes move to Cole, who still has his arm around me, and I'm pretty sure I just figured it out. I stand to greet him and he smiles, more with his eyes than his mouth.

"Good morning," he says, taking me in his arms.

I look up at him, still not able to believe he's here. "How did you…"

He grins and interrupts me, "I made a few phone calls."

"Of course you did."

I take a step back and nervously straighten his tie. He cocks a brow and watches me curiously. God, he smells delicious. Manly, but not overdone, and clean, like he just showered. I take a step closer to breathe more of him in as I picture him naked with the warm water running over his body. Suddenly I'm very jealous of that water.

"I just wanted a reason to touch you," I say with a shrug.

"Simply wanting to, is reason enough don't you think," he answers with a smirk. *Is it just me or is it getting hot in here?*

Cole clears his throat and stands. He places his hand on the small of my back. "I could use something to eat. Can I bring you anything?" he asks.

"No, thank you," I reply. I'm too nervous to eat right now.

Shelly hops up from the sofa. "Well I'm starving." She grabs Cole by the arm and drags him toward the door and away from me. "We'll be back." She stops short and turns back to face us. "Good morning, Nick. It's nice to see you here," she says with a wink, then she leads Cole out the door and down the hall. I haven't had a chance to fill her in, but I'm sure by now she's figured out I took her advice.

Nick is sitting next to me on the sofa. He's taken off his jacket and tie and rolled his shirt sleeves up to his elbows. He's got his arm around me while I lean my head against his shoulder and mindlessly watch television. My stomach has been screaming at me since Shelly and Cole got back from breakfast thirty minutes ago. They both keep asking me if I'm sure I'm okay and I keep telling them I'll be fine. Finally, Nick chuckles and looks over at me. "You need to eat, baby."

"I'm not leaving. He might be done soon," I inform him.

"Then I'll go get you something," he says, kissing my forehead as he stands.

When Nick returns with a cup of fruit, a bowl of oatmeal, and a bottle of Simply Orange, my insides stand up and applaud. I didn't realize I was so hungry. While he was gone, Michelle, Cole's wife, showed up and is now blatantly staring at Nick as he walks across the room. If she were a dog, she'd be panting.

"I'm sorry for taking so long," he says as he sets the food on the table in front of us. "It's a hospital, so naturally people have questions about healthcare," he explains.

It begins to dawn on me what he's talking about. Nick is a United States Senator. He's on national news channels and all over billboards across the entire state. He does radio interviews and magazine articles. Of course people are going to recognize him. How could anyone forget a face like that?

I suppose because we don't talk about his job much, paired with the fact that I've been lucky enough to have him mostly to myself, I forget who he is to the rest of the world sometimes. I only see who he is to me. And I know if the world had just a taste of who he really is, they would be begging for his attention even more than they do now.

I finish my breakfast just as Dr. Collins enters the room. We all stand, but she stops short when she sees Nick. I see in her the reaction I see in every woman when they first see him. The loss of breath, the step back to regain their balance, and then the swallow or the deep exhale to regain their breath. Her eyes stay fixed on him as she searches for her words. *It's okay, doctor. I know exactly how you feel.*

Everyone watches as she stumbles out of her fantasy and back into the real world with the rest of us. "Senator Knight.....I...I didn't realize you were friends with Ms. Lemaire," she stammers.

And I didn't realize filling out a friend list was a requirement for treatment of your child's heart condition these days.

Nick tilts his head and watches her in disbelief. *Yea, I think it's pretty unprofessional too, baby.*

"I mean I guess I just assumed she and Mr. Lemaire were....Nevermind." She looks away from Nick and over to Cole and Michelle.

"A common mistake, I'm sure," Nick says, his jaw twitching. "If you don't mind, I'm sure *Ms.* Lemaire would really like to know how her son is doing."

She looks a little embarrassed. I can't say I blame her. I would be too if my lady parts had just publicly taken over my brain. She turns her attention to me, finally. "He did great," she exclaims. "No complications. The surgery went very smoothly. He is in recovery now and you should be able to see him in about an hour."

"An hour?" I repeat.

She looks at me apologetically then over to Nick, then back at me. "He's not awake yet and we need to monitor him for a while. Give me thirty minutes and I'll see what I can do."

Monitor him? For what? She said he was okay. My heart starts racing and I'm freaking out inside. I know I won't feel better until I see him. "Okay," I say simply. What else is there? She's the doctor.

"Thank you," Nick tells her. She nods and leaves the room.

It's over. He made it through the surgery. His heart is fixed. He finally has a chance to be a normal little boy. The rest is up to me. Hudson will leave the hospital in a couple of days. Then it's up to me to keep him safe and help him heal. He can't get an infection. He can't have any contact to his chest. He'll need sponge baths until the stitches come out. And I'll need to watch for symptoms of complications. The next few weeks are critical. I'm suddenly very overwhelmed.

"What if I can't do it? What if I can't take care of him? What if I screw it up?"

I look up at Nick, who takes me in his arms and pulls me close. So many emotions all at once. I'm relieved, and excited, and nervous, and afraid. I'm so incredibly happy for my little boy. And at the same time I'm still waiting for something to go wrong. It's too good to be true. It can't be this simple. It never is.

"What was it you told me last night?" he says. "It'll come to you, baby. You love him. The rest will follow."

He's right. Just because I'm not a nurse doesn't mean I can't care for my child. I can follow directions. And I know his body better than anyone. I know when he isn't feeling well or when he's getting tired.

I can do this. I look up at Nick just as a single droplet of water falls from my eye.

He takes his thumb and wipes it away, bringing that same thumb to his lips and into his mouth. "You don't need those. Give them to me."

Did he just taste my tears? Holy shit. That was.....very emotional and strangely erotic. I close my eyes and exhale the breath I've been holding. "God I...." My eyes pop open and I immediately stop myself. What the four-letter-word? Did I really almost just say *it*? No way. I didn't almost tell Nick I love him. Because I don't. It's just been a really intense morning and my mind is messing with me. There's no way that's what I was going to say.

He brings his hand back to my cheek and looks me deep in the eyes. I can see his chest heaving underneath his shirt. He brings his head down so that his forehead rests against mine. "You what, baby? Tell me what you're thinking."

I usually give in to this request but there's no freaking way I'm telling him what I'm thinking this time.

"I am really glad you're here," I say.

He lets out a huff and smiles shyly. "Me too."

I lift my chin and let my lips touch his. His hand moves to my hair and he pulls me closer. I wrap my arms around his neck as he slides his other arm around my waist. My lips part, anticipating his kiss.

"Um. You do realize there are other people in the room, right?" Shelly blurts out.

Actually, I forgot about them. It happens a lot when I'm with Nick.

Dr. Collins holds true to her word and thirty minutes later, she comes to let Cole and I know we can go see Hudson. She informs us he is still in the recovery room so we can't stay long. We have to wear a suit that feels like it's made of napkins and cover our shoes. I don't care as long as I get to see my baby.

Okay, maybe I should have waited. He looks so tiny in that big bed, hooked up to an IV, and wearing a Spiderman hospital gown. He's still sleeping so we make sure to be quiet, although I doubt we'd bother him. He's so pale. He has dark purple circles under his eyes and his eyelids are the same, only a shade lighter. He looks so fragile.

I want to climb in that bed and hold him. To rock him in my arms. My baby boy.

I just stare at him in silence. I think even Cole is in shock at how delicate Hudson looks right now.

"He's going to be alright. He's just sleeping," Cole says and I'm not sure if he's trying to comfort me or himself.

He reaches over and grabs my hand and I quickly cut my eyes in his direction. "Relax, Heidi. I'm harmless."

This isn't the time for taking trips down memory lane. "Cole...." I start, but he quickly interrupts.

"So this thing with the politician. It's serious?" he asks, moving his hand from mine.

"No. I don't know. Maybe."

"But you're definitely sleeping with him," he states, although I'm not sure if it's a statement or a question.

"That's...not your business." My face backs up my response. What in the world is he thinking? Cole has never acted this way. Then again, I have never shown interest in another man in front of him. He, however, has spent the past year rubbing Michelle in my face. Not that I care. It's just rude. But that's classic Cole. I guess it's true what they say about knowing you can't have something makes it more appealing. That's the only way I could explain his behavior. He certainly doesn't want me back. Michelle is his perfect match. She doesn't mind being ignored for a basketball game or a phone call. She doesn't mind being left alone for days at time so Cole can hang out with old high school buddies. And she doesn't mind wearing the pants because he's doesn't care enough to put them on. No, Cole definitely doesn't want me. He just doesn't want anyone else to want me.

CHAPTER TWENTY-FOUR
Nick

Less than twenty-four hours ago, it felt like life had just delivered me a swift kick in the balls. The lab called to inform me they had mailed my results. Fuck that. Someone better find a fax machine. Call me impatient. You would be too.

I knew when I showed up at Heidi's apartment that would be the last I saw of her. Not because I thought she wouldn't accept the fact I have a daughter, but because of the fact I've been practically living with her and her mother for four fucking years. I don't expect Heidi to believe there's nothing going on. I know I wouldn't. I had this big ridiculous speech ready and everything. But there she went, proving me wrong yet again.. Just when I think I've got her figured out, she throws me for a loop, and I fucking love it. There are so many layers to Heidi Lemaire and I don't care if it takes the rest of my life, I want to know them all.

This morning I had no idea where she was. What I did know was that I had to be there. Two phone calls was all it took to figure it out. I wasn't sure what I would be walking into or if she would even want me there. If she wanted to be alone, I'd leave her alone. But something told me she wouldn't want to be alone, even though she'd never come out and admit it. When I walked into that waiting room and saw that mother fucker's arm around her like he owned her, I almost lost my shit. That feeling went away the moment she touched me though.

The way she let me hold her while we waited for the doctor to come in, letting me persuade her to eat, and comfort her when she was upset, made me feel closer to her than I've ever felt to anyone. She makes me feel...needed, something I've wanted from the day she walked into my office. When I saw her crying, I couldn't stand it. I want to take away her pain, her fear, and her doubts.

She's in the back with the asshole who can't keep his hands to himself. I'm not jealous. I'm possessive. It's not that I think Heidi wants anything to do with him. It's simply that I don't like to share what's mine. That includes the random dumb ass who thinks he's at a fucking petting zoo.

I'm answering twenty questions for Handsy's curious wife when the doctor walks in. Shit. Too late for me to pretend to have a phone call. She is beaming from ear to ear. Her long blonde hair is pulled into a low pony tail. She's not unattractive. I'm just uninterested.

"Senator Knight, I'd like to apologize for my behavior earlier. I was just caught off guard, I guess," she attempts at an explanation.

Why is this woman apologizing to me? "While I appreciate the gesture, I'm sure your apologies would be more appropriately directed to Ms. Lemaire. Wouldn't you agree?"

Again, she looks embarrassed and I feel the need to ease her tension, so I return her smile. "We are all very grateful that Hudson is in such capable and caring hands." Compliments usually do the trick.

Her cheeks flush and she immediately looks away. God, I hope she doesn't think I'm flirting with her. I glance over at Shelly for help but she just shrugs and smirks at me.

"Do you remember meeting me?" the doctor asks just as I was about to resume my position on the sofa.

"Excuse me?"

She smiles awkwardly. "At a fundraiser for the hospital. About a year ago. We spoke briefly."

Her sentences are choppy, like she wants to add more to them but is afraid to. Shit. I hope I didn't fuck her. "It's okay. I'm sure you meet so many people. It would be impossible to remember them all," she adds, interrupting my shuffling.

I dismiss the whole "one-night-stand" thought. Her demeanor is way too shy for someone whom I've already seen naked.

"Well, I will certainly remember meeting you this time, doctor." I give her a polite nod, then pull my phone out of my pocket and prepare to make that imaginary phone call. I laugh to myself at the scene. Here I am, alone in a room with three beautiful women staring at me like I'm the last man on earth, and I am about to pretend to make a phone call. If that's not what you call pussy whipped, I don't know what is.

The doctor smiles and extends her hand, which I proceed to shake. "It was nice to see you, Senator. Who knows? Maybe we'll run into each other at another fundraiser," she says. Then she leaves the room with a satisfied smile and a confident sway in her hips.

I look over at Shelly, who has been watching the interaction with amusement. "So, Senator," she says, being overly dramatic with her use of my title, "is this a recurring hot guy problem? Or did we just witness an isolated incident?" she mocks.

I shoot her a candid glare. "You're referring to being recognized, I assume?"

"She's referring to the way you make grown women lose their ability to form a complete sentence, simply by being in the same room with them," Heidi interjects.

She bites her bottom lip and arches an eyebrow at me while her eyes twinkle with a hint of mischief. Damn, she's beautiful. Her hair is in that messy pile on top of her head. She's wearing baggy jeans that she has folded up at the cuff. They hang low on her hips but do nothing for her amazing ass. Which is fine by me. I don't have a problem saving that for my own personal viewing pleasure. The loose black button-up shirt she has on hides her curves too, but I know what's under there so it doesn't keep me from imagining ripping those buttons off, one by one. Especially when she looks at me like she's looking at me now. It's playful on the outside, but on the inside, I know her thoughts are as dark as mine.

"It doesn't seem to have affected you one bit," I say, retaliating with a half curve of the lips. She swallows hard just about every time I do this. The other times, she either licks her lips or stares at me through hooded eyes, letting me know she likes it.

Heidi approaches me then slowly brings the hem of my collar between her two fingers. She pops up on her tip-toes and looks me in the eye. "Well, Senator," she says, and it's my turn to swallow hard. I hear the title at least a hundred times a day, but never has it affected me the way it does when it comes from her lips. Because I know when she says it, she's not referring to my political presence. She's letting me know, in her eyes, there's not a man alive with this kind of power over her. And that is a fucking head rush like no other. To know she is mine. "I'm immune to your powers," she says then she taps me on the nose and shrugs like I'm some little kid she just put in their place.

If we weren't in the middle of a hospital, in a room full of people.....

I am glad she's relaxed and playful again though. The visit with Hudson must have went well.

Heidi convinced me to leave long enough to get some things taken care of at the office. I think she mainly just wanted to be alone with her son when he finally got a room of his own, because she convinced Shelly and Cole to do the same thing.

I stopped by the office long enough to let Candace know I wouldn't be relocating. That's right. You heard me. I can't leave. I can't leave Olivia. I'm not going to be a part time dad. Once Monica and I figure out the best way to explain the situation to her, I plan on being the best father possible to that little girl. Then there's Heidi. I've never been a *plan for the future* kind of man when it comes to women. Hell, I don't even plan for a second date most times. But with Heidi, it doesn't even feel like planning. It's just....there. I can't see a life without her in it. Everywhere I look, she's there. Whether it's planning a career move, or buying a house, she's a part of it. I've opened the door to this brand new universe. A universe with her in it. And I don't plan on stepping back outside of it. That door closed on me for two long weeks, and I was a fucking train wreck because of it. And that was before all of this. Before she opened up to me. Before she let me inside. Before *I* let *her* inside. There's so much more I have to give her, so much more I want to show her. It's fucking crazy how she has flipped my entire world upside down.

Monica is in my kitchen when I get home.

"I see you got the test results," she says.

Okay, I'm busted. Yesterday when I got the results, I didn't want to tell her. I didn't want to talk about it. I didn't even want to face it. Which is why I researched the accuracy of these tests, got drunk, then ended up at Heidi's.

"You were in my office?" I know this is something we need to talk about, but that doesn't keep me from being a little fucking frustrated that she makes herself at home with my shit.

"I am still your housekeeper, am I not?" she asks defensively.

"Oh don't keep pulling that card, Monica. Tuesday is laundry day. Now tell me why you were in my fucking office." I'm tired of her playing the victim. If we are going to be parents, she's going to have to own up to her role in this whole thing.

"Fine. I was looking for the results. I was just as anxious as you were, Nick," she says.

"That's odd. Considering you already knew who her mother was. I'd say the stakes were a little higher for me. Unless....Is there a player number three out there? If my results were negative, what then?" I'm trying not to be upset, but this is a child we're talking about. What if I hadn't been her father? Does she have a list she's marking off as she goes? How can one woman be so irresponsible? Don't give me that look. I always use protection. Yes, even with Monica. It's not like I put the condom on and hoped it would bust. What guy does that? Heidi is an exception. Heidi is *the* exception. Mostly because I know we're exclusive. Partly because there usually isn't much planning involved. Partly because I fucking love the way she feels when I'm bare. Okay, *mostly* because I love the way she feels when I'm bare. And partly because I can't imagine anything better than part of me becoming part of her.

"I swear you can be such an asshole sometimes," Monica exclaims, distracting me from my train of thought.

Maybe I am being an asshole, but I never claimed to be a nice guy.

"I'm not trying to be an asshole, Monica" I admit. "All I'm trying to say is you can't keep treating this like it's *your* home." I wait, hoping that didn't come out asshole-ish. I feel like Monica and I have a good enough friendship to be straightforward with one another though. Even though it is a little awkward right now.

She starts to move toward me. Oh shit. What's that look? Don't do it. For the love of Pete, do not fucking touch me. Too late. She reaches out and takes my hand in hers. Then she touches the side of my face with her other hand. "It could be," she says, half questioning, half suggesting.

You've got to be kidding me. Did I spray on a shit ton of *eau de fuck me* this morning?

I take her wrist and gently remove her hand from my face. She's confused and I can't blame her. This is a fucked up situation. "Monica..."

She licks her lips and looks up at me, "Nick," she whispers.

I close my eyes and shake my head. I don't want to see the strong independent woman I've grown to care about become this desperate.

"We could be a family. We practically live together now. You wanted me once. I can make you want me again," she pleads.

God, I don't want to hurt her but I can't pretend something is there when it isn't. A few months ago, it wouldn't have bothered me one bit to fuck Monica right now. Because a few months ago, that's all it would have been. Fucking.

But since Heidi, it's so much more. I don't crave the empty pleasure of a random fuck anymore. I crave her. I crave the way it feels to be inside of her, hearing how much she needs me there, the way she tastes on my tongue, and the fire that burns in my soul when I take her.

I let go of Monica's hand and step away from her. "Don't do this to yourself. This isn't what you want. It's just what you think is right."

"So that's it? Just no? You don't know what I want or how I feel. If you don't care about me then what have you been doing for the past four years?" Her voice cracks as it raises.

"I never said I don't care about you," I explain. She is staring at me and I can tell she is trying not to cry. "Because I do. But not like that. Not the way you need." I take a deep breath and pinch the bridge of my nose. "I will be here for Olivia. I promise you that."

"And me? What do I do?"

"You will find someone. Trust me. But I am not that someone. And when you do find him, you'll see that."

She lets out a sarcastic huff. "Yea, because there are tons of men out there waiting to fall in love with a single mom," she quips.

"I did," I confess.

She stops basking in her self-pity and looks over at me as if I just spoke German. "What?"

"Heidi is a single mother," I tell her, not caring whether or not it was something she already knew. I assume by her expression, she didn't. I pull my bottom lip into my mouth as if that will stop my next words from spilling out. It doesn't. "And I fell in love with her."

The room suddenly feels smaller. Darker. I can hear my pulse pounding in my eardrums. I can feel my heart beating in my chest. Every single one of my senses is keenly aware of what I've just spoken out loud for the first time. I've known I was in love with Heidi from the moment I bumped into her at Jefferson Street Square. She was very drunk and very openly flirting with me. Not caring that I had Taylor Montgomery on my arm. I should have taken her home that night. I fell even more in love with her listening to her read her dirty bedtime stories to me, passionately explaining how she felt a deeper meaning behind them. Then, if there were ever any question of the spell she had on me, the day on my boat sealed the deal. She fell apart in my arms before either one of us ever even took out clothes off. I can dig up as many memories as you like, but I can't pinpoint one particular moment that made me fall in love with Heidi. Every moment I have with her makes me fall in love with her. Every time I see her with Hudson, showing him the unconditional love of a mother. Every time I see her fight for something she believes in. Every time I see her as the confident business woman that had the guts to walk in my office and call out the great Graham Batiste. Every time she opens her smart mouth to talk back to me, and then later wraps that beautiful mouth around my dick. Every time she gives me that mischievous look that tells me she doesn't want to say it out loud, but she really wants me to fuck her. Every time she sings my name while I make her come to pieces. Those times and many, many more, are the times I fall in love with Heidi Lemaire.

It's scary as fuck to finally say it out loud, yet at the same time it's like a part of me I've been keeping to myself is finally free.

Monica stands silently in the doorway for several minutes while we both process what just happened. "I should go," she says, finally.

"We need to talk," I say.

"I really should go," she repeats. Then she turns around and walks out the door, heading to the pool house where she stays.

Well, that didn't go the way I planned.

When Cole and I left Hudson, he was still sleeping. I knew it would be at least a couple of hours before he was ready for a room full of company so I talked everyone into taking a break. You're freaking crazy if you think I'm going anywhere. I could use a little time inside my own head anyway.

I can't even blame Dr. Collins for reacting the way she did to Nick. What woman in her right mind wouldn't? I guess it's just something I'll have to get used to if I am going to be with him. Am I going to be with him? Is being with him even an option? I'd like to think we're a little past the wondering stage. Nick's showing up at my apartment last night and being so transparent and then coming here today without me even asking him was a huge step in the "this could be serious" direction.

The nurse lets me know Hudson is in a room and ready to see me. I can't get there fast enough.

There he is, still hooked up to his IV, lying down with his eyes fluttering between sleep and wake. The moment I walk in the room, his eyes pop open and his scratchy little voice yells, "Mommy!"

And all of the sudden, that scratchy little voice is my favorite sound in the whole world, and those bright blue eyes jump start my heart and allowed it to beat again.

"Hello there my little superhero," I tell him with a kiss on the cheek. "Guess what?"

"What?"

"My new heart loves you just as much as my old one did," he says like the thought surprises him.

I can't help but chuckle at his revelation. "Of course it does, monkey butt," I say. "It's the same heart. It just works a lot better now."

The hospital has the room set up for parents to stay comfortably. The walls are painted a light beige on the bottom half and covered in a patterned wallpaper full of different color circles of all sizes on the top. On the east wall in between two honey colored wood cabinets,

193

is Hudson's bed. Next to his bed is a rolling tray on one side and his IV on the other. On the south wall, in front of a large window with red, tan, and blue striped curtains, is a tan sofa and glass-top end table. Across from the sofa, on the north wall, are two red reclining chairs and a table with a lamp. Then, on the west wall is a big screen television and all sorts of medical gadgets. The sofa makes out into a bed and there are blankets and pillows in one of the wood cabinets. Off to one side of the chairs, next to Hudson's bed, is a door that leads to the bathroom. Next to the two recliners is the entrance to the room. Even with all the available seating in the room, I sit beside Hudson on the bed and we watch television until a delivery disturbs us.

Two men bring in buckets full of plastic superheroes and hot wheels attached to matching balloons. There is a Star Wars balloon attached to a spaceship and two very large storm trooper figures and a jedi. Hudson's eyes grow wider with each new set of toys. This is crazy. Cole enters after the last gift is being delivered and I shoot him a glare.

"You know I'm still his favorite parent, no matter how much you bribe him," I tease. I'm not really mad. Actually, I'm quite the opposite. If anyone deserves to be spoiled, it's Hudson.

Cole looks around the room at all the balloons. "I was just about to say the same to you."

The nurse brings Hudson a tray of food and as soon as the scent hits me, I realize I'm starving. I guess Cole hears my stomach growl because he laughs and tells me to go eat. When I get back from the vending machine, Nick is sitting comfortably in a recliner, chatting it up with Hudson and Cole. Now that must have been awkward. Shelly stops by for a visit, as well as Meghan and Ashton, Cole's parents, and Michelle. I can tell in my little man's face he is getting tired but doesn't want to disappoint anyone so I politely let them know he could probably use some rest. He looks up at me with a smile and says an unspoken thank you with his eyes.

Nick was the perfect gentleman the entire evening. He charmed the pants off Mrs.Lemaire…and Mr.Lemaire too it seemed. And Hudson was amazed at all of his stories about the White House and the different things they do there. Not to mention the fact that throughout the evening, it became obvious that Nick had sent all the cool gifts and balloons. And now here he is, feet propped up in a recliner while I lie in bed next to my son and we all watch Star Wars Rebels, the cartoon. The room is quiet except for the tv and I can't help but smile when I look around and see what the rest of the world must see...a family. Even in his designer suit and unnaturally good looks, Nick belongs here. He belongs with me. And Hudson seems to approve of him too.

I'm not sure when we fell asleep, but the nurse wakes me for the eleven o'clock shift change. She's checking Hudson's pain medicine and vitals so I get out of her way, taking the opportunity to use the bathroom. I don't think I've peed in half a day and my bladder is about to explode.

When I come out, I stand beside the sleeping man in the chair, my sleeping man. I admire his face and the peace that covers it while he sleeps. I'm so used to seeing him contain his emotions and radiate power and control, it's nice to see him at rest. Even so, I can't keep from touching him. I run my fingers through his hair, hoping I don't wake him. But I do. Damn.

He looks up at me, a sexy grin slowly spreading across his face. "I was just dreaming of you."

I sit on the arm of the chair and continue to play with his hair. "A nice one, I hope."

He leans his head back and licks his lips. "I wouldn't exactly call it *nice*," he says.

I have to remind myself that one: my son is asleep ten feet away, and two: we're in a children's hospital.

I lean forward and softly place my lips against his and hold them there for just a moment. I just want to feel him, to breathe him in. I don't need to part my lips and have his tongue, even though my body is begging me to do just that. I just want this small yet intimate part of him in this moment.

"You should go home. You'll get more rest there. People will be in and out of here all night," I tell him.

"And you think being alone in my bed will be any better?"

"Oh, your bed is definitely better with me in it, but it would make me feel better to know at least one of us is well rested," I say with a wink. I have learned the only way to appeal to Nick Knight is to put a flirty twist on everything you ask. He's not an easy one to sway, this one.

"Since you put it that way, how can I argue?"

He reluctantly stands, pulling me close as he does. His hands cup the sides of my face as he tilts my head back. His mouth twitches and his eyes twinkle. "I'll see you tomorrow, Heidi." Then he kisses me the way I wanted to kiss him earlier.

Wednesday, July 23

The pain medicine helped Hudson sleep most of the night. Cole showed up before breakfast with a cup of much needed coffee. Shortly after that, I get a text from Nick.

Nick: *Up and ready to show you how just well rested I am*

Me: *I think there may be rules against that sort of thing here*

Nick: *Well then I'll just have to wait until I can get you away from there*

Me: *Anticipation…..*

Nick: *is the best foreplay. See you soon Heidi*

They're just words on a screen but they have my heart racing and body temperature rapidly rising. I don't even hear what Cole is saying. All I can think of is the next time I'm alone with Nick.

An hour later, Nick walks in wearing his tilted smile and tailored suit. His charcoal gray slacks hug his body in all the right places and the white button up shirt makes his tan skin glow. He's wearing a matching charcoal gray vest and black tie, no jacket. I could just lick him right now.

"Hello Mr. Nick," Hudson calls from his bed.

"We're friends now right?" Nick replies.

"Best buddies," Hudson says with a smile and a thumbs up.

"Then, it's Nick. Just Nick."

Hudson looks over at me then back at Nick, as if he's trying to decide which one of us holds more power at this moment. "My mom says it's rude to call an adult by their first name," he says, finally.

Nick cocks his head and ponders for a moment. I can see in his expression he's amused. He smiles at Hudson and ruffles a hand through the little boy's already messy hair. "Maybe I can convince her to make an exception." Then he looks directly at me and smirks. "What do you say, mom? Can we make an exception?"

The way he places emphasis on the word *mom* makes my ovaries explode. I would have his babies in a minute. Woah. *Did I seriously just think that?*

And if he thinks that look is all it takes for me to say yes.....okay so that look is all it takes for me to say yes, usually. But I can't cave right here, right now, in front of my child. I still have to be the authority figure here. Damn you, Nick Knight.

"We'll see," I say, causing Nick to chuckle.

"That means yes, but she's gonna make you wait for it," Hudson states, matter-of-fact.

"Hudson!" I exclaim, eyes wide and mouth open.

He just shrugs and smiles slyly. "What? It's true. You say it to me all the time."

The room laughs at his acute observation and I just shake my head.

"Well then I guess I need to start saying no more often, huh?" I say as I put on my best "I'm mom and I said so" face.

Cole takes the opportunity to give his input. "Awe come on mom, he's got a point."

He attempts to shadow Nick's earlier flirtation but...yeah, that one did nothing for my ovaries.

I roll my eyes at the fact that they're obviously all going to gang up on me now, then take a seat on the bed next to Hudson. I give him a kiss on the forehead and smile down at him. He's been so brave through all of this. He's kept his sunny disposition and optimistic outlook the entire time. And he's managed to keep the rest of us smiling and entertained in the meanwhile. I am one blessed momma.

"Maybe if you weren't so stinking cute, I'd actually be able to say no."

Shelly shows up while Hudson fills us in on the latest books he's read and a couple of movies he can't wait to see. She walks in with an oversized, stuffed, yellow Minion and sticks her tongue out at Nick as she walks past. "He's not the only one with gifts," she announces as she places the stuffed doll on the other side of the bed with Hudson.

She gives him a kiss on the cheek then walks over and leans into Nick. "Mine's bigger," she whispers loudly. That's my Shelly. She just couldn't help herself. I've learned there's nothing you can do with her so it's better to just watch and be entertained. Nick doesn't appear offended by her comment. Actually, his lips twitch, fighting a grin, and he arches one eyebrow in amusement.

"Mine doesn't require batteries," he responds.

"Why does it need batteries?" Hudson asks as he inspects the stuffed Minion, flipping it upside down and on its side. "Does it talk?" There's a hint of excitement in his voice as he asks the last question.

"No, baby. Mr. Nick was just being silly," Shelly says, shooting Nick a glare.

I am going to have my hands full with these two.

Michelle showed up and the group as a whole has convinced me that it would be okay for me to leave long enough to shower and change.

"I love you and all, but you kinda stink. Two days in the same underwear is just nasty," Shelly informs me. She has such a way with words.

"I think between me, Michelle, and the entire hospital staff, we can handle it for a couple of hours," Cole adds.

Hudson is sleeping now so it doesn't actually seem like a bad idea. I could use a hot shower. And a glass of wine. Just one. For my nerves. Nick wraps his arms around me from behind and whispers into my ear, "I second the underwear remark. We should probably get you out of those."

I feel an instant flush as my cheeks warm. I mentally add a heavy dose of *Nick* to the list of things I could use.

"Hello, other people in the room," Shelly interrupts.

I clear my throat and narrow my eyes at her. "Okay. Okay. I'll be back in a couple of hours," I concede. "Promise you'll call if he needs anything," I say to Cole as I gather up my purse and keys.

"He'll be fine," he says and I give him an insistent stare. "I promise. Go."

It takes me another five minutes to actually leave. It just doesn't feel right. I know I have obligations to my hygiene and all, but I don't want to leave my baby. What if he wakes up and wants to know where I am? What if something happens? What if the nurse has a question and Cole doesn't know the answer? Finally, Nick assures me it will only be a couple of hours and Hudson is in good hands. It's not like I'm leaving him at home alone. He's in a children's hospital for crying out loud. So I let go of the reigns and let Nick take me home. For now.

My exhaustion takes over and I fall asleep on the drive, so I'm surprised to wake up as we're pulling in to Nick's garage. He opens the door and leads me inside. "I don't have clean clothes here," I argue.

"You don't need them right now," he says as he stalks toward me. The temperature in the room instantly rises ten degrees. Every time with Nick feels like the first time. My heart races and my stomach flutters as my body anticipates his touch. My lips part intuitively as he comes closer. He looks into me with dark eyes that fall to my mouth when he takes my hand in his. He licks his lips and pulls me close. His free hand grips the back of my neck as his head dips. "I've been waiting forever to taste you," he breathes against my lips. I get lost when he kisses me. The gentle way he caresses me with his tongue. The softness of his lips. The urgency he possesses when he wants more. It all leads up to the formula for perfection.

I playfully take his bottom lip between my teeth when he begins to pull away.

"Careful," he warns when I release him.

"More orgasm torture?" I quip.

He graces me with my favorite tilted grin. "We don't have time for that baby."

Damn. "What do we have time for?"

He chuckles and takes my face in his hands. "You have time for a shower. I have to make a phone call," he states flatly.

I let out an exasperated sigh. Can't he see my body is one big bubble about to pop? Why does he do this to me?

"So you'll be joining me then? After your very brief phone call?" I ask while I begin unbuttoning my shirt.

Nick watches me intently until I have completely undone every button, teasing him with a sliver of exposed flesh and cleavage. He walks over to me and slips a hand inside my open blouse and around my waist. "I'll be inside you before the water gets warm."

My insides clench at the mere hint of his promise and I know my skin is scorching beneath his touch. I feel his grin widen against my neck, then he places a gentle kiss right beneath my ear before he moves away.

And Nick did not disappoint. I no sooner than finish undressing and turn the water on, than in he walks, throwing his vest on the bed as he loosens his tie. I walk over, nothing but a towel wrapped around my body, and finish undoing his tie. I start working on the buttons of his shirt and he hooks a finger in the towel and pulls, causing it to fall at our feet.

I slip the shirt off his shoulders and admire his impossibly perfect body with my hands, gliding them over every crease and bump of his chest, abs, arms, and shoulders before bring them up the back of his neck and into his golden brown hair.

His hand slides between us and grazes my heat. I didn't realize just how badly I needed him until he touched me. My legs feel like jello, boneless and weak. I moan as he slips a single digit inside. I close my eyes and tilt my head back as he delves deeper into me, his palm creating delightful pressure against my throbbing clit each time he dips his finger inside. His other hand is wrapped in my hair, where he is tugging gently to create the perfect threshold between pleasure and pain. His teeth graze my neck just before he scatters kisses across my bare skin. It's all too much. Too many sensations at once. I'm coming undone. It all feels so good.

Nick kisses me intently while I ride it out.

As soon as I can feel my legs again, I open my eyes and find him watching me. "Not exactly what I was thinking, but it will do," I tease.

He picks me up and carries me to the shower. I stick one hand in to test the water before he sets me inside. My senses are still on alert from the orgasm so the warm water feels like heaven. Nick stands just outside the shower, removing the rest of his clothes. His glorious cock springs free the moment he pulls his boxer briefs down. My mouth waters at the sight of it.

He steps inside, a sly smile spread across his face. "You were thinking something more like this?" he asks, wrapping his hands around his erection.

Oh god. He's standing less than a foot away from me, one hand braced on the tile wall of the shower, the other stroking his flesh. His eyes never move from mine as he becomes more focused on his actions. His breathing picks up pace and I notice the muscles in his thighs flex as he holds on to the pleasure. Holy shit. I am speechless. I can't pull my eyes away from him. I wonder if this is what he looks like when he talks filthy to me on the phone. I have heard Nick give himself pleasure, but seeing it is a totally different story. He is magnificent in every way.

I immediately fall to my knees and begin to kiss the insides of his thighs. I have to be close to him. I want so badly to touch him. To taste him. He continues stroking and pulling even when my mouth finds his balls. The minute I take them in my mouth, he lets out a loud sexy grunt. Then his hand moves from his erection to my head. He doesn't have to ask because I want nothing more than to have him in my mouth.

He allows me the pleasure of tasting him, but only for a moment. Soon, he takes me by the arm and pulls me off my knees. He has me backed against the shower wall, hands above my head, breathless and wanting more. I can see he wants it just as much as I do, but he reaches to the side and takes the soap and begins to lather my body. God, this man has superhuman control. There's nothing outside of willpower keeping him from screwing my brains out right now.

He takes his time soaping me up. My breath hitches when he runs the sudsy liquid across my nipples and he chuckles. He pulls my arms above my head and covers me in suds. He spreads my legs, getting down on one knee to make sure every inch is covered. Then he detaches the main showerhead from its place and begins to rinse me off, achingly slowly. He holds the nozzle a bit too long in front of my most sensitive areas, almost causing another orgasm. The man definitely knows his way around a woman's body.

Once we've finished what is considerably the most erotic shower I've ever had, Nick hands me a t-shirt and a pair of boxers. It's quickly becoming my favorite outfit. Although, there's no way I'm wearing this back to the hospital. "I enjoy seeing you in my underwear," he says. "It reminds me I've gotten you out of yours," he adds with a smile.

I walk over to the chest of drawers where he is slipping into a pair of athletic pants, minus the underwear, I should add. I'm reminded I haven't had all of him yet, and my body is going into withdrawals. "Does that mean when we're at my apartment, you get to wear mine?"

He looks at me like I have two heads. "I was joking. I doubt you'd…um…fit..in my panties, anyway," I say, running my hand over his crotch.

He backs me up until I am back against one of the thick posts of his bed. I haven't had a chance to get dressed yet, the clothes he handed me still bunched up in one hand. My body is very aware of his hardness pressing against my bare belly.

"Why do you keep his name?" he asks.

Huh?

Almost as if I had said that aloud, Nick continues, "Cole Lemaire. Heidi Lemaire. Why do you keep his name?"

Ohhhh. That. Really? You're thinking about that? Now? I fumble for the answer. Not because I don't have one, but because my head is nowhere near that vicinity now. Not even in the same time zone. "Because I don't want Hudson to have a different last name," I explain. And it's the truth. "Why? Does it bother you?"

"It's like part of you still belongs to him," he says. His hands find my face and he forces me to look up at him. "What if you were to get married? What then?"

Married? Is he kidding me? The laugh I tried to contain spills from my lips. "Married? I guess I never planned on getting married."

He presses himself against me and my knees get weak. "Some things you just don't plan for, baby."

"Like you," I say, my voice barely above a whisper.

"Like *you*," he replies. He leans forward, his bare chest against my bare chest, and speaks softly into my ear. "I want to know your fairy tale, Heidi. What do you wish for when you're all alone?"

You.

"Fairy tales are for children," I tell him, knowing it's a bold faced lie. I wish for him. I lie in bed wanting him. He is my fairy tale.

He runs the tip of his nose along my neck, his breath leaving a trail of fire everywhere it touches. "You don't really believe that," he says, his smooth confident voice sending chills down my spine.

I'm losing it. My guard. My apprehension. My denial. "Darcy," I say simply.

He brings his face around to meet mine. His flawlessness leaves me breathless. His golden eyes shine as he gazes at me. His tongue runs over his full lips. "I want someone to love me as much as Darcy loves Elizabeth. A timeless love. With no barriers."

Nick runs his thumb over my lips and I close my eyes, hoping he'll kiss me soon.

"What if I told you I can't do that?" he asks boldly.

I open my eyes and find him still looking at me, expecting the truth. "Then I would say I'll take whatever you can give."

What is he doing? Why is he asking me this? I never expected him to love me. I'm not even asking him to love me. Even though I'm pretty sure I've fallen in love with him. But I'm woman enough to keep those emotions tucked carefully away in a tight-lidded little box. I've been very careful to guard my heart up until now. I can handle it.

He kisses me softly, slowly. "Because I can't," he says when he pulls himself away. "I can't love you as much as Darcy. Or Rochester. Or Heathcliff. Or any of those men."

I open my mouth to tell him that's okay, that I want him just the way he is, but he interrupts.

"I can't love you *as much as*....anything. Because no one has ever loved anyone like I love you. I can't love you like Darcy. I can just fucking love you. Way too goddamn much."

My heart just fell to the floor. I can't breathe. I can't speak but I want to scream. I can't move but I want to jump out of my skin.

"I won't let another day go by without you hearing it." He lifts me up and throws me back onto his bed. He climbs between my legs and presses against me. "And I promise you baby, I am far more real than your Mr. Darcy."

Yes. Sweet lord yes, you are.

My hands grip the waistband of his pants and slide them off his body. He enters me slowly and makes love to me like it's the end of the world. My hands massage his back as he rocks into me, deeper, harder. I feel my body climaxing and I wrap my legs around his as I return his urgency to fill me completely. "I love you Nick," I tell him just before we both fall over the edge.

CHAPTER TWENTY-SIX
Heidi

Thursday, July 24

We get to go home today! Hudson is responding very well to the surgery and Dr. Collins feels very confident that in about six months, the tissue will have grown over the patch and his heart will be completely healed. Of course, no one is more excited about this news than Hudson.

Nick offered to drive us home, but I asked him to give us time to get settled in and adjust to being home and all the changes we'll have to make for the next few weeks.

Yesterday still feels like a dream to me. A man who couldn't be more perfect if I had created him myself, is in love with me. And I am ardently and completely in love with him. This man. The man who opened his office doors and stole my breath, has now stolen my heart.

Later that night, I'm relaxing on the sofa with my second glass of wine. Of course this is after Hudson helps me cook and I read him two books and give him a bath. He fell asleep in my bed sometime during the third story. Maybe I'm being overprotective, but I'm not ready to sleep in separate rooms just yet.

I'm just about to turn on the television and prepare to get all wrapped up in a Lifetime movie when there's a knock on my door. *Weird.*

Nick always texts in lieu of knocking. Shelly left for Florida this afternoon with Emmett. Surely Cole wouldn't be checking on Hudson this late. I can't think of anyone else. So you can imagine my surprise when I open the door to find Alex standing there.

"Hello beautiful."

I'm sure I look as if I've just seen a ghost. I dig my heels in and find my composure. I haven't seen Alex since I left his loft with Nick. He still finds the charm to compliment me, even though I am far from deserving it in my polka dot pajama bottoms and oversized t-shirt.

"Hello there handsome," I say with a genuine smile. "Come in."

He walks into the living room, looking around nervously. "It's just me," I assure him.

Alex is dressed in his usual post kickboxing class attire. It's easy to forget how hot he is after looking at someone like Nick every day.

I take a seat on the sofa and pat the empty spot next to me, inviting him to have a seat.

"How was the surgery?" he asks as he sits.

"Fine. He's home." I nod my head in the direction of my bedroom. "He's sleeping."

"Good. That's really good."

The conversation is littered with half sentences and casual comments. I wish we could go back to where we were just a little over a week ago. It seems like so much has changed in such a short period of time. I miss the comfortable silence. Now the silence is deafening.

"Look, love, I don't mean for this to be uncomfortable. I just came to say goodbye," he says.

Goodbye? NO. I mean, I knew he was leaving. I knew it was coming. I know I can't expect him to stay here and be a part of my life like he was before. That doesn't mean I won't miss it. That I won't miss him.

"Alex," is all I manage to say. He drapes one arm around my shoulder and pulls me into his chest.

I sit like that, my head against his chest just listening to his heartbeat, matching my breathing to his, comforted in the warmth of his arms, for what seems like hours before either one of us speaks.

"Nick is a very lucky man," Alex says finally. "And I have no doubt he knows that."

And somewhere out there is a very lucky woman, although she doesn't even know it yet.

"Promise me you'll keep in touch," I plead. I can't stand the thought of what it would be like not knowing if he's happy or if he's well. I want to know about his new partnership. I want to hear about

Miami. I can't fathom the thought of having him just disappear completely from my life.

The hand he had running through my hair stops moving, causing me to pull my head from his chest and look him in the eye. "Alex?"

He moves his eyes from mine, consciously focusing on anywhere but my face. I bring my hand to his chin and force him to look at me.

"Alex? You will keep in touch? Right?" If I sound anywhere near as frantic as I feel, I'll be surprised if he even understands me.

"I came here to say goodbye, love," he says, almost apologetically. The water in my eyes begins to blur my vision. This is it. I'm really losing him. Is it possible to love one man absolutely, yet let another one have the power to break your heart?

"Like….*goodbye* goodbye? Disappear and change your number goodbye?" My voice cracks.

He swallows hard and begins to stand. I stand in front of him. Like I could actually block him from leaving.

"Can we at least talk about this?" I beg as I blink back the tears that are rapidly building up.

A sad smile crosses his handsome face in place of the usual Cheshire grin I've gotten so attached to. "We never were very good at talking," he says, attempting to soothe my mood with humor.

"So that's it then," I say as the harsh realization hits me square between the eyes.

He takes my face in his hands and looks into my eyes. I blink back more tears. Alex kisses each one of my eyelids. "Don't waste those on me," he tells me, then he lovingly places a single soft kiss on my lips, lingering there for several seconds.

There's nothing sexual or uncomfortable about it, yet it's still sensual and intimate. And it's definitely goodbye.

I spend the rest of the night holding Hudson and convincing myself I won't really miss Nathan Alexander.

CHAPTER TWENTY-SEVEN
Heidi

Tuesday, August 5

It's been two weeks since Hudson's surgery and he is healing wonderfully. Today he had his post-surgery check up with Dr. Collins. We left with a good report. I can't believe the way things have worked out. It's been twelve days since Nick told me he loves me and he has held true to his promise of not letting a day go by without reminding me of that. It's also been eleven days since Alex said goodbye and like Nick, he has held true to his word. I haven't heard a peep from him since he walked out my door. I can't say I don't miss him. But in no way do I question my choice.

The first week after Hudson's surgery, he slept in my bed so I could keep an eye on him. Nick would stop by with lunch most days. He has definitely found his place in Hudson's heart. And I'm pretty sure the feeling is mutual.

The past week has been especially challenging for my hormones. The first week was tough, with Nick simply stopping by after Hudson fell asleep to tell me goodnight. A stolen kiss against the wall now and then is all we took. This past week, however, Hudson has been sleeping in his own bed. Which means Nick has spent the past five nights torturing me with some serious dry humping and making out. I feel like a teenager hiding in my bedroom from my parents. We have finished the first and second books of the series I started reading to him not long after we first met. His outlook on the characters has changed and he has expressed significant interest in the playroom idea. When I asked if he'd prefer a big silver pole in the middle, he threatened to turn me over his knee. Is it bad that part of me wished he weren't joking? I am in serious need of some skin on skin action. Soon.

During the day, we have been looking online at possible locations for my new office, and Nick has been driving by and scouting them out.

We have it narrowed down to three, which we will be checking out together this afternoon.

Shelly shows up to keep an eye on Hudson for a few hours. He is recovering well, but I'm still not comfortable with him leaving the house just yet. One more week. He's going stir crazy. We have done everything from making our own indoor bowling lane to building a giant fort in the middle of my living room and playing knights versus evil kings.

Nick has adjusted well to fatherhood and according to him, Olivia couldn't be happier with the news. One night he even showed up with hot pink toes, warning me, *"Don't ask,"* he said. I thought it was adorable.

I'm showing Shelly what I have laid out for lunch when Nick arrives. I have seen him every day for the past three weeks but he still takes my breath away the very moment he flashes that sexy little tilted smile my way.

He greets Hudson, who is in the living room building an airplane out of legos, first. Then he approaches the kitchen where Shelly and I are busy discussing how long it's been since I've had any.

Nick slips a strong arm around my waist and pulls me into him. "Are you ready?" he asks calmly.

You have no idea how ready. "For you? Always," I flirt.

Shelly pretends like she has to throw up, but I know the truth is, she's loving it. She has told me...more than once...how happy she is that I *"finally came to my senses and hooked this man."*

I give Hudson at least a hundred kisses before Nick finally drags me out the door.

Our first stop is a space located in a large brick building in the warehouse district. It's three stories high with the top floor being set up as a residential loft. The building itself sits on an entire corner off Julia Street and is home to a couple of restaurants and art galleries. The black shutters and iron balconies stand out against the red brick. The floors are stained concrete and the architecture is true New Orleans style, with exposed ductwork and brick walls. I'm in love. The loft is a huge bonus because Hudson and I could live there and I wouldn't have to worry about working late. I'm walking around looking like a kid at Disney World when Nick comes up behind me and wraps his arms around my waist. "I take it you like what you see?" he observes.

Here we go. Just the sound of his voice filling the room and I'm taken away from this place. As much as I love this building, I love his touch a thousand times more.

"It's okay," I reply.

"Just okay?" he says as he pulls my hair to the side and brings his face to the crook of my neck.

Please kiss me there. Now.

"It's growing on me," I say and I feel him huff out a quiet chuckle against my skin.

He presses into me from behind, his erection very apparent. "So it is," he says.

"Nick," I moan. God I need him. My body has been a short circuit for two weeks and I am about to die. Can you die from sexual frustration? I'm pretty sure that's a thing. Because I'm right there. His hands slide up the sides of my body, bringing the material of my white, cotton, strapless dress with them. He starts placing a line of kisses along my bare shoulder and I can't contain myself. I can't think straight. His hands. His mouth. The way he smells. Oh my god. My body instinctively backs into his, begging for another caress from his hard flesh.

He turns me around, holding my head in his hands, and kisses me. *Finally.*

Then he backs me against an iron spiral staircase in the far corner of the room, until I have no choice but to fall backwards and sit on one of the steps. He is holding on to the railing on either side of me, between my legs. He leans into me and licks his lips.

He lets go of the rails so his hands can slide up the sides of my thighs as he pulls my dress up. "What if someone comes?" I ask, not sure exactly how much I really care if they do.

Nick's mouth turns up in his tilted grin. "Someone's definitely coming," he says.

"Nick," I reply flatly and he rolls his eyes.

"We're alone. I made sure we wouldn't be bothered," he says as he brushes my hair away from my face and looks me in the eye. "Tell me you need me as much as I need you."

"I need you," I tell him. Then I reach forward and unfasten his gray trousers and take him in my hand.

The sex on the stairs was amazing, but I want more. Ten minutes with our clothes still on satisfied a craving, but the hunger is still there. I will never have enough of him.

I pretty much decided I'm locked in on the building on Julia Street. It definitely had its perks.

"We can skip the next one. I think I've made up my mind," I tell Nick when we get in his truck.

He smiles and looks at me from the corner of his eye. "That quick huh?"

I shrug and smirk. "I kinda like the staircase."

He laughs and starts punching another address in his navigation system. "Let me show you one more," he requests. "I'm sure we can find something to like about the next one too."

I'm sure we could find something to like about a run-down barn in the middle of Idaho. As long as Nick is part of the package.

We pull into a gated subdivision and I begin to wonder where he's going with this. I don't remember looking at anything in residential areas.

He stops at a very big contemporary style home at the end of one of the streets, and turns off the ignition.

I eye him curiously. "Kind of big and out of the way for an office, don't you think?" I question.

He just grins and leads me to the front door.

The home is perfection. The architectural details are a perfect combination of modern amenities and traditional touches. The crisp white kitchen cabinets and glass subway tile backsplash offset the travertine tile floors and painted gray kitchen island. There are floor to ceiling windows along the entire north wall, allowing a perfect view of the jetty that leads to the lake. The living and dining rooms are divided by a double sided fireplace with a slate tile surround. And there is a staircase. A much wider, and likely more comfortable, staircase, right as you enter into the foyer. There are square columns designating you have left the entrance area and are now in the living area. And a giant waffle ceiling in the living room with beautiful geometric detail appliqued within each square. Although there is a pool, I notice the absence of a pool house. There is one bedroom and an office downstairs. Along with a sunroom and two bathrooms. And there are three bedrooms and a media room upstairs, along with two more bathrooms. The master bath has a huge jetted tub in the center of the room, with the shower located directly behind it.

"It's beautiful," I say as I look around the kitchen.

I assume Nick has been house shopping. He told me he decided even though he's not moving to Washington D.C, he still needs a change of scenery. And Monica needs her independence. Which is most likely why there is no pool house here. Close that door before it ever has a chance to open.

Nick lifts me up onto the kitchen island and settles between my legs. He guides his hands up my thighs, exposing flesh as he goes. "This," he says, "is beautiful. The house is nice."

I twist my fingers in his hair and lean my forehead against his. "The house is very nice," I agree.

"It's yours," he tells me.

I sit up straight and narrow my eyes at him. "I don't need a house. You do."

He takes the bottom tips of my hair and tugs lightly on them, pulling me back to eye level with him. He swallows hard then exhales a deep breath. Like he's nervous.

"Well, I will be living here too...if that's not a problem," he states.

Too? As in...*together*? *Living* together? Me and Nick. Oh. Wow. Oh my god.

"Nick," I start, but he interrupts.

"I want this. More than anything," he confesses.

I cock my head and watch him attentively.

"Not because you're beautiful, or smart, or funny," he continues, "or absolutely fucking adorable when you look at me that way." He takes his hand and runs a fingertip along my jaw. "No, Heidi, I want you here because there never has been, and never will be anyone else like you. And I don't want to wake up another single day without your face being the first thing I see."

I wrap my legs around his waist and lick my lips. I want to kiss him forever. This man is everything I ever wanted. He is more than I ever thought I deserved. And he is mine.

I don't know where we will end up or how hard it will be to get there, but I do know I can't imagine my life without Nick in it. Today is the beginning of a new world for me. For us. A happy world. A *hopeful* world. My business has a bright future in a perfect location. Hudson is on his way to living a normal, healthy life. And I will spend every night lying next to the man I love. And every morning waking up with his arms around me. It doesn't get any better than this.

"How does a girl say no to that?" I reply.

He grins my favorite grin, "So, you're in?" he asks.

I reciprocate his grin. "I'm all in baby."

"I fucking love you, Heidi Lemaire."

"I fucking love you too, Nick Knight."

THE END.
(I know. I'm sad about it too.)

Oh. My. Goodness! Thank you for coming on this incredible journey with me!! I hope you all love Nick and Heidi as much I do. They will forever be my first. And you just don't forget your first. ;)

Added Note: I have had SO much input from readers regarding wanting MORE of this story... soooooo There WILL be a novella for Nick and Heidi!! Coming September 2016! In addition to that, Alex will also have his very own HEA! YAYYY!!

Naturally, there will be more to come. I have characters screaming at me all day long to have their stories told. Sin With Me will be released late Summer 2016 and Amesbury Park in Fall 2016.
If you haven't figured it out by now, I'm just a girl who loves to write. And I am SO excited you have decided to tag along.
So buckle up boys and girl. The ride has just begun!

And as always- It would be FAN-FREAKING-TASTIC if you would leave a review!!!! Seriously, you'd be like my own personal superhero. And everyone wants to be a superhero.

Thanks again for all your support! Readers rock! For real. ;)

XOXO,
Delaney

Sin With Me
By Delaney Foster

```
My lips long for the curve of yours
  Craving the honesty in bare skin
   I want to breathe in all of you
     You are my sweetest sin

                    -Chrissie Pinney
```

Prologue

May 2016

My head is throbbing… and heavy. So heavy that I'm struggling to hold it up. There's music. It's so loud. A man's voice bounces off the walls in screaming echoes. *Is that Eminem?* My arms. I can't move my arms.

Deep breaths, Makenna.

As I inhale I realize the sweet smell is burnt into my nasal cavity. *Chloroform.* I didn't think this actually happened in real life. Panic threatens to overcome me and I'm fighting to stay calm. I draw in long, deep breaths through my nose because my mouth is covered with duct tape. My eyes flash wildly around the space. I'm in a garage. Or maybe a warehouse. I can't tell. The bright fluorescent lights force me to squint as I look around at the bare gray cinder blocks.

The left strap of my white sundress is torn at the seam, but that's the extent of any damage to my person. *Thank You, God.*

I look over my arms and legs, as much of them as I can see anyway, and note there are no bruises. No cuts. No scratches. Nothing. Other than the fact that my wrists are strapped to the arms of a wooden chair in the middle of an empty room, and my ankles are bound together, there's no indication of harm. Whoever did this to me must not have had much of a fight.

The last thing I remember is pulling into my driveway after Brynn's birthday dinner and now here I am. Tied to a chair. Surrounded by bright lights and loud music. The words of the song seem to be coming so fast I can hardly understand them. I feel disoriented and I'm starting to get cold. My bare feet brush against the concrete floor as I work to adjust myself in the seat. *Oh God.* I have to pee. As if things weren't bad enough already.

How did I get here? I'm the girl with a five-year plan. I always order the same thing off the menu and I don't take the scenic route home. Life has taught me, if anything, to play it safe. I'm a fighter. I'm a survivor. I'm strong. Strong people don't end up in abandoned warehouses strapped to wooden chairs. *Was that a gunshot?*

In an instant the room goes silent and I am surrounded by darkness. I close my eyes just as the tears silently spill over my cheeks. I'm very careful not to make a noise. I don't even breathe. The sound of slow, heavy footsteps gets increasingly louder as they get closer.

I've always heard that right before you die, your life flashes in front of you. In this moment, with my eyes closed and tears steadily falling, I fight to remember…

To be continued… July 2016

45602173R00123

Made in the USA
San Bernardino, CA
12 February 2017